REBEL REAPER

AN URBAN FANTASY

ANN GIMPEL

CONTENTS

Rebel Reaper v
Book Description: Rebel Reaper vii
Books in the Gatekeeper Series ix
Author's Note xi

1. Chapter One, Cait 1
2. Chapter Two, Liam 17
3. Chapter Three, Cait 33
4. Chapter Four, Liam 47
5. Chapter Five, Cait 61
6. Chapter Six, Liam 75
7. Chapter Seven, Cait 91
8. Chapter Eight, Liam 107
9. Chapter Nine, Cait 123
10. Chapter Ten, Liam 137
11. Chapter Eleven, Cait 155
12. Chapter Twelve, Liam 169
13. Chapter Thirteen, Cait 183
14. Chapter Fourteen, Liam 197
15. Chapter Fifteen, Cait 215
16. Chapter Sixteen, Liam 229
17. Chapter Seventeen, Cait 243
18. Chapter Eighteen, Liam 261
19. Chapter Nineteen, Cait 277
20. Chapter Twenty, Liam 291

Book Description: Untamed Reaper 305
Untamed Reaper, Chapter One, Cait 307

About the Author 323
Also by Ann Gimpel 325

REBEL REAPER

GATEKEEPER SERIES, BOOK TWO

An Urban Fantasy

By
Ann Gimpel

Tumble off reality's edge into myth, magic, and Death

Copyright Page

Edited by: Kate Richards

ISBN: 978-1-948871-58-7

BOOK DESCRIPTION: REBEL REAPER

Come fly with me. Catchy, huh? It works for airplanes. Maybe it will work for the dead once I launch my own Reaping business. Except my new tagline will be, come die with me.

Back when my life was simpler, I thought all I had to do was hold gateways for the dead to pass through. Silly me, I actually enjoyed Reaping. Almost like a drug or fine old whiskey, it made me high, filled me with delight, and left me glowing with the rightness of providing a last bit of compassion.

Good little Reaper that I am, I never examined any of it too deeply, just crafted portals, exactly as Death trained me. Ha! She neglected to mention I command way more magic than she'd let on in Reaper school.

Death smiled pretty to my face and then lied to me. Used me.

Me and all the other Reapers.

I can't not Reap. It's hardwired into me. But I can tell Death I quit.

Big words. I have no idea if I've got the guts to follow through, or what Death would do about open insubordination.

I've always liked to live on the wild side, though, so I guess I'm about to find out.

BOOKS IN THE GATEKEEPER SERIES

Shadow Reaper, Book One
Rebel Reaper, Book Two
Untamed Reaper, Book Three

AUTHOR'S NOTE

After a million dragon books, I'm branching out. Good to cross train that muse of mine. The concept of the Grim Reaper has fascinated me for years. I used to work for a residency program training newly minted doctors. A few of them were quite sensitive to supernatural phenomena, and they'd come into my office and talk with me about sensing Death's presence before a patient passed.

They'd also talk with me about the numinous aspect of both birth and death.

Fast forward the clock a few years to *Supernatural*. Sam and Dean dealt with both Death and Reapers—until Dean killed off Death in I believe season ten. Then it's mostly Reapers.

A Reaper tale has been running around in my mind for quite a while. I hope you enjoy the Gatekeeper Series.

CHAPTER ONE, CAIT

Air rushed beneath the Citabria's wings. Normally, I don't borrow airplanes, but I needed something with aerobatic capability. My student would show up in about two hours, and I was upstairs putting the plane through her paces.

Most people would never guess airplanes have personalities. Even the same model from the same manufacturer has its idiosyncrasies and will fly differently. Luckily, one of my fellow pilots owed me a favor, or I'd have had to turn down a previous student who wanted to try his hand at aerobatic maneuvers.

By the time I paid to rent the Citabria, any profit from my lesson would have gone down the proverbial tubes. I flew figure eights and did a few rolls. The right rudder felt mushy. Worse, one of the wing struts creaked alarmingly when I pulled out of the last roll.

A quick glance out my window was far from reassuring.

Bellanca, the company that made the Citabria, had gone out of business forty years back. All the Citabria models had issues, the worst being cracking struts. The original wood had been reinforced with a length of metal, but the bottom screws had pulled out of the body of the plane.

Crap.

So much for getting ahead of the stack of bills that had piled up since I got stuck Reaping Vampires. I couldn't use this plane for a lesson, not with knowing it had a mechanical issue. And Doug, the plane's owner, would probably insist I pay for repairs. I nosed the plane back toward the field. The gauges weren't reading what I wanted them to, either.

Damn it. Nothing I'd done during my short flight would have created this level of damage.

I slapped my forehead with my open palm. I'd been both gullible and a fool. None of the local pilots would willingly give me the time of day. I'd been pleasantly surprised when Doug had agreed to let me borrow the Citabria, thinking maybe my problems with him were over.

Yeah right. And pigs will sprout wings and fly alongside me.

The other pilots tolerated me. Their antipathy wasn't as "in my face" as it had been when I first set up shop as *Carrick Sky Sports*. The bedrock problem was they still believed I belonged in a kitchen or shackled to a bed. Flying was for men, and Amalia Earhart got what she deserved.

I am such a Pollyanna. Doug had known exactly what was wrong with his aircraft. And now he had someone to blame—and charge—for fixing it. I let go of the yoke and doubled up a fist. Yeah. Right. Punching the instrument panel wouldn't solve anything.

Doug must have added extra heavy hydraulic fluid so the plane's issues wouldn't become apparent until I was in the air. Ditto for the screws and the strut. I'd done a preflight. I always do. I walk around the plane jiggling things to make certain nothing is loose.

Apparently, I didn't jiggle hard enough.

I patted the yoke. None of this was the airplane's fault. "Come on, sweetie," I crooned. "We can do this."

And then I summoned magic and wove air beneath the wounded wing to keep the plane straight and level. More magic, heavy on water, kept the engine from overheating. Damn Doug to hell. I'd pitch nine kinds of fits if he opened his yap about sending any fixit bills my way. To hedge my bets, I opened a channel to Air Traffic Control. When they responded and cleared me to land, I told them the plane had a myriad of mechanical issues.

And listed them.

Nothing gets ATC's attention quite as fast as a plane that could turn into a danger to other aircraft—or ground crews. They directed me to land and taxi directly to one of the certified mechanics who maintain shops along the strip.

They didn't care which one, so long as I did not pass go or collect 200 bucks.

My headset crackled. "What in the hell did you do to my plane?" Doug demanded. He didn't identify himself, but he didn't have to. I recognized his voice.

"Nothing," I said succinctly, knowing we had ears listening in over on the ATC end of things. "Your plane was broken when you loaned it to me. It's a wonder I wasn't killed."

He shut up fast after that.

My wheels kissed the ground; I taxied to the shop I use. If I hadn't been so angry my blood was nearly molten, I'd have asked Doug which mechanic he preferred. As it was, I was determined to turn the Citabria over to someone I trusted.

I gathered up my shoulder bag with my logbook, phone, tablet, and flight computer and exited the plane. Most of the mechanics monitor radio channels, so Rick Dogris was waiting for me. Middle height and barrel chested, he wore his usual set of greasy gray coveralls. Bald as a pinball, he sported dark glasses that covered his shrewd blue eyes. I dropped the keys into his hand.

"Wouldn't fly it if I were you," I said and sketched out everything from the visibly busted strut to the mushy rudder and overheating problems.

Rick's worried expression deepened. "Christ, Cait. I'm glad you got her back on the ground. Did Doug authorize repairs?"

I shook my head. "Nope." I sucked in a breath and cut to the chase. "He must have known the plane had serious problems. I want to make certain he doesn't pin them on me."

Rick set his jaw in a tight line. "He's a slimy one. Wouldn't put it past him."

"Yeah. Which is why the plane is here and not with whoever signed her off as airworthy."

"Don't you worry. I'll chase that angle down too." Rick's

nostrils flared with annoyance. "Until I hear from Doug, I'll taxi her out back and leave her."

"It's as good a plan as any."

Rick patted the fuselage. "I really like these planes, but they never were as reliable as, say, a Cessna."

Awk. With all the excitement of almost crashing, I'd forgotten the whole reason I'd had the Citabria in the air. "Hold up," I told Rick and fished my phone out of my bag. A bit of scrolling yielded my student's number.

Xavier picked up right away. "Yeah, Cait. What's up?"

"We don't have a plane. I took the one I'd planned on using for a test ride, and it's not safe."

"Damn it." He hesitated, and I visualized his dark eyes narrowing in thought. 'I'm already en route. Is there anything else we could do today?"

I thought about it. "Do you have long-range plans to get certified in a twin engine plane?"

"Not really, but I suppose I could give it a go."

I smiled. "It's a lot of work. Today would only be the tip of the iceberg. And it would be expensive."

"How about if I just rent the Cessna 172 and fly around for a bit?"

"Sure. You can do that. Normally, I don't rent out my planes, but I trained you."

He chuckled. "I'll do my best to bring your baby back in one piece."

Before I could respond, he'd disconnected. I dropped the phone back in my bag, swiped sweaty hair off my forehead with the back of one hand, and glanced at the sun. It was early afternoon. My lesson may have gone up in smoke, but I had plenty to do.

I quashed a wry grin at my choice of imagery. I was damned lucky the Citabria hadn't caught fire.

"Want a ride back to your office?" Rick asked.

I shook my head. "Nah. Good to get the kinks out. I'll walk."

"Do you want my report once I've checked out the Citabria?"

I chewed my lower lip and hefted my bag over one shoulder. "She's not my plane. How about we do it this way?"

"Which way would that be?" he quirked a brow.

"If you find anything that could conceivably be my fault, let me know. I'm not overly fond of Doug Printz, but if I damaged his plane, I'll pay my share."

Rick punched my upper arm lightly. "I like you, Cait. Will do."

Coming from him, the bit about liking me was high praise. Rick was known for being a dour son of a bitch, but being an airplane mechanic is considerably more nerve-wracking than, say, working on cars. If someone screws up a car, you can pull it to the side of a roadway.

Not so much with aircraft.

I set off toward the Quonset hut where my office is. It's right next door to a hangar that shelters my three planes. It did feel good to walk the half mile or so back to my shop. The day was chilly, but clear, and the air had a bite to it that reminded me winter was just around the corner.

The sky was full of fluffy clouds, but they had gray edges. Rain was never far away in the Pacific Northwest, and I wagered it would pour sometime before dark. The drone of airplanes coming and going filled my ears. I loved flying, and I was damned lucky to have built a viable aeronautics business.

Eh. It had been viable, but that was before Death assigned Vampires to me. I'm a Reaper, one of many, actually. We all report to Death. She sort of un-assigned me, but the damage was done. Plus, I'm kind of in limbo. The Vampires don't give a rat's ass I'm not plotting their downfall at the moment.

I'm still on their hit list—or more accurately, their "let's make her just like us" project roster.

Death had rescinded her No Reaping edict, and a few other promises, until I had no idea quite where I sat.

My breath made plumes in the frosty air. My long legs ate up distance quickly as I crossed in front of the hangars and small businesses that catered to pilots and our specific needs. A month had come—and gone—since I'd seen Death. Liam, a Sidhe I'd fought side-by-side with, had been absent as well.

He'd had to go back to the Old Country. He'd asked me to go with him, but unless I wanted *Carrick Sky Sports* to truly go into receivership, I'd had to remain here.

Probably for the best. I'd halfway fallen in love with him, but getting closer wasn't a good idea. He and I had both spent the entirety of our lives—his immortal and mine not quite so bombproof—by ourselves.

The familiar whine of an engine snapped my head upward. My mouth dropped open. The goddamned Citabria was back in the air. Why? She was a flying deathtrap. My phone started ringing, and I dug it out. Rick's number flared across my screen.

Before I could even say "hello," Rick was screeching in my ear. "That bastard just up and grabbed his plane. How bad was it, Cait?"

"Bad enough to not be in the air. What the fuck do you suppose—?" The whine turned to a squeal. Metal scraped against metal, and something with all the subtlety of a sonic boom sent me to my knees. The wing with the broken strut fell off, and the Citabria turned into a whirling fireball.

"Call the fire department," Rick yelled at someone.

I got my feet back under me. Phone still clutched in my hand, I did my best to judge the plane's trajectory. Spinning, falling almost straight down, it would explode again on impact. Anything it touched would go up with it.

Humans don't trust anything magical. Usually, I sheathe my power. For most of my life, I didn't realize I could do anything beyond create and hold a gateway for the dead. Liam changed all that. He opened my eyes—and my magic—much to Death's annoyance.

She liked it better when her Reapers maintained their focus on Reaping. None of this fancy-schmancy magical shit. The plane was dropping fast. Not much time. Certainly not enough for me to make my next moves look accidental. I hurried closer to the touchdown spot and shot magic ahead of me to form shielding over people and cars.

I'm stronger than I believed I was, but magic has limits. Mine were rapidly stretching to their endpoints. I wheezed from effort and dug deeper. Half a dozen people were screaming and running, but there was no way for them to move fast enough. Satisfied my shielding was as robust as I could make it, I focused on the burning mess that was the plane I'd been in not an hour before.

The detached wing hit the tarmac and crumpled to matchsticks on impact.

Feet firmly planted on the ground, I drew Earth magic, mixed it with huge gouts of air, and gave the Citabria a hefty shove to the north where nothing would be beneath it. I'd built the protective canopy first, in case my current maneuver failed.

Power arced from my extended hands. I wound it around the doomed plane and guided it to where it wouldn't hurt anyone. It smashed against the asphalt with enough force to dig a crater a couple of feet deep. More explosions rocked the ground.

For the second time in a few minutes, I staggered and fell, ears ringing from the noise. My mouth and throat were raw from panting, but the only casualty was Doug—and his poor airplane. I felt far worse for the Citabria than I did for the man stupid enough to take her upstairs.

Footsteps pounded toward me from all directions. The shrill beat of sirens filled the air. I cut the flow of my magic. It had done its job. Before anyone else reached me, I felt the chill of the grave descend. It had to be Doug.

I cracked my Reaper magic open, but only a little bit. Sure enough, he shambled into view. "If you think I'm going to help you cross," I hissed, "think again."

I'd be damned if I'd do zip shit squat for Doug. Let him find another Reaper.

He barreled toward me, singed and stinking of greasy

smoke. "You bitch," he snarled. "Everything was fine. Until you fucked it up."

"And just how did I do that?" Without waiting for an answer, I kept chugging along. "Safety first, bud. Or did you forget that part? We don't fly planes that aren't safe. And we don't foist them off on our associates, either."

I could have said more. A whole lot more, but I didn't.

He launched himself at me, but he was dead, and so he passed through me. I slammed my grave vision shut and thinned my Reaper power to the barest glimmer. I'd meant the part about him finding another gatekeeper.

He threw himself at me again. And then a third time, ending up sprawled on my other side. "I have to get out of here," he yelped. "You're my ticket."

"Some people's," I agreed. "Not yours." With a flick of my hand, I dismantled the canopy I'd constructed. The people trapped beneath it had been panicking. I'd felt their horror and fear through my casting.

I had no idea what Doug would do next. "Be a good ghost," I purred, infusing my next words with compulsion. "Go away."

"I can't," he wailed.

"First ghost ever who couldn't leave the place they died." I mocked him, certain I was right. "You sidestepped the wrath of the FAA. They'd probably have stripped you of your certifications, but you'll have a lot of time to think about it."

"You don't get it." He was still snarling, but now he sounded more pathetic than anything. The transition to being, well, dead, takes a while. Ghosts don't exactly embrace a change that means they'll never be able to do anything again—except talk with a Reaper.

So long as I'd thought about it, I added, "Doesn't matter what I understand, no one but me can see you."

The first fire truck squealed to a halt fifty yards from me. Men jumped down, hustled the hose off the truck, and sprayed fire retardant around the burning wreckage. Its astringent scent polished off what was left of my throat, leaving it even scratchier than it had been before.

Rick reached me and wound a big hand around my forearm. "Cait. Thank god you're all right. Who are you talking to?"

The old me would have demurred, said I was talking to myself, but I was done concealing who I was. Over a hundred people had witnessed me throwing magic about. Denying I could command power was disingenuous and stupid.

I twisted until I met his blue eyes. "I'm a Reaper. Doug was lobbying for a way through the veil. I refused."

Rick's fingers tightened around my arm. "Now is not a time for jokes, Cait. I know you've had a rough time here, but—"

"I'm not joking."

Something about my tone must have gotten through. He dropped my arm as if it had turned into something that would poison him and crooked two fingers into the sign against evil.

I screwed my mouth into a grimace. "Really? You drank the Kook-aid, huh?"

"What do you mean?" He was still looking at me as if I might suddenly sprout another head. Or horns.

"Did you sign on with Humans Rule?"

He looked at his feet. "I might have, but only because Doug talked me into it. He's a big muckety-muck in the local chapter."

Meanwhile, Doug had switched to throwing himself through Rick's body. He was clawing at him, shouting in his face, and telling him to shut up.

"What part about 'he can't hear you' didn't soak in?" I asked.

Rick shifted his gaze from side to side. "What's going on?"

"Nothing much. Doug just walked through you for maybe for sixth time, and—"

"Ick. Make him stop. I never liked him very well when he was alive, but this has a huge creep factor." Rick sounded freaked, his voice shrill, and jumped back a step.

"I have no control over him, but he can't hurt you. Or anyone else. He's a ghost. A spirit."

"Fine." Rick was doing his damnedest to appear stoic. I swear, being a man comes with a shit ton of baggage. I'd have sent a thread of calming magic his way if he hadn't admitted to being part of Humans Rule. On the surface of things, they're a bunch of bigots who want people like me locked away. If you dig deeper, they're a front for humans who want to sling illicit magic around.

I'm certain most HR members are like Rick, horrified by magic, but some of the more highly ranked folk are dabbling in it. Vampires traded with them: magical tricks for blood.

Humans were never meant to wield power, so it's a big fat problem for the rest of us.

A crowd was gathering. At least Doug had faded from view. Maybe his new position at the sub bottom of the totem pole was sinking in. It always did.

"Ms. Carrick." A man called my name. Turning toward him, I recognized the airport manager. Tall, spare, and dressed in gray slacks and a wrinkled white shirt, he trained solemn brown eyes on me. His hair was black and cropped short.

I inclined my head. "Mr. Johnson."

He extended a hand, and I shook it. "That was incredibly brave of you," he told me. "Most people would have run the other way."

Pleasure at the compliment warmed me. I hadn't exchanged two words with him after signing contracts allowing *Carrick Sky Sports* use of the runway.

"She did something," a youngish woman with red hair shouted.

"Trapped us with magic," another yelled.

Bill Johnson turned his attention toward them. "She protected you while she made certain the plane came down where it couldn't hurt you or anyone else." Before others jumped into the fray, he raised his voice and said, "Everyone here owes Ms. Carrick a huge thank you."

"Not necessary." I projected my voice as well. Maybe it wasn't the smartest thing to do, but I rolled my shoulders back and announced, "I used the magic that lives within me to make certain none of you were harmed. I'm a Reaper, and damn it feels good to stop hiding what I am."

"Why didn't you kill us?" someone called.

I swallowed back a sharp retort and jumped on my first opportunity since the 1800s to educate humans. "Reaping isn't like that. I hold the gates for newly dead to cross over. We don't kill anyone."

Except maybe Vampires, but I didn't feel compelled to add that part. Besides, they didn't count since they were already dead.

The adrenaline was fading. Being a hero has never been high on my list. Before anyone got any ideas about a longer conversation, I threaded my way through the crowd, still intent on at least stopping by my office. Xavier had probably come and gone by now. Or maybe the crash had been on the news, and he'd turned around and headed back into Seattle. The strip would be shut down for at least long enough to clear the wreckage from the Citabria and patch the hole it had made in the runway.

I'd broken a few rules, the biggest of which was revealing what I was. Death didn't want us outed. As I covered the few hundred yards to my Quonset hut, my thoughts were a jumbled mess.

I'd check my messages and head home. Probably, I'd teleport. The last thing I needed to deal with was rush hour traffic. I skipped hunting for my keys and sent a shot of magic at my locked door. It sprang open, showering me with the decayed, rotten stench of Vampires.

Fuck. Crap. Damn it all to hell. There should be a quota for how many bad things happen to one Reaper in a single day.

The air near me shimmered and glistened. I unclenched

my fists and untangled my bag from around my neck. I knew who was coming, and at least her timing was good. Sure enough, Death sashayed through a silver-rimmed portal. Leather pants and a long leather tunic fit her like a second skin. Lace up high-heeled boots encased her lower legs. Her silver hair was loose and hung to knee level. A blood-red gemstone I hadn't seen before glittered from where it hung around her neck, and an ever-changing collage of the dead and dying played across her eyes.

"Come on." She clapped her hands smartly together.

"Come on, where?" I asked.

"Let's go get 'em." Without waiting to see if I'd follow like the obedient puppy she imagined me, Death surged into my office right into the middle of a pack of Vampires.

I might not want to Reap Vampires, but letting them run around free was far worse. Before Death could yell for me again, I warded myself and charged after her.

CHAPTER TWO, LIAM

I called my mage light closer to better illuminate a scroll spread across a dusty desk. The radiant globe—more blue than white—complied, but reluctantly. If I didn't know better, I'd have believed it missed Ireland as much as I did. The Sidhe had lived In Scourie, a hamlet on the northwestern coast of Scotland, long ago. Our castle dated back to 1200, and age hadn't improved it.

Its primary draw was no one lived anywhere close, which made it a perfect choice for our current needs.

We had to bide somewhere, and we'd burned more than a few bridges in Malin, an Irish village where we'd resided until our abrupt relocation. It hadn't been fair to continue to put Malin's residents at risk. Vampires had killed close to forty of them, not so much because of the Sidhe, but because of Cait Carrick, a Reaper assigned to keep them in check.

By tricking them into crossing the veil.

Something tantalizing hovered between Cait and I, and it

ran deeper than facing a common enemy. Her magic slotted nicely with my own—once she'd claimed a generous piece she hadn't realized existed. Ripping the lid off that can had done a stellar job alienating Death, but Cait deserved access to the full range of her power.

Not much point in explaining her Vampire assignment to Malin's villagers, though. As far as they were concerned, dead was dead. No reasons in the world would return their loved ones to them. I was certain they'd been glad to see the Sidhe leave. Our move wasn't permanent, but we'd be gone long enough to get the Vampire problem under better control than it was at the moment.

What about the dark gods and Humans Rule? An implacable inner voice nudged me.

Aye, well perhaps we'd be in Scourie a wee bit longer than my original estimate. As in we could be stuck here for a good long while. We had yet to untangle the complicated relationship between Vampires, half a dozen black magic wielding mages, and Humans Rule. Ostensibly HR was an in-your-face anti-magic coalition of humans, but some of them were slinging power about on the sidelines courtesy of an assist from black magic and Vampires.

Breath whistled through my teeth. I unclenched my jaw and returned my attention to the scroll. We needed a coordinated plan, which was why I was buried in old scrolls. The more we knew about Vamps and the dark gods, the better equipped we'd be to defeat them. Most of our library was still in Ireland. It posed a few logistics problems, but nothing that couldn't be addressed with a judicious application of magic.

I rubbed my eyes. The spidery runic script in front of me was starting to swim together. It came back into focus. Not many treatises on Vampires. Those I had found were old enough to be penned in languages that had fallen out of use centuries ago.

Material on the dark gods was even harder to unearth. Some enterprising soul had turned them into comic book characters around the late 1990s, comingling fact with fiction until truth became impossible to tease out.

I might long to get back to Cait, but my duty to the Sidhe came first.

She and I had exchanged emails over the last month, but the old Sidhe castle lacked anything resembling either cell service or Wi-Fi. She was too far away for telepathy, so the only time I could communicate with her was when I went into the village proper—or teleported back to Malin.

I slapped the open scroll with the palm of one hand, willing it to hustle and provide answers faster. Dust plumed, filling the air, and half of the page crackled into tiny bits. I reassembled them with magic. Once I was certain the ancient document would hold together, I pushed my chair back from the desk I'd been working at and got to my feet.

Frustration was getting the better of me. That and a need to reconnect with Cait. Surely, she missed me...

I grimaced. Maybe she did, and maybe she didn't. Her last few emails had held a decidedly impersonal tone, almost as if she'd fallen back on us being comrades in arms.

We were, but I wanted ever so much more.

Walking out of the basement room where I'd holed up, I trotted toward the nearest staircase. I could have teleported, but I'd been sitting so long my arse had practically glued itself to the damn chair.

I've never liked this castle, even when it was our chief base of operations, and age hasn't been kind to the structure. Older and moldier than when we abandoned it, it was cold and drafty. Scarcely the type of place I would have picked to sit out a storm, much less set up shop.

"Stop whining," I mumbled and made a sour face.

The windswept moors and steep cliffs surrounding our current abode have never been much of a draw for mortals. To ensure our privacy, we'd planted rumors the region was haunted. Despite being a superstitious lot, sheepherders had plied these hills back in the day, probably because grazing land was cheap. But even they'd moved away, seeking proximity to larger towns.

The sooner we eliminated the Vampires, the sooner I'd be free to return to Malin. Or maybe to Seattle to deepen my fledgling relationship with Cait. She might be backing away because we hadn't seen one another in several weeks.

I preferred that explanation to any other, and I piled other reasons on top of it. Chronic loners, she and I would naturally gravitate toward being by ourselves. Solitude had been a comfort zone through the lengthy years of our lives. Reapers aren't immortal like the Sidhe, but they live a long time.

If I had my way, I'd weave a Sidhe spell and see if I couldn't push her longevity in the immortal direction. But I was getting way ahead of everything. Myriad things could have happened in the weeks we'd been apart—from her deciding she didn't like me as well as I thought, to her meeting someone else.

Besides, my arguments were riddled with holes. I wasn't pining for solitude, and I'd totally bypassed the thorny issues of both the dark mages and Humans Rule. Vampires were only part of the problem, and probably not the biggest one. They'd never been all that bright under their pretty faces and knockout bodies.

Even if they all vanished in the sweep of a fantastic, knock-your-socks-off spell I had yet to come up with, I still wouldn't be free to pursue Cait. Maybe waiting until I'd totally cleared the decks of all the problems facing us wasn't realistic. By then Cait would have forgotten my name.

How long had it been since I'd visited the village with its scattering of hotels and an Internet café? Several days, at least. Once I dug into a project, I liked to keep chipping away at it. In this instance, no end was in sight. The more I read about Vampires, the less I liked them. One thing was abundantly clear, though. Eliminating them entirely would be nearly impossible.

They could make new Vamps faster than we could kill off the existing ones. Brand new Vampires needed the older ones to corral their bloodlust. It took years to learn to control that aspect of their makeup. My take-home message was sobering. If we chopped a broad swathe through the seasoned Vampires, the only ones left would be those who didn't pay attention to anything except sating the heat in their black, black souls.

Aye, they still possessed souls, but, according to Cait, they were riddled with rot.

I'd crested the stone steps long since, and I strode down the long central hall. Rooms opened to both sides with fires crackling at a dozen hearths. Fireplaces in old castles aren't terribly efficient. Most of the heat goes right up the chimney, but seeing the merry blazes was heartening.

"There you are," a voice called from behind me.

I turned and waited for Padhraic. Up until about a fortnight ago, he'd been a Leanan—the Vampire version of the Sidhe. The rest of his ilk were buried in a pit that I hoped held them forever.

Eh, forever was a long time for immortals. If it held them long enough to dispatch the Earth-bound Vampires, I'd be satisfied.

Roughly my six foot four height, Padhraic had abundant dark hair trimmed to shoulder level. An old-fashioned blue-and-green-and-black tartan wrapped around his body, covering an undyed linen shirt. He wasn't as thin as he'd been when he was a Vampire, so his new diet of food rather than blood must be agreeing with him. He smiled, and his silver eyes crinkled at the corners.

"Here I am," I agreed. "Why were you looking for me?"

His smile slipped a notch. "Um, it's your turn to keep an eye on me."

I've had lots of experience holding onto a poker face. Good thing. Padhraic was still fairly fragile, and I didn't want to out and out tell him I'd forgotten about him. It had taken the rest of us two passes to strip him of his fangs and the Vampire parts of his nature. The casting had been hard on him, but he'd kept up his end of the bargain.

No matter how much pain we'd caused him—and

there'd been times when he'd been in agony as we carved up his magical center and reshaped it—he'd never complained.

I clapped him across the shoulders. "Feel like a jaunt into the village?"

His face brightened. "I'd love one, but are you certain you trust me around mortals? I haven't left the castle since you brought me here."

"Do you trust yourself, mate?" I draped a subtle truth net over him and waited.

Frown lines formed between his thick, black brows, and he rocked from foot to foot. "I think so. I'd expected more in the way of blood hunger, but it seems to be gone."

His words beeped cleanly off my spell, so at least he believed his own hype. It was a start. "We'll take it slow," I told him. "A nice cuppa in a café, and then back here. Grab some footwear and meet me out front."

"Are we teleporting?"

I shook my head. "Driving. We're keeping overt displays of magic to an absolute minimum. No reason to alert the locals to our supernatural aspects."

Padhraic squeezed one eye shut as he made a face.

"What?" I nailed him with the question. My jaunt into Scourie would pull double duty. Emailing Cait and supporting Padhraic. It wasn't as if he could hole up in one Sidhe fortress or another for the next fifty years. He needed to jump back on the horse and figure things out.

"Humans recognize we're not like them. Even if we hide behind a glamour, we don't feel the same."

"How do you know?" I asked.

He raked curved fingers through his hair. "For obvious

reasons, I spent a lot of time talking with mortals while I was a Leanan. I needed to forge relationships with them to feed. We're not like the Earth-bound Vamps, who kill those they don't turn. We form an alliance with a mortal and remain affiliated with them..."

Color blotched his cheeks, darkening his fair skin. He sucked in a breath, nostrils flaring. "The bargain was for a year. At the end of it, the mortal was free to go. Most of them did, but a few wished to remain."

"What did you do?" I'd never known much about the inner workings of the Leanan for the best of reasons. The idea of any Sidhe taking to Vampirism disgusted me.

"Forced them to go," Padhraic said in a low voice. "I didn't begin that way. But I found out soon enough that mortal women turned into monsters if they overstayed their allotted time."

I slitted my eyes his way. "Monsters as in they became Vamps?"

"Aye, and they ran off and joined the Earth-bound type of Vampire, except they were stronger in many ways. They were the first to teach other Vampires how to walk in daylight and enter homes at will.

"'Twas a slow process," he continued. "So slow as to be barely noticeable for many a long year. By the time the rest of us threw our lot in with the other Vampires, the die was cast."

The already chilly hall grew colder still. Standing about discussing Vampire comings and goings made me wish they'd all die miserable deaths. I had lots of questions, now that Padhraic was in a sharing mood, but they could wait.

Perhaps once we returned he'd become a valuable asset to help with my research project.

I'd been hoping for a foolproof casting that would immobilize every Vampire on Earth at the same time—before they could panic and make new ones. Clearly, I'd need to lower my standards. The question was by how much.

"Meet you outside," I repeated and sprinted toward the imposing front doors. Twelve feet high and crafted of heavy timbers banded with iron, they'd been built to withstand a siege. Being careful to avoid touching the metal, I slid the wooden bar out of its holder and laid it aside.

Once freed, one of the doors opened on its own. We'd trained the castle to sense us when we first lived here. Apparently, it hadn't forgotten. I trotted down a series of broad flagstone steps and made my way to the carriage house. Some of the wagons were still usable, but we'd left all our horses in Malin, turning them over to the village stables.

Most Sidhe don't care for driving. I'm the odd exception. In the time since we'd moved here, I'd come up with an aged BMW sedan. It had a few dings and dents but was mechanically sound. By the time Padhraic emerged from the castle, I'd started the engine and driven around to the front doors.

He jumped nimbly inside, smiling. "Thanks for trusting me."

"Don't be too quick to thank me. This trip to town is self-serving on my part." I dropped the car into gear and started for the rusted wrought iron gates. Much like the castle doors, they opened and closed on their own.

Padhraic didn't question me. Perhaps he wasn't certain he'd like my answers. Regardless, we didn't speak until after I'd parked the car. The tiny hamlet was quiet. With winter approaching, days were quite short this far north. Tourists who flocked to Scotland's Highlands and islands in the summer had moved on to putting up holiday decorations at home.

All the buildings date back at least fifty years with many double that age. I led the way up a set of rickety wooden risers and into a cheery café. "Who's your mate, Liam?" a well-rounded woman swathed in an enormous white apron called from behind the low counter. Her gray hair had been tucked into a neat bun, and her blue eyes gleamed with curiosity.

Not many strangers visited Scourie outside tourist season.

Padhraic touched the top of his head as if he wore a hat and inclined his head. "Padhraic McGleen, ma'am. I'm Liam's cousin. Pleased to make your acquaintance."

I quested about for her name and came up with Deidre, but I'd let her introduce herself.

"Och. Another Irish," she exclaimed. "Well, I'm Deidre, and it looks as if I'll have to start stocking Connemara for the two of you."

"Whatever you have will be wonderful." Padhraic smiled disarmingly. "Never had a bad cuppa."

Deidre turned and busied herself with tea leaves and hot water. Midway through filling two generous white ceramic mugs, she twisted and glanced my way. "Shame on me, I didn't ask. You'll be wanting the usual, right?"

I nodded and took stock of the small selection of bakery goods in the display case. “Anything look good to you?” I asked Padrhaic.

“It all does. Just get two of whatever you’re having.”

I motioned him to join me toward the back of the medium-sized tearoom and sat in front of a computer. Deidre kept three terminals for customers. They were connected via ethernet. No wireless in this café, although some of the hotels had Wi-Fi servers.

Padhraic settled next to me. I’d rather he sat across, but I didn’t have anything particular to hide. “How’s that Reaper?” he asked, keeping his voice pitched very low. The café was empty other than us, but it paid to be cautious.

Shrugging, I said, “I’m about to find out.”

A few keystrokes got me into one of several email accounts I keep. Scattered amidst the junk mail were three messages from Cait. The first two were newsy. Reading between the lines, she hadn’t had any problems with Vamps or Humans Rule. *Carrick Sky Sports* was doing well enough to break even this month. Death hadn’t shown up since I left, and Cait wasn’t expecting her.

She referred to Death as “my boss,” but I knew who she meant.

Toward the bottom of email number two, she asked why she hadn’t heard from me. Guilt jabbed me in the gut. She hadn’t heard from me because I’m an inconsiderate sod.

Padhraic tapped the screen. “I’m beginning to understand what we’re doing in town. Why haven’t you kept in better touch with her?” He turned the full force of his silver gaze on me. I saw him for what he was, but it's because I can pierce his glamour.

Deidre bustled our way with a generous tray. After leaving two steaming cups, sugar, cream, a teapot, and a plate of assorted cookies and cakes, she hurried back toward her kitchen. "Be sure and let me know when you're ready for more," she called over one shoulder.

The tea was too hot to drink, so I went hunting for my last email to Cait. Shock buffeted me. Had it really been ten days since I'd written to her? I turned my hands palms up. "Time got away from me. We need Wi-Fi at the castle."

Padhraic snorted and picked up one of the mugs, blowing on its surface. "Some endeavors are beyond the reach of magic. I suspect that's one of them." He took a slurpy sip of tea, said "Damn, that's good," and regarded me through slitted eyes. "You care for her, right?"

"I do. Not much has passed between us. The first little while, we danced around one another. She didn't trust me, and I'd never spent enough time around Reapers to know what to expect."

No reason to tell him we'd gotten off on the wrong foot because I'd lied to her about who I was and why I'd shown up at *Carrick Sky Sports*. The way events fell out, her suspicion of me had been a good thing. It saved us both from landing in the midst of a Vampire onslaught.

Too bad the mortals in the vicinity hadn't been quite as fortunate.

I opened the last email. Three times longer than the others, it described an incident at the airfield, one where another pilot had knowingly loaned her a defective plane. I ground my teeth, determined to kill the bastard until I read further and discovered he was already dead.

She'd refused him passage across the veil.

Good for her.

"What are you going to do, mate?" Padhraic asked.

I shook my head. "About what? He's dead."

"Not that. This." He pointed at the last few paragraphs, which I hadn't yet read.

I focused on them.

ONCE I FINALLY GOT BACK TO my office, my boss showed up. I figured it was because I'd nearly died. Or maybe because I'd come out of the closet about what I am. That was until I kicked my door open, and we waded into the midst of a huge fight with Vs. If it weren't for that trick my boss has where she just kind of sucks them up like a vacuum cleaner, we'd have been hurting.

As it is, she's as depleted as I've ever seen her. I'm doing some cleanup around here, and then I'll head home.

I know you're busy, but is there any way you could break loose for a couple of days? I'm not feeling very optimistic. This last batch of Vs were, eh, I don't quite know how to describe them.

Vicious. Single-minded. They weren't after my boss, but after me. I'm wondering if there's not some connection between the dude who owned the plane that crashed and the V attack. They were so close timewise, it can't have been a coincidence.

I'm certain they'll return, and sooner rather than later. My boss might not show up because she's not very happy with me.

And now I'm rambling. Let me hear from you, please, either way. If you can't get here, I'll need to make other plans.

CC

~

I DID a quick check of the date. Yesterday. Not as bad as I'd feared. And then I added a time correction and came up with another few hours. I typed quickly, told her I'd be there as soon as I could, and signed off. That done, I exited my session on the café's computer.

Padhraic had inhaled his half of the bakery goodies. I didn't have much of an appetite, but I slogged through the rest of them. It would hurt Deidre's feelings if any were left. Once I'd washed everything down with tea, I said, "Best get you back to the castle."

"You could take me with you," Padhraic said. "And I mean to the States."

My eyes widened. The thought hadn't occurred to me. "Not without clearing it with the others," I told him firmly. Catching a lift into town was one thing, teleporting across an ocean quite another.

He gripped my forearm. "I want to come." Switching to telepathy, he added, *"I understand Vampires a whole lot better than any of you—because I was one. If they're waging war on Cait, you need me."*

I dredged a few pound notes from my jacket pocket and slapped them on the table before I stood. Padhraic followed me out of the tearoom. He didn't say anything else. He didn't have to. He'd pitched his case. What happened next was up to me and the other Sidhe.

By the time we turned in at the castle gates, I'd made up my mind. Bringing Padhraic was a risk, but when could I start trusting him? If not now, would tomorrow work? How about next year?

We'd shackled his teleport ability—for obvious reasons. If he came with me, we'd have to correct that. I pulled the car into the carriage house and turned to him.

"No promises. I'll have a quick chat with as many council members as I can find."

"Thanks, mate. I appreciate it more than I can—"

"Save your words," I snapped. "If the others agree about you being restored to your full power and you fuck me over, I will hunt you through this world and whatever other ones you run to."

A corner of his mouth twitched into a somber smile. "You're forgetting something, Liam. I know you. Once we were as close as brothers."

I got out of the car. So did he. "Aye, and that niggling point bothers me," I muttered. "As in fuck me once, shame on you—"

"There won't be a twice," he said and loped toward the castle.

I considered yelling after him to ready himself to leave—just in case—but I knew him too. And it was precisely what he'd be doing.

When the rubber met the road, he understood all too well I couldn't resist his inside-track information, bits and pieces that could well mean the difference between success or failure the next time Vampires surrounded Cait.

If Death's appearance yesterday had been accidental, Cait might not fare so well next time. Determined to get my part of this show moving, I raised my mind voice and called for Krin, Dena, and a few of the other higher ranking Sidhe. If they weren't in ready agreement about Padhraic accompanying me, I'd go by myself.

CHAPTER THREE, CAIT

A *Few Hours Earlier*

It was dark before Vampires stopped leaching out of the walls and the floor and through my open office door. I was almost too trashed to recognize the irony of nighttime bringing the end of a Vampire siege, rather than the beginning. Death sank to her knees, sucking air in panting gasps that worried the living fuck out of me.

She was a goddess. How could she have run her magic down to fumes?

I tried to come up with a question she wouldn't react negatively to and finally gave up. There's no politically correct method of asking someone who outranks you how much magic they have left.

Especially someone like Death.

I sent a jet of magic to shut my door and switch on the overheads. And then I worked my way through piles of fallen Vampires, pushing what was left of their souls past the gates that seal the realm of the dead off from Earth. It was hard work, like I was struggling uphill on sand that kept collapsing beneath my weight.

The half-light of the nether world pushed against me, not welcoming for once. I kept going anyway.

Thank all the bloody damned gods Death had managed a gateway for maybe the first half of them. Once they were out of the way—and the flood just kept on rolling—she probably began to conserve her power. Not that these Vamps hadn't already been dead, but their souls milled around my office like displaced moths. Instead of battering themselves against my bank of fluorescents, they ran into each other. And me.

They gave Death a wide berth.

A blistering sigh rattled from her, and she pushed upright. "Are you nearly done?"

No "gosh, we did good work here," or "how are you doing, Cait?" Death was all business. She wanted to be finished here, but for that to happen, she needed to obliterate the stacks of bones that decorated my floor, turning my office into something that looked like a meat-packing plant.

They stank of decay and mold and rot, but my nose had quit reacting to the stench hours ago.

"Cait?" Death's voice cut like a whip, making me flinch beneath its implacable tones.

I scanned the Quonset hut and took stock. "Yeah. Almost done. Just two more groups." I tried to sprint and gave it up for as quick a shamble as I could manage. It's easier to dispatch reluctant souls when I'm touching the bodies they vacated.

Or in this case, the bones. Vampires mostly leave bones since they revert to what their bodies would have turned into after a few hundred years of being dead. Only the younger ones have much in the way of remains.

Time ticked past. Maybe another half hour before I reeled in my Reaper magic. My vision swirled back to normal. I nodded Death's way to let her know my job was complete. A month ago, she'd forbidden me from Reaping at all, and then she'd rescinded her edict. The last time I'd questioned her, she told me I'd misunderstood.

Ha! As if any part of "no more Reaping" wasn't crystal clear.

She given me hope and then jerked the rug out from under me. The situation annoyed me so much, I kept my mouth shut. Neither she nor I were at our best right now. So far, we'd avoided an argument, but that could change in a New York second.

Magic flared from her as she rounded up Vampire carcasses until they were stacked from floor to ceiling in two mounds. I was pretty sure what was coming next, and she didn't disappoint me. Mage fire crackled from her fingertips, and both piles ignited. They'd burn quick and clean with very little smoke and zero residue.

That type of magical fire was a neat trick. I wondered if it was one Liam could teach me. It was a sure bet Death wouldn't. Once the pyres were well underway, the place Death had stood shimmered to nothingness.

"Goodbye to you too," I called to the empty room.

I strode to my door and opened it. There wasn't much smoke, but I wanted every shred of Vampire residue out of my office. I killed the overhead lights. My night vision is excellent, and my eyes felt hot and gritty and strained. While the fires reduced themselves to nothing, I sat in front of my computer and brought it out of sleep mode.

Liam hadn't answered either of my last two emails. Phooey. Maybe all my worries about us getting too close were just me spinning my wheels. Our brief romantic interlude had been real enough, but anything beyond the kiss and dinner we'd shared was looking more like wishful thinking on my part than reality. He sure wasn't acting like a man who was smitten. Sheesh. His last email had been something like nine days ago. No, ten.

I'd have called him, but he doesn't own a cell phone. Besides, where he is in Scotland doesn't have cell service. Cripes. Who doesn't have a phone these days?

Didn't matter. I'd already begun typing. It was cathartic, but I was careful not to reveal too much. Cyberspace was easily hacked. So I called Death my boss and used a V to denote Vamps. Because I had no idea who else I might turn to, I asked for his help but couched it in a way he could easily demur.

My fingers stilled. I'd run out of words, and I scanned what was on my display before clicking send. The hard truth was Reapers didn't have magical buddies. Death showed up when I needed her, but something huge and irreparable had changed in our relationship.

That something was when Liam made certain I understood I'd barely tapped the surface of my magical potential. Death had been furious with him for removing my blinders. She probably still was. Regardless, she'd forbidden me to tell any other Reapers.

Like who would I tell? In Death's army, we all worked alone. I recognized most of the other Reapers, but it was rare for me to run into others like me.

I put the computer back to sleep and rubbed the heels of my hands down my face. I was tired. I needed to go home and try to rest. My relationship with Death would never be the same. I didn't fully understand why she'd shown up today—unless it was to read me the riot act because I'd said the word Reaper out loud in front of a crowd of people.

That type of thing gets her attention fast.

The more I thought about it, the surer I was that I was onto something. My big mouth had placed her where I needed her, but if I'd followed Reaper Rule #14 and kept my trap shut, I'd have been on my own battling all those Vampires.

I'd have called for her, but she might not have arrived in time.

From her way of looking at it, Vamps capturing me could be a veiled blessing. It would ensure my knowledge about the extent of Reapers' hidden magic died with the last of my humanity. Once Vampires turned me, the last thing I'd care about was Reaping.

A shudder racked me, followed by several more.

The twin pyres had winked out. Past time for me to leave. As I summoned a teleport spell, I remembered what Liam had taught me about how to mask my destination, and built strong warding into my casting. If someone had told me I'd learn more about magic from a Sidhe than from Death, I'd have laughed in their face.

But that was a while back.

What if Liam didn't answer me? His lack of communication might have nothing to do with him changing his mind about me. Something bad could have happened in Scotland.

"And then, what?" I muttered. My business was turning a profit because I'd actually been front and center to run things this past month. If I raced off to Scotland, *Carrick Sky Sports* wouldn't fare as well.

Again.

One month in the black was welcome, but it didn't erase all the months I'd sustained a loss.

I told myself not to borrow trouble. I needed to wait at least a day or two. If I still didn't hear from Liam, then I could decide what to do next. Meanwhile, if I didn't get some food into me and a few hours' sleep, I wouldn't be good for anything except staring into space like a zombie.

Something poked at the edges of my casting. I blinked stupidly, certain I was imagining it. After today's carnage, there couldn't possibly be any Vampires left within a hundred mile radius. I waited, hands raised, magic flowing.

Not very fast or very strong, mind you, but I couldn't afford to be picky.

I didn't have much juice left after all those broken souls had passed through me. Newly dead mortals enrich me. Vampires are a total soul suck. Maybe because they've been dead for so long. Maybe because they're just plain evil.

Regardless, I felt as if I'd been licking the bottom of a parakeet cage.

Cautious with my newly uncovered magic—since I didn't understand how to employ it very well—I sorted out a seeking thread to track whatever was dicking with my spell. It tangled with my teleport casting until I couldn't tell one from the other.

Fuck.

My chest hurt when breath whistled from my lungs. So did my throat. I'd inhaled too many toxic fumes from the Citabria—and the Vampires. The combination had left my nose and throat raw and scratchy.

I reeled in all my magic. The effort left me shaky—and told me how worn-out I was. Sheesh. I'd even left my shoulder bag next to the door instead of wrapping it around my body. It felt like another lifetime when I'd dropped it on my way inside to take on the Vampires.

Trudging to the door, I snatched up my bag. Before I could dissect my next moves, I walked out the door and shut it behind me, tossing the deadbolt into place and the key into my bag. My aged Toyota SUV was parked around the corner next to the hangar that houses my three airplanes. I never locked my car—in hopes someone would steal it, and I could collect on the insurance—but I'd have to alter that practice.

Or not. Locks never deterred anyone with even a flicker of power, and mortals didn't worry me. Not even the zealots in Humans Rule.

I scanned the darkness with magic and my scratchy eyes. I was jumpy as a cornered alley cat, but nothing untoward showed itself. Even though I was almost certain I was alone, part of me was surprised when I made it into my vehicle without incident.

My heart thudded hard against my chest, and my breath came in little panting gasps. I locked myself in and wrapped my fingers around the steering wheel so hard my knuckles turned white.

"Get a grip," I muttered. If I was this spun out over nothing, what chance would I have if a real bogeyman showed up?

I set my bag on the passenger seat and fished around for my keys. Once I located them, I started the engine and nosed the car toward home. It wouldn't be nearly as fast as teleporting, but at least nothing magical could interfere with the Toyota's engine.

Magic and mechanical items didn't play well together.

My phone pinged and beeped and chimed. I ignored it. The shape I was in, I didn't dare take my attention off the road. Traffic in the Seattle area is hideous. There is almost no time of any day when my drive to or from the airfield doesn't involve at least one stretch of road where traffic has come to a complete and total halt. Sometimes it takes a quarter hour for it to get moving again.

My heart rate was settling back to normal. I popped a lemon drop into my mouth to help with my abraded throat and did my damnedest not to think about anything. I couldn't fix my shattered relationship with Death. I couldn't suddenly become an expert with my brand new magical ability. I had no way to find out what was going on with Liam.

I shook my head and loosened my death grip on the wheel. Pretty pathetic that I had almost no friends. No one I could call and chat up about my current spate of problems. A few mortals know what I am—eh, maybe more than a few after my performance earlier—but none of them actually understood what a Reaper does.

They got it that my power was wound up with what happened after a person died, but the whole topic wasn't something anyone bought up in polite company. It's not like the olden days when mortals had plenty of rituals surrounding death and dying. Nope. Modern humans expended hundreds of millions of dollars on doctors and medicines in an attempt to stave off the inevitable.

They died anyway, despite pulling out all the stops.

After putting up a pitched battle to avoid being Reaped, they scarcely welcomed me. It's not accidental more ghosts roamed Earth, but the longer they remained, the more confused they became. Nemed—leader of the third race to occupy Ireland—was an exception, but from what Liam had said, he'd been an extraordinary man.

I got off the freeway and wound my way toward my houseboat. My slip included two parking spots. Good thing. Otherwise, I'd never have anywhere to leave either my SUV or my car. Street parking costs money, and I'd easily blow through more than I made.

Not that I make all that much.

Flying can be lucrative, but I had to be front and center every day to teach people how to fly, rent out planes—but only to carefully vetted pilots—or take care of the occasional load of freight that exceeded someone else's weight and balance allotment.

I slipped the SUV into its too-narrow space and killed the engine. Once I had the keys and my bag, I hesitated before unlocking the car. And kicked myself roundly. I had to live in this world, goddammit. Living didn't include skulking in shadows expecting Vampires or evil mages to make an end run that would erode my freedom.

Or finish my life.

After a few steadying breaths, I got out of my car—locking it behind me—and covered the ground to my houseboat. I'd resurrect my warding as soon as I was inside. Lights from other houseboats and the street beat back the night, made it feel less intimidating. Not that I've ever been afraid of the dark.

But bad things walked at night.

"And in the daytime," I said out loud just to make certain I was clear about that. A quick fumble produced more keys, and I let myself inside, dropping my bag in its usual spot in my tiny mudroom.

I had a whole lot to do. Instead, I stood rooted in place, too dead on my feet to even start the process of warding my home.

"Come on," I urged and rolled my eyes. Had it come down to having to cheerlead myself?

I started from scratch and began the incantation to seal out the rest of the magical world. My power was sluggish, slow to respond, but I can be determined. No matter how many times I had to start over, there'd be no food or rest for me until I'd made myself as safe as I could.

Finally, after the third time my spell frittered to streamers around me, I visualized it as bricks and stacked them one atop the next until I had a wall. For whatever reason, it worked. The small electrical zing of the casting snapping shut was music to my ears.

And my soul.

Sweat slicked my sides and dripped down my forehead despite the fifty degree temperature inside my home. One thing about living on the water is it's usually cold. And damp.

I flipped the switch on an electric heater set in the far wall. Each room had one. If all of them were engaged, it ate an ungodly amount of electricity—and money—but at least I was warm.

Moving slowly, I passed through my living room into my tiny kitchen. I'm not much of a cook. Never have been. A quick look in the freezer yielded a choice of pot stickers, pizza, or a couple of varieties of frozen dinners. Going for comfort food, I unwrapped a meatloaf dinner and popped it into the oven.

While it cooked, I stopped by my bedroom and stripped out of my clothing. Spattered with blood and gore and stinking of Vampire, everything needed a couple of turns through the washing machine. I'd have chucked them, but new clothes weren't free, even from the thrift store.

I squeezed my eyes shut. Money was a perpetual problem, but when had I developed this unholy focus on my finances? It made no sense. So what if my business went under? I'd start over somewhere else. When you lived as long as I did, nothing was permanent.

I might enjoy running my aeronautics venture, but constant pressure to make ends meet eroded the joy I felt when I sat behind a yoke. It was as good a place as any to turn my brain off. I dropped my clothes into the washing machine and stepped into the shower. By the time I was clean, my dinner was done.

It might be premade and chockful of chemicals to make it smell as good as it did, but so what? I wrapped my dripping hair in a thick white towel, my body in a threadbare terrycloth robe, and plucked my supper from the oven.

Nowhere to sit in the teensy kitchen, so I carried my bounty to the card table pushed into a corner of my living room. A quick return to the fridge for a beer, and I settled in to eat, congratulating myself for holding onto the pleasant blankness that kept me from thinking about anything.

It held a Zen aspect. No past, no future. Just now. A reluctant grin split my face as I envisioned myself holding my hands over my ears and chanting, lalalalala.

My plate—actually, the aluminum pan that had held my dinner—emptied out fast. The next time I picked up my beer bottle, it was empty too. I remembered all those beeps and chimes when I'd been driving and got up, intent on checking my phone.

Just in case there was something I had to attend to.

So much for my "live in the now" mindset. Someday, I wouldn't own *Carrick Sky Sports*, but as long as I did, I had an ethical obligation to my clients and students.

After a mental eye roll, I lurched to my feet and headed for my bag. Phone in hand, I sank to the sofa and started in on my emails and messages. Damn, but there were a lot of them. None from Liam. Double damn. I was worried about him and trying not to envision the many things that might have gone wrong. I'd respond to the emails come morning. It was pushing midnight. No one expected me to be quite that driven.

Pep talk about ethics aside, my main motivation had been to see if Liam had responded. No reason why he would have. I'd only written a couple of hours back. Maybe three. He couldn't intuit my email was waiting. Magic didn't work like that.

But what about the other emails I sent?

I shushed my inner voice. Neither of the earlier ones had requested a reply.

I'd worked my way around to messages. I wasn't certain why, but my finger hesitated over the green square with the white cloud floating in its center. Telling myself I was being ridiculous, I tapped it smartly.

Messages scrolled past. My eyes widened, and the world slowed until it may as well have stopped. I scrunched my eyes shut, but when I opened them, the messages were still there.

Yeah, where would they have gone?

They ran the gamut from, "Die, bitch," to "Brave woman," to, "We know who you are now."

What in the hell did the bit about knowing who I was mean?

I set the phone aside and dropped my head into my hands. Maybe Death's prohibition about outing ourselves had its roots in something deeper than her being a control freak. It didn't matter. I couldn't undo what I'd done. People had snapped pictures of me. They were all over social media and attached to some of the messages.

I couldn't run far enough to escape. Earth wasn't that big a place. I didn't have enough magic to construct and hold a glamour 24/7. From its abandoned spot next to me, my phone rang. I stared at it as if it had grown tentacles but snatched it up.

I'd be goddamned if I'd go into hiding.

"Cait Carrick," I barked.

"Oh good," a rich female voice purred. "I was afraid you wouldn't answer."

"I almost didn't. Who are you?"

"Someone just like you. Can we meet?"

I shook my head to clear my jumbled thoughts. "What? You're a Reaper?"

The connection clicked off. I stared at the screen where "private number" had flashed moments before. I couldn't call her back. Had it been wrong to utter Reaper out loud?

Confused. Tapped out. Beyond caring about much of anything, I switched my phone to airplane mode and tottered down the short hall, turning out lights as I went. If the mystery caller wanted me badly enough, she'd call back.

If she didn't, I had plenty to deal with without one more layer of complexity.

CHAPTER FOUR, LIAM

When I returned to my chamber, Padhraic was waiting for me. He'd changed from his tartan into dark slacks, a blue shirt, and a cable knit ivory sweater. A black jacket was slung over one shoulder and scuffed boots graced his feet. His black hair had been gathered into a thick queue low on his neck.

He'd been perched on the edge of the room's only chair, but he bolted upright, an expectant look on his face, as soon as I swung through the door.

"You're in," I told him, "but with caveats."

"You were gone so long, I figured there'd be some. It's all right." He rolled his shoulders straighter and kept his unwavering gaze trained on my face. "What I did was worse than wrong. That I clung to my poor choice as long as I did was unconscionable. Allowing me to return was generous."

He stopped there, clearly waiting to hear what restraints the Sidhe council had imposed. He was correct about me being gone a while. Arguments had flown fast and loose. Tempers had run to boiling. In the end, Padhraic's inclusion had hinged on a single vote. Those who disagreed had left in a huff muttering dire predictions under their breath.

Prophecies I hoped to hell didn't come true.

"You must remain with me at all times." I drew a dirk from its sheath and a small vial from a pocket.

He reached for them, intuiting he had to leave some of his blood behind. It would allow us to track him, should he go back on his word and make a break for freedom. While he chopped a gash in one finger and bled into the vial, I changed into traveling clothes much like Padhraic's. Slacks, shirt, vest, jacket. Neutral colors. The last thing I wanted was for us to stand out in anyone's memories.

Krin stepped through the door and held out his hand for the blood-filled vial. Padhraic gave it to him, and he nodded curtly, sweeping curved fingers through his close-cut red-gold hair. He narrowed his dark eyes Padhraic's way. "You agree with our terms?"

"So far, he's only heard two," I clarified and dropped items I thought I might need into a leather satchel.

"What beyond this?" Krin tapped the glass vial with an index finger. Leather garments hugged his lanky frame, and he was barefoot.

Padhraic wiped the dirk with a bit of cloth and handed it back to me. "I'm to remain within sight of Liam. What else is required of me?"

Krin drew an oblong crystal from one of his pockets and gave it to Padhraic. "This is—"

"I ken what it is well enough," Padhraic cut in. "It will

allow you to see where I am at all times." He shrugged and curled his fingers around it. "Seems like overkill, since you already have my blood, but I will do whatever I need to. Eventually, you will trust me again."

"Emphasis on eventually," Krin growled.

"I wouldn't trust me, either," Padhraic agreed affably. The stone left his hand and made a dive for his pocket. Obviously, the bit of quartz had been spelled not to leave his person.

I drew my brows together. Padhraic was being an awfully good sport about this. Did he have something up his sleeve? I'd be a fool not to keep my guard up. A spate of second-guessing my decision to include him circled through my head until I felt like a cat chasing its tail.

Krin glanced from Padhraic to me and back again before addressing Padhraic. "Liam has a softhearted side, and the two of you used to be friends. He may not tell you this next part, but I want to make certain you know not all of us were in agreement about you leaving. Many believe it's far too soon, that your commitment to lay your bloodlust aside should be tested in smaller ways."

He blew out a tense breath. "Were it not for your pervasive knowledge of Vampires, we'd never have agreed to Liam's plan."

"Regardless of your reservations," Padhraic began, "I appreciate—"

"I wasn't done," Krin spoke over him. "If you deviate from Liam's instructions by so much as an angstrom, your tenure among us will end. You will be imprisoned once again. This time, we will ensure you cannot escape. Do I make myself clear?"

"Abundantly." Padhraic's pleasant demeanor slipped a notch, and my suspicions soared.

Was his expression of bonhomie a front? Was bringing him with me a mistake? Or was he simply chafing at being talked down to?

I could interrogate him here and glean at least some of his knowledge. It would take time, though. After Cait's last email, I wasn't certain I had much of that.

Krin planted himself in front of Padhraic and dropped one hand on a shoulder; the other rested on his head. The air around the two of them turned fluid with the muted shades of Sidhe power. Blues and purples and greens. The scent of winter greenery, wet and piquant, thickened.

Krin shouted a power word that drove Padhraic to his knees and made me struggle to keep my balance. The shackles we'd erected around his magical center chimed discordantly as they fell away. "Do not make me sorry I restored your full power." Krin ground out the words.

Padhraic closed his fingers over Krin's forearm. "The one who has the most to lose if I backslide is me. Just so we're clear on that little point."

"Pretty words, but talk is cheap." Krin yanked his arm loose. "Let us know if you have need of reinforcements," he told me and left the room.

Padhraic shook himself from head to toe and muttered, "Guess that spying stone could come in handy."

"It could, indeed." I finished tossing magical

accoutrements into my satchel and turned to face him. "Are you certain?"

"Quite the open-ended question, mate." He frowned and hesitated, maybe organizing his thoughts. "You and the others removed Vampire essence from my magical center, but it left a hole. So far, I haven't felt tempted to fill it, but the first time I've left here was when you and I went to the village."

I made come-along motions with one hand. He understood me and kept talking. "The primary challenge to my resolve will be from Earth-bound Vampires."

"Why them? Wasn't it the dark gods who turned you?" Shock ratcheted through me. I'd been certain the Leanan shared the Sidhes' antipathy for Earth-bound Vampires. Before he could answer, I tossed out, "Maybe this is a bad idea. We will run into Vampires, and you'll have to raise magic against them."

Padhraic nodded; his smooth veneer cracked along with his voice. "I understand. It's why I volunteered. You don't trust me, but neither do I trust myself. Not completely. How will I know how strong—or how weak—I am until I face temptation? To answer your question about why the attraction to the other breed of Vampire, the closest I can come is when we're feeding, there's no difference between us.

"I don't want to be like them anymore, but I have no idea if my steadfastness will hold up in the face of a bunch of Vamps with their mouths glued to mortals' necks. The dark mages may have turned us, but they didn't stick around afterward. They're not driven by blood hunger."

Something, maybe his tone or his posture—shoulders rounded, and forehead crinkled with concern—reassured me. “All right,” I said, “let’s do it this way. If anything threatens your barriers, speak up right away.”

“Fair enough. Look, mate, I don’t want to fail. This is like a first battle where I have no idea how I’ll fare until I’m in the thick of it.”

It was as good a note to leave on as we were likely to get. I strapped my satchel to my body, built a travel spell, and draped it around both of us. Should I aim for Cait’s office or her home? It was morning on the West Coast of the U.S., so I opted for the Quonset hut and narrowed my spell to hit its interior. No handy evening shadows to shield Padhraic and me.

Cait’s disclosure about being a Reaper had to have riled more than a few mortals. Humans Rule would be up in arms, for certain. “Be ready for anything,” I told Padhraic.

“You always were a master of understatement,” he said, sounding more like himself as we waited out the spell. Surely, Cait would have received my message when she woke this morning and checked in with her phone. I’d missed her. The thought of seeing her soon was exhilarating—before a dose of reality crashed over me.

I reminded myself to keep my expectations within reason. She’d reached out because she was frightened and had no one else to turn to. I’d damaged her relationship with Death, and Reapers were lone wolves. Death had set things up to maintain several degrees of separation between their assigned territories.

Probably so they couldn’t compare notes.

That would be especially true now that Cait knew how much magic she possessed. Death had forbidden her from disclosing anything about it. The prohibition might work—for a while. Death might limp along for another century—perhaps even two—but eventually Cait would tell someone. The more Reapers who knew the truth, the harder it would be to keep under wraps.

Surely, Death understood that part.

Question was what she'd do about it.

The edges of my casting developed shimmery edges. I double-checked my destination. We seemed to be right on target. Next to me, Padhraic stiffened. "I smell Vamps."

"There was a battle here yesterday."

"I remember the Reaper's email. These scents are fresh."

I readied defensive magic. "Silver stakes are in my satchel," I told Padhraic. "Along with a few syringes of dead man's blood."

"Brilliant! When did you have time to put them together?"

"I didn't. Dena gave them to me when the council was arguing over you."

"I'll thank her after we get back." He mixed air and fire, blending it into my defensive spell.

The decayed stench of Vampire reached me, along with the coppery tang of fresh blood. Cait's cries pierced my teleport channel next. I punched through and landed on my feet, blessing the instinct that had pushed me to come here first. If I'd gone to her houseboat, we might not have arrived in time.

Padhraic emerged next to me.

“You weren’t invited,” one of the dark gods—Adva?—skinned his lips back from his teeth and snarled. Red curls had been cropped short. Green-gold eyes sparkled from beneath a high forehead. A blue linen shirt covered his broad shoulders, and brown woolen pants hung low on slender hips. Shiny black wingtips lent him an uptown lawyer look.

Cait stood in a corner—thank all the gods she’d had the sense to not let herself be surrounded. Power streamed from her, along with fury. Blood dripped from a gouge down one of her arms. Her cheek had been scraped down to bone on one side. Fury surged through me, running hot and savage.

Besides Adva, three Vamps and four mortals faced off against Cait. I wanted all of them deader than dead.

Horrible odds. Or they were until we got here.

“Great timing!” Cait called, trying for jaunty. Her courage smote me and made me proud of her.

“We aim to serve,” I retorted.

Unclipping the satchel straps, I burrowed into the outer pocket where I’d tossed a dozen silver stakes. When I grabbed one, the fucking thing burned my fingers, but I chanted through the pain and turned it into a homing pigeon keyed to one of the Vampires. No matter how far he ran, the stake would follow him until it buried itself in his heart.

While I was intent on my spell, Padhraic located a syringe. The blood within it was so dark it appeared black. He seemed to be holding his own, which was a plus since I couldn’t split my attention too many ways.

The Vampire I’d targeted ran out the door with my stake

right behind him. He didn't get twenty paces before it stabbed him in the back and on through his heart. I missed exactly how Padhraic ended up scrabbling with another of the Vamps on the floor, but he was quick and efficient. The thing about dead man's blood is it doesn't matter where you stab the needle in. It won't kill a Vamp, but it causes excruciating pain and slows them down enough to either stake or behead them.

I snatched up another silver stake. My right palm was bleeding, but it didn't take much to toss the stake to Padhraic. He filleted the Vamp already writhing in agony between the ribs and tossed the stake back my way.

Smart.

We couldn't replace them, and we'd just arrived.

I called the other one back with magic. It clattered to the floor next to my satchel. Both Vamps had turned to piles of bones. The third one had vanished. Guess he saw the writing on the wall.

I'd never realized they could teleport. The Leanan could, of course, but apparently they'd taught their Earth-bound counterparts how to launch journey spells. Once things slowed down, I'd have Padhraic make me a list of everything the Leanan had imparted to the other Vampires.

Adva dove for Cait. For one heart-stopping moment, I was afraid he'd slice right through her warding, but it held. I sprinted toward her. The humans formed a line between me and her. Between their hissing and snarling, I made out words like abomination.

A bitter snort rolled through me. "Hey there, mates," I

told them. “You can’t have it both ways. Either you hate everything magical, or you decide it’s handy, after all.”

“You can’t tell us what to do.” A rawboned fellow with a bald head sneered my way. A wrinkled suit suggested perhaps he had some type of office job.

Weak, pathetic magic flickered around him. A perversion of everything power should be. This batch had Humans Rule stamped all over them from the man-atop-mountain logos on their shirts or jackets to their caps. They also sported fang marks in their necks.

I’d deal with them later.

“Bind them,” I told Padhraic.

Power flashed from his hands, and netting dropped over the men amid cursing and screaming. Adva was clawing at Cait’s warding. I skirted around the men and kicked the dark mage in the small of his back.

He spun to face me exactly as I’d hoped he would. Nothing pretty was left of his face. He looked ancient and wicked and furious. Exactly like any predator who’d had his prey well in hand—until competition showed up.

Cait loped to my side and joined her power with mine. We’d worked as a team before; our magic was strong when we combined it.

“You will leave and never return,” I told Adva.

Laughter burst from his throat. “I scarcely take orders from the Sidhe,” he choked out between gales of harsh-edged mirth.

“What did you want with me?” Cait asked.

“Vampires have had a rough go of things lately,” Adva

purred. "Once you're out of the way—" He dusted his hands together.

It was Cait's turn to laugh. "Death will just assign another Reaper."

"Aye, but they'll be like Jake or Maxwell." Adva shrugged. "So far, you've been the only one who turned into a thorn in our sides. And an impediment to our plans."

"What might those be?" Padhraic called from where he was holding the mortals captive.

"You." Adva narrowed his eyes. "You escaped. What are you waiting for? Help me with her." He jerked his chin at Cait.

Padhraic shook his head. "Look closer, portal-boy. Things have changed."

Adva snorted. "Nah. You're pretending. No one lives on blood as long as you did and forgets how intoxicating it is." He lowered his voice to a seductive whisper. "Did those pesky Sidhe strip you of your gifts? I can give them all back to you. Just ask."

"I'd rather be dead."

The finality in Padhraic's words warmed me, made me certain I'd chosen well.

"It's an open offer," Adva cried. He jumped higher than I'd have thought possible, even with a magical assist, and vanished.

"What the fuck?" Cait stared above us.

"He controls portals," I reminded her. It wasn't worth mentioning I'd never seen anyone disappear quite so quickly. It's good to know what your enemy is capable of.

"What do you want to do with them?" Padhraic called my way.

I assessed the men. They'd quieted, but if expressions could kill, they'd have done away with us and not looked back. Their sick version of power still sputtered around them.

I crafted a hasty spell and loosed it. The men squealed like gutted pigs.

"Not that I care, but what did you do?" Cait asked.

"Stripped their magic." I raised my voice to make certain it would penetrate their pain and said, "If you decide to dabble in what was never meant for mortals again, it will mean your deaths. Do you understand me?"

Padhraic reeled in the magic holding the men in place. It took a moment before they realized they were free and stumbled out the door. One fell over the pile of bones left by the Vampire.

Without warning or fanfare, Death jumped through a gash in the ether and glared at Cait. "In trouble again, girl?"

"If I am, it's your fault," Cait shot back.

"Watch your mouth, missy. I'm not the one who announced to the world you were a Reaper."

"No. You just made certain every Vampire on Earth knew."

Death narrowed her eerie eyes. "Clean up those souls."

"Do it yourself," Cait said in a voice I'd never heard from her before. "I'm not your *girl*. Neither am I your lackey. I quit."

Shock rolled off Death in palpable waves. "You can't."

"Oh yeah? Watch me." Cait stalked through the open door, snatching a set of keys off a board on her way out.

Death rounded on me. "This is your fault," she sputtered.

"Nice try." I should have stopped there, but I didn't. "If you want her back, try treating her like something other than a scullery maid."

The muted roar of an aircraft engine filled my ears. Good. Cait didn't need to hear any of this.

Death crossed an arm beneath her breasts and shook a finger at me. "You'd best plan to be here a lot, Sidhe. Because I'm done. You hear me? Done! Cait wants to quit? So be it. Let's see how far she gets on her own."

Before I could tell her what a selfish bitch she was, how she should rise above her hurt feelings and show a little respect for her Reaper, she was gone.

Padhraic started to laugh. "Same old Liam," he sputtered. "Insert foot in mouth. Rinse, repeat."

At first, it pissed me off, but soon I was laughing right along with him. Death wouldn't stay gone. I'd bank any amount of money on it, but having her out of the way for a while might actually work in our favor.

Too many cooks, all with different magic, only muddied the water.

CHAPTER FIVE, CAIT

I taxied the Cessna 172 out onto the runway and pinged the tower for permission to take off. I needed space. Time to think. Liam would wait for me, and I didn't plan to be gone long. What the hell was Padhraic doing with him? When I'd seen him, I'd been afraid maybe Liam had switched sides, but I'd buried the thought deep.

I was already up to my ass in quicksand, and I couldn't believe Liam would have brought Padhraic if he didn't trust him on some level. As events played out, the former Leanan had actually been helpful, so maybe the Sidhe version of rehab had worked.

I had no idea what got into me, telling Death off like that, but it had to be cumulative. I'd dealt with not one, but two Vampire fights in a fifteen-hour span. Adva perched in the middle of my office like a black widow waiting to snare me in his web hadn't helped. The mortals weren't more than an inconvenience, but a woman can only fight so many nasties at once.

The morning had actually started out pretty decently. I'd slept like a dead thing for seven hours, gotten up to Liam's note saying he'd arrive as soon as he could, and made myself a pot of coffee.

It didn't take long before I was suited up for the day, bag in hand, and driving out to the airfield. Breakfast from my favorite to-go café sat on the passenger seat. I'd returned yesterday's emails, and today was shaping up to be busy with lessons and a two-hour stint as backup air ambulance.

Doug had had that job, and the service was scrambling to fill his slots. Since he'd tried to kill me with the defective Citabria, I didn't feel the least bit guilty profiting from his suicide-by-airplane stunt.

My happy space had shattered around me when I walked into my office.

Crap. You'd think I'd be smarter after all the shit I've lived through lately, but nope. I'd waltzed through my door as if I didn't have a care in the world, coffee mug in one hand, breakfast and my shoulder bag in the other.

"Who in the fuck are you?" I'd growled. It was a generalized question since beyond knowing three of the men in my office were Vampires and four were mortal, the other dude remained a mystery.

"I'm Adva." The pretty man sitting at my desk as if he owned the joint got up and faced me. A smile graced his face, but it was feral rather than warm. "I believe you've met two of my associates, Perrikus and D'Chel."

God of portals, eh? my inner voice inquired acidly. At least mystery-man wasn't a mystery any longer. Out of all the choices, facing one of the dark gods didn't even make last place on my preferred activities list.

"Explains how you got in here," I muttered and backed toward the nearest wall. No chance to grab the special Vampire-killing saber that lived in my locker. Maybe I should start keeping it in my car. Somewhere between untangling myself from my bag, breakfast, and coffee, two of the Vampires surged toward me.

I'm not great yet with all my recently discovered magic, so it took me a moment to build a ward. Because I wasn't fast enough, one of the Vamps tore a gash in my cheek with his filthy, broken nails. The other ripped a long, jagged wound down one arm. The scent of my blood is like an aphrodisiac to them, and the one nearest me made a dive for my neck. It lit a fire under my fledgling spell. I shelved doing it by the book, opting for expediency instead. I could fine-tune any problems later.

Vamps hate water, so I poured it into my casting, gratified when they jumped back hissing like scalded rats. As soon as I had a little breathing space, I took stock of what I faced. My best bet would be to teleport out of here, but timing would be dicey. I'd have to ready the travel spell and dismantle my warding all in the space of a couple of breaths.

In the brief time after my ward came down, I'd be vulnerable—to all of them.

Could I pull it off?

Liam and Padhraic chose that moment to show up. My out-of-control heartbeat slowed a little. We weren't out of the woods by any means, but the odds had just improved by a good big bunch.

On our side.

Adva didn't look worried, but his kind probably never did. A sick magical patina coated the mortals. It was eroding what was left of their souls. And then I saw the marks in all their necks. They hadn't been turned. Not yet, but the Vamps were feeding from them, polluting their humanity.

By the time Death showed up, the fireworks were over. She needn't have bothered to make an appearance at all. Unless she craved an "I told you so" moment. The thought made me sick. When she'd called me "girl," and then ordered me to clear the Vampire souls, something inside me snapped.

Not that I hadn't considered standing up to her before, but no one was more surprised than me when the words, "I quit," bellowed from my mouth. They felt right, righter than any of my interactions with her had for a long time.

It was why I marched out of there and into an airplane before I had second thoughts. In many ways, Death has been like a strict, relentless parent. She's been the only constant in my long life, and I was certain I'd mourn slamming the door in her face.

But I could do that on my own time. Not when I might weaken and do something truly stupid, like apologizing. I flew a couple of touch-and-goes before taxiing back to the hangar. It had been kind of Liam to drop everything and show up, doubly so since he'd plopped right into the middle of yet one more Vampire attack.

I didn't want him to think I didn't appreciate him prioritizing me.

After hurriedly buttoning up the plane, I walked briskly back into the Quonset hut. Everything stank of Vampire. Big surprise. They were spending as much time in my office as I was. The Vampire bones were gone.

Padhraic inclined his head. "Good to see you again, Cait. I wish the circumstances were more favorable."

I walked toward him and extended a hand. He shook it. "The Sidhe cure worked, I see. Excellent."

He smiled, and it lit his gaunt features from within. "Seems to be, but I'm not taking anything for granted until I have a wee bit more time under my belt."

"Well, you look a thousand percent better than when I last saw you."

"I suppose you'd notice things like that," he murmured.

"Yeah. Your soul is whole again, not riddled with rot."

"How are you feeling?" Liam arched a white-blond brow my way.

I rolled my eyes. "Trying not to think about how I told Death to fuck off. It's why I left, so I wouldn't have a change of heart and throw myself at her feet begging forgiveness. Um, did she say anything after I stormed out of here?"

Liam snorted. "Aye, she blamed me, and then she left."

"Makes sense," I murmured.

"How so?" Liam asked.

"Well, she can't blame herself. It goes against her principles. Blaming me is tantamount to admitting she failed." I shrugged. "You turned into a convenient fall guy."

He snorted again. "Good to have a purpose. On a more

serious note, apologies it took me so long to get here. I've been hunting for a way to disable Earth-bound Vamps in one fell swoop."

"Bet you didn't get very far."

"Why didn't you ask for help, mate?" Padhraic asked Liam.

"I was getting around to it. You may recall, it took you a while to recover from...eh, your reprogramming."

"Such a modern term for such an ancient ritual," Padhraic muttered.

I looked from one to the other of them curious to know more, but not wanting to rip scabs off healing wounds. A tentative knock on the door I'd left ajar brought my head whipping around.

"Am I in the right place?" A middle-aged woman with short russet hair smiled uncertainly. Levi's hugged her slender legs, and a zip-up purple hoodie covered her torso.

Damn it. She had to be part of my day's schedule. Of course, I'd hoped everyone would show up, but I'd been expecting a bevy of no-shows in the wake of yesterday's news.

"If you're my ten o'clock lesson, then indeed you are," I replied.

"Are you sure you're not too busy?" She glanced at Liam and Padhraic.

I looked at them too, grateful they were dressed in twenty-first century garb rather than hunting leathers or armor or robes. Hustling to my computer, I brought up the program where I collect information on all my students and motioned her to come sit.

"Fill everything out," I told her. "You'll need your student pilot registration number."

"I brought it with me." She walked toward my desk, and I hunted through my memory for her name. Nothing materialized.

I smiled and said, "Welcome. I'll just step outside with these gentlemen for a moment, and then you'll have my undivided attention."

Liam nodded at me, and then he and Padhraic walked through the still-open door.

The woman's brown eyes skittered toward me, and then away. "Yesterday can't have been easy for you. I wasn't even sure you'd be here. I tried to call, but you didn't answer, so..."

I stifled a wince. I'd checked phone messages, sort of, but hadn't returned any calls. I'd planned to do that once I got to my office. By the grace of Danu, my student had missed Adva and the Vampires. They would have made short work of her.

"I'm glad you're here. Once you're all registered, we'll go over a few basics and take our first flight."

A shy smile curved her mouth. "I'm excited. Learning to fly is a gift I've been promising myself for years." She sat in front of my monitor and began to type.

"Thanks for picking me for a teacher," I told her. "Back in a few minutes."

She twisted her head and made eye contact for the first time. "I, uh, did try once before. Thought it might be easier with a female instructor."

I bit my tongue. So many of the male flight instructors fancied themselves a reincarnation of Tom Cruise in *Top*

Gun. Any display of timidity on the part of a student was met with derision. Being scared responds better to compassion than mockery. Not everyone is cut out to fly, but it doesn't make them any less human.

"I'll take good care of you. Promise." I patted her shoulder and trotted outside to join Liam and Padhraic.

Padhraic pulled the door shut, and Liam built a sound screen around us. I dragged my phone out of a pocket and brought up my schedule. The woman sitting at my terminal was named Lisa Greenstone. Good to know. I drew my brows together. "I have another lesson after the gal who just arrived. And then I have to be here because I'm on call for the air ambulance, but I can cancel that obligation."

"No need," Liam said. "You had no idea when I'd get here until this morning. What time will you be done?"

"Three." I chewed my lower lip. "It's not safe for me to have students here, is it? What if Lisa had come earlier?"

"Nay, it's not." Liam skirted my question about Lisa's fate had she run into the Vamps and Adva.

"Things should be all right if you or I remain here," Padhraic said to Liam. "The dark mages and Vamps won't be quite so quick to break through if they don't believe they'll score a quick victory."

I shook my head. "I can't ask you to do that. Best thing would be for me to shut down for a while."

The admission cost me. A lot. Closing my doors for a week would mean trouble. Longer than that, and I may as well give up and sell my planes. I couldn't go for an extended period without income. I'd been playing catchup for the last six months. My balance sheet was an unholy mess.

Students, the air ambulance, and the odd air freight job would migrate to other firms. Other pilots. By the time I got around to picking up the pieces, there wouldn't be anything to work with. My shoulders slumped, and I gave myself a boot in the rump.

Feeling sorry for myself wasn't productive. I'd play the ball where it had come to rest. Keeping my business going was ridiculous if it meant innocent mortals might end up Vampire fodder. I needed to get my head on straighter.

Liam dropped a hand onto my shoulder. "Don't."

"Don't, what?" I asked dully, and then I remembered he was skilled at reading minds. I shook my head. "Leave a woman some privacy."

A corner of his mouth twitched downward. "Asking questions takes time, a commodity we're shy on." He tightened his grip on my shoulder. "Vampires have to be our first priority. It's handy they like to congregate here, but clearing the decks of humans is important. I told you once before, I'll help with *Carrick Sky Sports*."

I opened my mouth to say absolutely not, but he waved me to silence. "We're a team, Cait Carrick, an unusual one since Reapers and Sidhe aren't known as associates, but we can rewrite the script, eh?"

"You said one more student after this one?" Padhraic asked. When I nodded, he said, "Liam and I will remain close, but we won't be visible. Unless you need our help."

"At the end of today, we need to return to Scotland," Liam said. "All of our lore materials and the other Sidhe are there. The most prudent path will be for you to come with us."

I've always been stiff-necked. Proud and stubborn could have been my middle names. "I'll let you know my decision at the end of today," I mumbled.

"Good enough." Liam moved his hand off my shoulder. The place it had sat felt cold, and I craved his touch, wanted him to rest his palm in the crook of my neck again.

Christ on a bloody crutch. What was wrong with me?

I turned and headed back inside. My inner landscape was a jumbled mess, but it wasn't an excuse for being rude. Liam had shelved his duty to the Sidhe so he could be here when I needed him. Embarrassment churned along with all my other confused feelings. Before I rethought my motives —again—I turned and said, "Thank both of you so much. For everything."

There. At least I'd dredged up a few manners, but I didn't feel any more settled. Within the span of a few hours, I'd have to make a decision that would alter my life in major ways. Not that I hadn't already forced one major alteration by flipping Death off.

Maybe it was why I was loathe to change anything else, but I didn't have much of a choice in the matter. Liam had been kind enough not to rub my nose in that niggling reality. He hadn't punched holes in my fantasy that I had any options left.

Pasting a smile on my face, I strode inside determined to make Lisa's flight a positive experience for her.

LISA'S LESSON went off without a hitch. She had the makings

of a decent pilot, and I told her so. I could tell my assessment pleased her. Her first flight instructor had drilled holes in her self-confidence. Big ones. My next student was a man I'd worked with before. I kept expecting Vampires to jump out from behind every cloud, but perhaps Liam's and Padhraic's presence had a modulating effect. Surely by now, the Earth-bound Vamps knew about the demise of the Leanan.

At the hands of their Sidhe kinsmen.

And me.

I made good use of my air ambulance downtime and updated the spreadsheet that tracks my students. I took a stab at how long I'd be closed and stared at a calendar. Two weeks wasn't enough, but if I spun my absence out farther than that, all my gloom-and-doom predictions about my business would come to pass.

No matter which way I told myself everything would be all right, that I could start over somewhere else, I kept coming back to one hardline fact. I didn't want to start over. I wanted my current business and my airplanes and my messy Quonset hut.

I'd have to start over someday, but that wasn't supposed to be for another twenty years or so.

I've never been one to perseverate over decisions. It's what makes me a decent pilot—the ability to assess a situation and pick a direction and stick with it.

"Two weeks it is," I said out loud as if hearing the words would cement my decision, imbue it with rightness. I'd just finished constructing an email and batch-sending it to my students when the distinctive scent of Sidhe magic—rain-wet greenery and sandalwood—filled my nostrils.

I inhaled hungrily. The smell reminded me of being in Liam's arms with all those acres of hard-muscled body pressed against me.

My nose twitched. Something else magical was with the Sidhe. My eyes widened when I recognized the heather-and-wildflower scent common to those like me. I'm so used to smelling myself, it took longer than it might have for me to sort it out.

I half expected a gateway to form. Instead, my door opened, and Liam, Padhraic, and a Reaper who looked vaguely familiar walked through.

"We found her skulking about outside," Padhraic said without preamble.

"Aye, she said she knows you," Liam added. Suspicion sharpened the edges of his words.

I turned my chair around and got to my feet, never taking my gaze from the Reaper as I sifted through my memory banks. She was dressed in nondescript tan slacks, a faded-red stretchy shirt, and a hooded black pullover. Socks and sandals graced her feet. On the shortish side, she had bright-red hair that fell to her shoulders and blue eyes. Freckles dotted her nose.

"We all more or less recognize each other," I told Liam and walked closer to the other Reaper. "Stacia?"

She nodded enthusiastically and smiled. "I knew you'd remember. We went through Reaper school together."

"Yeah, and I haven't seen you in hundreds of years," I replied, and then I remembered my mystery caller from the night before. "Last night. It was you, wasn't it?"

"It was her, what?" Liam demanded.

Stacia kept on bobbing her head. "It was." She lowered her voice. "We need to talk, but not where anyone can listen in." The feel of her magic thickened as she worked to construct a primitive privacy screen.

"We'll take care of that part," Padhraic said. The prickle of Sidhe magic displaced Stacia's paltry attempt, and the weave of a sound shield settled around the four of us.

"She called me last night," I told Liam and Padhraic. "The minute I said the word Reaper, she hung up."

"Death is keeping a very close eye on all of us," she said. "It has something to do with you—and probably with Vampires—but none of the rest of us can figure it out. Jake is missing, and Maxwell has turned into a ghostly prophet of doom who refuses to cross. He says a Harpy killed him, but the rest of us think he's gone mad."

I let her words percolate for a bit, and then said, "I'm confused. We don't talk with each other."

"Some of us do," Stacia said. "Death never cared until a few months back." She stood straighter. "A few of us decided someone had to contact you. What's going on, Cait? Since when do we team up with the Sidhe? Or any other magic wielders?"

I exchanged a pointed look with Liam. His response was a miniscule shoulder shrug. If I read him right, I was on my own here. Reapers were my people, my kinsmen. What I disclosed was up to me.

I wanted to tell Stacia to come back tomorrow, but it wasn't fair to her. Goddess only knew how far she'd traveled to reach me. And Reapers didn't teleport—except me.

If my brain had been a tumbled mess before, its current

state made my earlier spate of indecision pale by comparison. “It’s hard to know where to begin,” I said at last.

Stacia continued to stare at me, an expectant look on her face.

“Shall we move to your houseboat?” Liam spoke up. “It’s easier to ward than this spot.”

“Good idea,” I agreed.

Could I trust Stacia? She might be a spy for Death, but Death and I were on the outs. It was hard to imagine bigger fracture lines in our relationship than I’d already put there.

“Alrighty.” I tried for a smile, but it wasn’t in the cards. “We’re teleporting to where I live.”

“Honey, it’s not part of our magic.” Stacia’s voice tone took on the aspect she might have used with a child who didn’t understand quite why it had died, what it meant, or why it needed to cross over.

“You only think it isn’t,” I retorted. “Death kept a whole lot of things from us.” I stopped and blew out a breath. “You’re at a crossroads, Stacia. Do you really want to know? Because once I start talking, there won’t be any going back.”

CHAPTER SIX, LIAM

When we'd found another Reaper doing her damnedest to hide behind a totally inadequate invisibility casting, Padhraic and I had discussed what to do about it. Should we ignore her? Should we tell Cait and let her decide?

We'd opted for a wait-and-see approach when the other Reaper crept around toward the back of the Quonset hut. It seemed sneaky enough, maybe ignoring her wasn't the best approach.

Perhaps Death was up to something, and this Reaper was on a mission.

Regardless, we'd come up on either side of the Reaper and caught her between us. Apprehending her had been ridiculously easy, until I remembered how little of their own magic Reapers were aware of. Fear sheeted from the woman, but I hadn't been inclined to soothe her.

Not until I was certain she didn't mean Cait harm.

“I’m an old friend of Cait Carrick’s,” she’d told us as she tried to wrest herself out of our grasp.

“Shall we see if she remembers you?” I’d asked.

“What? You think I’m lying?” The woman displayed a burst of spirit I wouldn’t have believed her capable of.

“I’m keeping an open mind,” I replied.

“In you go,” Padhraic had said almost cheerfully as we’d half walked, half dragged the Reaper inside the Quonset hut.

I’d been relieved Cait actually knew the other Reaper by name. Stacia. But it was clear she didn’t know her well and hadn’t seen her for a very long time. Because it’s not my nature to trust anyone, I added a truth weave to Padhraic’s sound shield.

When Cait glanced my way, clearly unsure how to proceed, I was noncommittal. This wasn’t exactly my problem, nor was I the best judge of how much to divulge. Granted, I’d been the one who ripped Cait’s blinders off, but I wasn’t about to compound my sins by making sure every Reaper I came across knew the extent to which their mistress had lied to them.

When you cut to the heart of things, it was Death’s job to educate her minions. Light was leaching from the day, so I suggested moving to the houseboat. It was easier to protect, plus up until now there hadn’t been any direct attacks there.

What would Cait decide?

I admit to curiosity. She’d walked out of Death’s army a few hours before, but the door was still open a crack. Would she slam it the rest of the way by revealing the extent of Reaper magic to Stacia?

After agreeing her home was a more defensible location,

she announced we'd teleport. Stacia had jumped in and reminded her Reapers couldn't do that. She'd done it carefully, with warmth and compassion. Clearly, she figured Cait had lost her mind and needed support from the Reaper community.

Intriguing there was one. Cait had been convinced her kin never talked with one another.

Stacia hesitated after Cait told her to think long and hard before hearing anything further. She did stand at a crossroads, one where she could still chalk up Cait's comment about teleporting as budding insanity. Once Cait swept her up in a teleport spell, that door would shut forever.

"I— I'm not sure," Stacia said at last. "I mean, I'm here to gather intel, so I suppose I should jump on it, but why do I have this eerie premonition what you have to tell me will run ever so much deeper than any of us could have imagined?"

"Because it will," Cait said. Softening the set of her shoulders, she went on. "Intuition is part of Reaper magic. It helps us read the newly dead so we can offer what they need to encourage them to cross over."

"I know as much," Stacia said.

Cait raked hair back from her face. "One thing I can tell you—because you'll find out anyway—is I quit today."

"Huh?" Her blue eyes rounded into moons. "What do you mean? We can't quit. Reaping is etched into who we are."

"Oh I didn't quit Reaping," Cait clarified. "What I did was

quit working for Death. I'll still be a Reaper, but on more of an, erm, freelance basis."

"Whoa." Breath whooshed from Stacia; twin vertical lines formed between her russet brows. "What did she do when you told her?"

Cait shrugged and jerked her chin my way. "Ask the Sidhe. I walked out of here and took an airplane up."

Stacia's gaze shifted to me, entreaty in every line of her body.

"She didn't hang about long," I told the Reaper. "She blamed me for Cait's rebellion and then left."

"Why you?" Stacia's eyes skittered back to Cait seeking answers as to why Death would blame a Sidhe for a Reaper leaving the fold.

"What did you decide?" Cait asked.

"About?" Stacia's voice shook.

"About knowing more," Cait answered. "There's no way to give this to you in dribs and drabs. I've told you the only thing you can know as an independent fact: me leaving. Everything else is interconnected, and actually my defection is as well, but it can stand on its own."

Stacia clasped her hands in front of her and stared at them. When she finally scraped her gaze upward, she said, "Aye. I wish to know. Things have been...strange for many months. We've all felt the change in Death. And in the dead. They're less cooperative."

"No shit," Cait muttered.

"Shall we move, then?" I prodded. Dusk had fallen, and my instincts had been activated by something. I didn't hear or see anything untoward, but the hairs on the back of my neck prickled unpleasantly. My first guess was one or more of the dark mages were lurking nearby. Not so close I could know with certainty, but near enough to pounce and exact maximum damage.

For all I knew, they were just waiting for a critical mass of Vampires to materialize.

Cait nodded, and Padhraic said, "We should have been gone a while ago. Something feels off to me."

Stacia twisted her head about, probably hunting for what we sensed, but she'd never find it. Her current sensitivity was to the dead, not the living. In the interest of not totally freaking her out, I draped a travel spell over all of us and fed in coordinates for Cait's houseboat.

"Hold up a moment while I lock the hangar," Cait called and ran out the door.

I almost raced after her, but it was a better use of my time to finish my spell so we could leave as soon as she returned. Moments later, she was back, locking the Quonset hut from the inside and dropping things into the leather shoulder bag she never went anywhere without.

"Something feels...strange out there," she said.

"We'll dissect it later," I told her and loosed my spell. The walls of her office faded, replaced by the living room of her houseboat. First thing I did was check the warding, reinforcing it in spots.

No one had been here, which was a huge relief.

Stacia hadn't said a word after her comments about the dead being harder to control. She glanced around Cait's living room and murmured, "This is nice. You've done well."

"Are you still in that basement in Prague?" Cait asked her.

Stacia shook her head. "Uh, no. That whole section of town was bombed during one of the big wars. I'm still in Prague, but in a walkup flat east of town. It's just one room, but it isn't like I spend much time there."

"What do you do besides Reaping?" Cait asked.

A shocked look bloomed on Stacia's face. "Nothing. Why would I?"

"So you can eat and pay rent on that flat," Cait replied.

"Death covers everything, or someone does. I always assumed it had to be her," Stacia said.

"Really?" Cait doubled up a fist and punched the back of the sofa.

I caught her arm before she put a hole in the wall. "You made your choice," I reminded her. "Stacia just corroborated it was the right one."

Cait yanked from my grip. "Does Death—or someone—support the rest of you?"

"I think so," Stacia said. "Why?"

"Because she's never offered me so much as a farthing."

"I'm sorry, Cait. I had no idea. Maybe it's a geographic thing. All the Reapers I know are on the other side of the Atlantic."

Cait shook her head. "It doesn't matter."

It did, though. The news had rattled her. Nothing like finding out firsthand that every other kid in the family received better treatment than you. I headed for the kitchen intent on brewing tea for all of us.

"I'll make tea," Padhraic said and pushed past me.

I turned back to catch Cait saying, "Makes what I'm going to tell you easier because right now I'm so furious at Death, it's all I can do not to chase her down and confront her."

"She only shows up when she wants to," Stacia reminded her.

"Oh, she'll want to see me," Cait snarled. "By the time I'm done talking to you, she'll be planning my demise."

"She wouldn't—" Stacia began.

"Yeah, she would. Let's see, where shall I begin?"

I listened and ferried tea from the kitchen as Cait sketched out her Vampire assignment, the links with Humans Rule, our battle with the Leanan Sidhe, and how we believed the dark mages were involved. By the time she got around to her public announcement about being a Reaper, most of the color had left Stacia's face, leaving her freckles standing out in bas-relief.

Somewhere in betwixt and between, Padhraic rejoined us.

"So, anyway," Cait continued, "Death dropped by yesterday to read me the riot act about outing myself. My office happened to be full of Vampires, so she hung around to deal with them."

"I see," Stacia said. "How'd you get from there to quitting?"

"I'd been considering it for a while," Cait told the other Reaper. "Liam floated the idea, and I poo-pooed it, but it got me thinking. Anyway, when I showed up for work this morning, my office was full of Vampires, mortals who'd been playing with magic, and Adva, god of portals."

"Awk. You poor thing." Stacia set her tea down and patted Cait's arm.

"I would have been a very poor thing if Liam and Padhraic hadn't happened along. By the time Death arrived, it was all over but for the crying. She mocked me, and then ordered me to Reap the Vampires' souls."

Cait turned her hands palms up. "Something snapped. I told her I was done, turned on my heel, and walked out. But there's more you don't know."

"I'm gathering as much." Stacia nodded slowly and listened as Cait described the rough extent of Reaper magic.

"How could we have all this extra ability and not know about it?" Stacia sounded thunderstruck.

"Because your mistress planned it that way." I stepped into the conversation for the first time. "She admitted to me that she manipulated Reaper school to steer all of you away from spots where you might discover your untapped skills."

"Whoa." Stacia sank to one end of the sofa and pinched the bridge of her nose between her thumb and forefinger. When she looked up, she said, "I see what you mean about no going back."

I'd spent enough time inside her mind to know she wasn't spying for Death, so I dismantled my truth net as unobtrusively as I could. I don't think she noticed. Understandable since Cait had just dropped several bombshells that occupied more than her full attention.

"I, uh, guess I should leave," Stacia said. "The other Reapers are waiting to hear back from me."

"What are you going to tell them?" Cait squatted in front of Stacia and skewered her with an uncompromising gaze.

"Not sure." Stacia licked her lips. "I mean, it's either go back and say I couldn't find you or spill everything. Right? It's not as if I can weave my way through that minefield of information and cherry-pick bits of it to make Death look a little less polluted."

"She's always been demanding," Cait pointed out.

"Not open to compromise." Stacia nodded knowingly. "But holding our magic secret boots her sins into a whole other arena. Some of us have had close calls lately. Dead passing through us have caused pain, confusion. We lost one Reaper to the nether regions. He grew disoriented and couldn't find his way out."

"If he's lost there, how do you know?" Padhraic asked.

"Other dead have told us there's a Reaper loose among them," Stacia replied. "We put two and two together."

"Did you ask Death to rescue him?" Cait pursed her lips into a thin line.

Stacia nodded. "She said she was certain he was fine."

"When she knew damn good and well he wasn't," Cait sputtered. "Fuck. Whose side is she on, anyway?"

"Her own?" I suggested. "It's not worth your time to second-guess the gods. They play by their own rulebook."

"One that left decency by the wayside?" Cait arched a dark brow. "I'm glad I'm free."

"I'm beginning to wish I was," Stacia muttered.

"No reason you can't be," Cait blurted, and then clapped a hand over her mouth. "Oops. That just slipped out. Forget I said it."

"Not sure I can do that," Stacia said.

Cait rolled onto her haunches until her butt was on the

floor and crossed her legs beneath her. "Our situations are different. If you thumb your nose at Death, you'll have to get a job or move or something."

A corner of Stacia's mouth twisted into a wry grin. "Not much money to be had from the dead... Wait a minute. Their families used to leave offerings for us."

"Yeah and provided places to live," Cait agreed. "Food too, but those days are long gone."

"No reason they can't come back." A determined note ran beneath Stacia's words. She dug a phone out of her purse.

"Who are you planning on calling?" I asked. I thought I knew, but it paid to offer her the benefit of the doubt.

"Why, the rest of our group," she said. "They deserve to know everything."

"Not over the phone they don't," I said. "Anyone could tap into your conversation, including Death."

Cait turned her hands palms up. "We can't keep secrets from Death. She lives in our heads. It's how she knows precisely where we are."

I thought about it and frowned. I'd known that part, about Death keeping tabs on all her Reapers, but I'd never considered the magical underpinnings of it.

"We might be able to alter the linkage," Padhraic said slowly.

"It's a two-edged sword," Cait told him. "Maybe not as big a deal for me since I already cut the umbilical cord, but Death does manage to show up to bail us out of trouble."

"She used to," Stacia corrected her. "I do need to discuss this with the others."

"How many?" Cait asked.

"Six, including me."

"Wow!" Cait's mouth rounded into an O. "Given that I haven't said ten words to another Reaper until you showed up, it seems like a lot."

Stacia nodded solemnly. "It is. Among us, we Reap all thorough Eastern Europe, Russia, and China. We're always stretched far too thin, but Death hasn't created a new Reaper in the past 200 years."

"What would happen if you quit Reaping?" I asked.

"Now there's a concept. Death would have to pick up the slack." Stacia made a snorting noise. "Maybe. Beyond that, it would be almost impossible to stop Reaping, but nowhere is it written we have to Reap under Death's watchful eye."

"Do you remember when you talked about a dynamic balance where mortals and their good counterbalanced Vampires and their evil?" Cait asked me.

"Aye, I recall that conversation."

"Unless this is one more of Death's lies, the rationale behind us Reaping souls also comes back to a matter of balance."

Stacia bobbed her head. "I recall those lessons. If too many ghosts are stuck on this side of the gateway, it puts Earth in danger from wicked forces, not from the ghosts *per se* but from the energy they unleash."

She still clutched her phone. "If calling is a bad idea, then I have to return home. It took me three days to get here, and—"

"We were going back to Scotland, anyway," I told her. "We can see you returned to Prague."

"Piss on that," Cait said. "Let's teach her to teleport on her own. I did it. No reason she can't."

"I— I'm not sure I'm ready for such a drastic step," Stacia mumbled.

"Do you want stronger magic?" Cait asked point blank.

"Not sure about that, either." Stacia winced. "Sorry. I don't mean to be a wimp, but all I know is Reaping."

"It's a lot to take in," Padhraic said. I sensed a soothing spell threaded in with his words.

"How did you manage?" Stacia asked Cait. "Did you just glom onto the additional magic?"

"Not exactly. I was at Liam's in Ireland. Death showed up, and Liam confronted her about withholding information from her minions. She blew up. While they were shouting at each other, I snuck upstairs and dug into Liam's lore books to find out for myself. It was probably stupid, but as soon as I thought I could manage it, I set a teleport spell in motion."

"Worked for you." I kept my tone as neutral as I could. "But I admit I was worried until I located you."

Cait grinned crookedly. "That's me. Go big or go home. In this instance, I did both." She turned to Stacia. "How about this. I'll come with you to Prague. That way, I can walk you through the magic to make it happen. We'll join our ability. Actually, we have to because you'll be who fashions our destination."

"Oooh, and then you can tell everyone what you told me."

Cait shook her head. "Nope. I'm already on Death's shit list. I'll see you safely back, and then I'll travel to Scotland. How about it? Are you in?"

Stacia chuckled. “I remember you saying those exact same words in Reaper school when we were about to break some rule or other.”

Cait winked broadly, not looking the least bit chagrined. “Guess I haven’t changed.”

I was proud of her. “Would you like me to come with you to Prague?” I asked. “Not that I don’t trust your magic, but just in case.”

“We should be fine,” Cait said. “What about it?” she repeated her offer to Stacia.

“It’s a good way to get my pinfeathers wet,” Stacia said. “I’m in.” She got to her feet. So did Cait.

I wrapped an arm around Cait’s shoulders and held her against me, not for long but enough to let her know how important she was to me. “You haven’t been to Scourie,” I said, “so I’ll meet you at my home in Malin.”

She leaned into me before dipping from under my arm. “I like it. We have a workable plan. I didn’t have a chance to tell you, but before you and Padhraic and Stacia came inside, I cleared my schedule for the next two weeks. It was as long as I dared, so we’re going to have to make as much headway as we can.”

“We won’t waste a minute,” I reassured her. “Padhraic and I will do some spade work while we’re waiting for you.”

“You won’t be waiting long,” Cait said. “How much extra time could one more journey spell take?”

“Probably not much.” I kept my concerns under wraps. Cait had to believe in herself. Her magic was still so new, the last thing I wanted to do was offer up a laundry list of everything that could go wrong.

"We'll take care of the warding here," Padhraic told the Reapers. We'll punch a hole in it for you to teleport through, and then Liam and I will repair everything."

"How will you leave?" Stacia asked.

"From outside," I told her.

Cait picked up her shoulder bag and, in the same voice she'd used to teach me about airplane instrumentation, she began talking with Stacia, detailing how to access the power that had been denied her.

Hesitant at first, Stacia warmed to the ideas quickly. By the time Cait's spell swept them away, her enthusiasm was palpable, but magic was like that. It snatched you up and dug its claws in deep.

"What do you think, mate?" Padhraic asked.

"About?" I went to work resurrecting the warding around the houseboat.

"Looks as if Cait might end up at the head of her own regiment of Reapers."

"Best not say that too loud," I muttered. "You think Death was put out today? We haven't seen anything if Cait goes rogue."

"She already has," Padhraic observed. "It's just a matter of what she does with it."

"Right you are. Shall we?" I headed for the door, and we slid through, closing the warding—and the door—behind us. We'd go to Malin and research the fuck out of the dark gods until Cait showed up.

Then we'd head for Scourie and plot war on the dark gods. D'Chel had my blood. Adva probably wanted a chunk of me too after I'd sent him packing this morning.

"Get in line," I muttered.

"Huh?" Padhraic quirked a dark brow.

"Nothing. Let's get out of here." We'd stopped in the shadowed alcove of Cait's deep front porch. It was a decent place to build and loose a teleport spell. Quiet and out of sight of passersby.

Padhraic opened his magic to me, and we made haste for Ireland. Two weeks was no time at all, but I vowed I'd get Cait back to her sky-sports business before there was nothing left to salvage.

CHAPTER SEVEN, CAIT

I've always loved Prague with its old buildings and cobblestone streets, but I wasn't going there to sightsee. Stacia latched onto her nascent magic like a newborn puppy grabbing onto its mother's teat. It erased one worry: that a taste would scare her so badly she'd run the other way.

While I fed instructions to her, my mind was busy. I couldn't stop thinking about her cadre of Reapers. Reapers who'd banded together despite Death's prohibition against doing just that—in any manner whatsoever.

"Why that last step?" Stacia asked. "I mean, we've already done it."

"If you don't keep feeding information about your destination into the spell, you'll end up somewhere else." I blew out a breath. "My first try, I skipped several steps and didn't get very far."

"I see. Did you tell Liam?"

A snorting laugh rustled through me. "What do you think?"

"Good enough. Your secret is safe with me. Wow, Cait! This is unimaginably awesome. The others will be stoked. I just know it."

Her use of language made me curious. "You've spent time in the States, and fairly recently." I didn't pose it as a question.

She nodded. "Busted. I love California and the whole West Coast. I've snuck off several times." After a hesitation, she added, "One advantage of there being a few of us is we cover for each other."

"But Death always knows where to find you," I protested.

"Yes and no."

I rechecked our coordinates, pleased we hadn't drifted off course, and I waited for Stacia to clarify her statement. When she didn't, I asked, "What's that supposed to mean?"

"There are a lot of us—and only one of her. We've tested just how, erm, present she is and discovered we can get away with a few days out of her gunsights. Sometimes. Depends on her mood and what she's looking for."

I digested the information. I was lucky to steal a few hours' respite, let alone days.

"What?" Stacia quirked a red brow.

"Guess I'm jealous."

"Of?"

"Lots of things." I shrugged. "You have a circle of Reapers who are friends. Death only looks in on you occasionally." I stopped there. No reason to throw myself headfirst into a pity party because I'd been on my own—except for Death, who never left me alone for long enough to do much of anything. And she'd apparently provided for everyone else while letting me swing in the wind.

Stacia threaded an arm around me and gave me a quick hug, but moving a hand interrupted her spell. She felt the fluctuation in the magic circling us and made corrections.

"The others would welcome you—" she began.

I shook my head. "The thought is appreciated, but I have a lot to get done. If I could hang around in Prague, get to know everyone, it would be different. Between Vampires, the dark gods, and Humans Rule, I…"

I, what? It wasn't fair to lay my burdens on Stacia or anyone else. Liam had chosen to support me. Padhraic too. The other Sidhe, not so much. Their interest had been corralling the Leanan Sidhe—their very own brand of Vampire. I supposed some of them had a stake in quashing Humans Rule and maybe the dark gods, but beyond that I didn't expect much.

They weren't doing it for me, the dumb fuck Reaper who'd been unfortunate enough to draw the short straw and end up on Vampire patrol. No. Any efforts on their part would be so they could move back into their compound in Ireland. I'd gathered the ancient castle in Scourie left a lot to be desired.

Another thought occurred to me. "If I so much as darken your door in Prague, it will move Death's lens closer. She won't appreciate any Reaper who offers me zip squat, and you do not want to be under her microscope. Believe me on that one."

"It's an open offer," Stacia said, followed by, "Something feels different."

My heart slammed into hyperdrive before I understood what she'd sensed was our spell winding down. The edges had developed the silvery aspect that meant we were almost in Prague.

"Everything is fine. What you felt means we're nearly to our destination. Next up," I said briskly to conceal my reaction to her "something different" observation, "we ward ourselves."

"We shouldn't have to. I visualized my room."

"We might get lucky and hit it spot on," I told her, "but often these spells lack that level of accuracy. We'll end up in Prague, but maybe a few streets over."

"Got it. What do I do next?"

I walked her through the last part of the spell, proud of myself for adding a cushion of air so we didn't splat ignominiously onto the ground. When the mists cleared, we were in the midst of thick foliage.

"That worked unexpectedly well." I kept my voice low as I unraveled the rest of our spell, including our ward.

"It did. We're in the park a few blocks from my home." She gripped my hand and tugged.

"Nope. Not coming with," I reminded her.

"I was hoping maybe you'd changed your mind."

To cover how closely she'd skirted the truth, I gave her a quick hug and detached my hand. I wanted to at least lay eyes on the other Reapers. I was certain I knew all of them. My longing for the companionship of my own kind shocked me. It wasn't as if I'd stayed up nights aching for another Reaper to share things with.

Why would I? My inner voice was bitter. *Death practically lived on my doorstep.*

"I'll be in touch," Stacia said and melted out of the thicket. Eagerness streamed from her, and I could tell she was anxious to round up the others to share her newfound knowledge.

I sank to a crouch with my back against a thick, old tree trunk to catch my breath and clear my thoughts before I set another teleport spell in motion. This one would be far quicker since I wasn't going all that far.

A chill ran through me, followed by another as my vision opened to the half-light of the realm of the dead. Damn it. A ghost had located me. My heather-and-wildflower scent draws them like a potent drug. But there were plenty of Reapers in this region.

In truth, one had just left my side.

I've grown understandably suspicious when a ghost appears to have picked me out of the pack. Twice now, Vampire minions—not turned, but dead nonetheless—had tried to pass through me with disastrous results. If enough of them succeeded, I'd be stuck in the realm of the dead with no way out.

Death wasn't about to lift a finger to save me. Not after I'd flipped her off and told her I was done.

The chill deepened. Great. More than one ghost. I cast my gaze from side to side and saw spectral forms streaming toward me. Clearly, the Vampire in charge of this mission was hedging his—her?—bets. Damn it. I should have told

Stacia about this particular wrinkle. So she and the others could be on the lookout for ghosts that were only pretending to want to cross over.

Had the Vampires and dark mages figured out some neat trick that turned my gateway into a revolving door? Or had they just offered empty promises. Something like, "Go ahead. We'll bring you back." When they could do no such thing.

Last I checked, there was no chance of communication from the far side of the veil, so those who'd been tricked couldn't warn anyone.

Feeling vulnerable, I got my feet under me and snapped my grave vision shut. Tried to snap it shut. I managed to close myself off from the realm of the dead, but it took twice the magic I expected it would.

The old me—the pre-magic-discovery me—wouldn't have been able to manage it. I could still see the ghosts, of course I could, but they were barely there.

"Let us pass," one cried.

"Aye, you're a Reaper. It's your job," another chimed in.

Arms passed through me. Bodies too, as they threw themselves at me to no avail.

I shook my head hard. What the fuck was I doing hanging about? Eventually, the crowd of spirits would drill chinks in my resolve. As it was, my Reaper side was screaming at me to open the damn gateway.

Reaping is hardwired into me. I can't not Reap. What I can do is control when I open the gateway, but the amount of magic I was pouring into keeping it shut was draining me fast.

Did I have enough left to teleport out of here?

Guess I'm about to find out.

I hadn't built a ward, but it might be a good thing since I'd only have to take it down to teleport. Closing my mind to everything but concentration on my next travel spell, I built it brick by brick as an army of shades formed around me, all crying piteously.

Their voices smote my soul. No matter if they'd turned into Vampire tools, they were still dead. The dead were my responsibility, and—

"Not now." I spoke out loud and kept my tone stern.

"If not now, then when?" a woman squealed as her hand punched through my side.

"I'm not like the rest," another woman garbed in business modern whispered.

A closer look showed gunshot wounds to her chest and a red-stained blouse. Maybe she hadn't been sent by Vampires, but I wasn't willing to chance it.

My cowardice made me ill.

Two more steps and my journey spell would be complete enough to get me out of here. My mouth had gone dry, and my heart pounded like a tripwire, banging against my chest. Sweat slicked my palms and my sides despite a temperature that hovered near freezing.

I had to make this work. I didn't have enough magic for another go. I could always chase down Stacia and the other Reapers, but it wasn't part of my plan. Best not to focus too much on what I'd do if this didn't work. I might sabotage my efforts if I looked backward.

One more step, the one to kindle my spell. I shut out

everything. Shades. The thick greenery. The woman with bullet holes above her heart who'd begun to cry. The ancient feel of Prague tugged at me. A city this old had to be full of ghosts, but not this full.

Vampires must have imported this batch, or most of them anyway. It pissed me off, and I latched onto my anger. I needed the energy, and I turned it into the linchpin to ignite my casting. I didn't try for elegant, like when I'd taught Stacia. What I aimed for was quick.

My spell punched me in the guts, but the forest turned liquid, traded for the blackness of my travel channel. Breathing as if I'd just run a race, I gathered my thoughts. I'd done it. None of the dead could follow. The only magical gateway open to them was the one I controlled, the one allowing them access to the next stage in their soul's existence.

I was still panting when I dropped onto the cobblestone streets in front of Liam's flat. I'd aimed for his living room, but this was close enough. I'd also been so rattled I'd forgotten to cushion my fall. Before I could pick myself up, Liam's door flew open, and he gathered me into his arms, lifting me handily.

I wanted the comfort he offered so much it embarrassed me. What the fuck had happened to Ms. Independent?

"What the hell, Cait? What happened?" He meant to sound soothing, but his tone was so sharp, he reminded me of Death.

I cringed, and he said, "Sorry. Sorry. I felt your energy barreling toward us, and then it just stopped. Thank Danu you're here."

"Is she all right?" Padhraic bolted through the open door, his dark brows drawn into a worried expression.

"I'm fine." I tried for as much dignity as I could muster. It wasn't easy since shutting out the world and leaning into Liam were hella tempting.

"You're not looking fine," Padhraic said.

"Let's go inside." Liam didn't couch it as a request, despite his choice of words.

He carried me through the door before putting me down. Padhraic followed us and shut it. The scents of wet greenery and sandalwood rose as the Sidhe built a ward. I started to tell them not to bother. No ward could keep Death away, and then I remembered she wouldn't be riding to my rescue.

I untangled my bag from around me and dropped it onto a chair.

Even though I resented the hell out of Death's intrusiveness, still her absence felt like a loss. Kind of like I imagined things with an abusive parent might be. Can't live with them, but living without them leaves a hole and takes some practice.

The men had been settled at the table. I took a seat, and Liam poured me a cup of tea fragrant with cinnamon and cloves. It didn't take long to catch him and Padhraic up.

"'Tis a blessing you've come to recognize that particular trap," Liam growled. "When I figure out who's responsible, I'll make them think twice before doing it again."

Padhraic narrowed his eyes into a thoughtful expression. "There seemed to be some lag time between when you realized you were under attack and when you marshaled the magic to leave. Why?"

It was a good question. “No easy answer,” I said and drained half my cup. The tea had a stabilizing effect. Hot and strong and sweet, it fortified me. “Reaping is my go-to place. When the dead come knocking, my first instinct is to open a gateway for them. To have to stop and think why I shouldn’t doesn’t come naturally.”

“What tipped you off these weren’t normal dead?” Liam asked.

“Stacia had just left. If they’d been garden-variety ghosts, they’d have been drawn to her too.” I blew out a long breath. “Just like with Maxwell the first time spirits tried to snare me in Malin. When it happened, I thought it odd they hadn’t latched onto him.”

“Aye, and now we know why they didn’t.” Liam’s tone could have carved glass into splinters.

I splayed both hands on the table. “Enough about me. What happened while I was gone? You can’t have been here that long.”

“We weren’t,” Padhraic said.

“Mostly, we were upstairs in the library selecting books and scrolls to bring back to Scourie,” Liam added. “Your stack is on that table.” He pointed at a respectable pile of mostly old books.

“Why mine?”

A corner of his mouth twitched downward. “So you can learn more about how your magic operates.”

“Aye, you’ve barely scratched the surface,” Padhraic said.

Hot words of protest crowded the back of my throat. I was doing fine, thank you very much. We had more important tasks than my magical side. I'd been figuring things out, and I'd continue to do so.

I felt Liam's gaze on me. Damn it, he had to be inside my head again. "Stop it," I growled.

"Nope. Not going to happen."

His words didn't leave much space for negotiation. "Why? I never signed up for a guardian."

He reached across the table and dropped a hand atop mine. "When I opened your eyes to your magic, I took on the responsibility of making certain the knowledge didn't get you into trouble."

"But I teleported halfway around the world my first time."

A snort rolled from him. "Aye, and when I figured out what you'd done, I was stunned."

"Why?" Erg. I'd been reduced to a one-word vocabulary.

"Most of us experimented with teleporting one village over," Padhraic answered in Liam's stead. "Gutsy to take on a journey spell as long as the one you directed."

"At first, I assumed you'd done something sensible," Liam went on. "Death disabused me of that notion damned fast. She knew exactly where you'd gone. And then she said a number of things that made sense."

Crap. There it was again. Death was a whole lot like a mother, someone who knew me better than I knew myself. The crater I'd carved into my being when I told her I was done grew deeper.

"What did she say?" I asked. Part of me didn't want to know, but a bigger part did.

"That you'd been casting magic for a long time, and your

days of testing the waters with teensy spells were a product of the distant past."

I nodded reluctantly. She did, indeed, have my number. "What happened after that?" I pressed.

"More sparring," Liam said. "She knew where you were, and I asked why she hadn't left to make certain you emerged unscathed. Regardless of her plans, I gathered power for a teleport spell of my own."

"What did she say about not leaving?" I snared Liam's gaze, not willing to let him off the hook."

"That she was trying to make a point, teach you a lesson." He hesitated for a moment, perhaps reconstructing their conversation. "She said something like mistakes would teach you more than successes."

It was very like something Death might have given voice to.

"This isn't productive," Padhraic muttered.

I agreed with him, so I glanced from one Sidhe to the other. "We should be on our way back to Scourie, shouldn't we?"

Liam nodded. "We were just waiting for you."

"Has anyone checked Malin village lately?" I asked, concerned there might be more innocent casualties. Souls I'd need to Reap.

"We did," Padhraic said. "Right after we arrived, we warded ourselves and walked the village. All appeared to be in order."

"As in, neither of us sensed Vampires or the dark mages. Kilkenny Green was back to normal. No bodies scattered about. What were all over the bloody place were people sporting Humans Rule logos. On caps, shirts, briefcases. You name it, that depiction of a man perched on top of a mountain with his arms raised has become ubiquitous."

"Oh-oh. Not good," I murmured.

"Nay, 'tisn't," Padhraic agreed.

"Not much we can do to stop them," Liam said. "We're the enemy. Any effort on our part to intervene will be viewed as interference."

"We can force those using the magic they profess to disdain out into the open," I suggested. "Kind of a *hoisted with their own petard* approach."

"We're not there yet," Padhraic said.

"We can't fight on too many fronts," Liam agreed. "Our first priority has to be taking a chunk out of the Vampires. To do that, we have to also target the dark mages."

"What we were discussing before you showed up," Padhraic told me, "was who to go after first."

"Makes sense to discourage the dark gods," I replied. "If they're lending power to the Vampires, getting rid of them will cut the legs out from under the Vamps."

"Same conclusion we came to," Liam said, but he didn't sound happy about it. "The dark mages have been around for a long while. They're canny and persistent. We can't kill them, so we have to somehow persuade them to go back to whatever they were doing before they got excited about helping Vampires."

I closed my teeth over my lower lip, thinking. "We might not have to go it alone," I murmured.

"What are you considering?" Padraic asked.

"When you were still Leanan Sidhe..." I began and grimaced. "Sorry. Didn't mean to be quite so blunt."

"It's all right," he said. "Go on."

"Death and some of the other deities helped us defeat you by holding off the dark mages for a while," I said.

"Means they have a dog in this race," Liam said. "Or they'd never have offered."

"Exactly." I nodded.

"Leaves us with two choices," he continued, sounding thoughtful. "We can dig around and try to ferret out what their stake is—"

"Or we can invite them to a council meeting and ask them," Padhraic broke in. "I favor that approach. It's cleaner and a whole lot faster."

"I agree." I finished my tea and rolled my shoulders back.

"Two votes out of three has it," Liam said.

"How would you have cast yours?" I asked.

"Not sure. Dealing with deities has always been tricky. They're never honest with one another, and certainly not with those like us whom they consider inferior, but it's worth a shot. Our lives could become considerably simpler if they signed on to help."

"They did before."

"Aye, but that was before you told Death to piss up a rope." Liam sent a pointed glance my way.

"I can't have been her only motivator," I countered. "I'm just not that important to her."

At least, I didn't believe I was. It wasn't as if she'd always singled me out for "special" treatment. That had only happened after she dumped Vampire duty into my lap.

For the millionth time I wondered why she'd chosen me. Out of probably hundreds of us, surely she could have found a more malleable Reaper. One who would have been more like Jake, my predecessor who'd smiled pretty to her face and gone back to doing nothing as soon as she left.

Why did Death have what appeared to be a vested interest in Vamps all of a sudden? They'd been around forever, and she'd never singled them out before. Yeah, there were lots more of them, but surely she'd seen waves of evil come and go since the dawn of time.

I got to my feet and wandered over to my pile of assigned reading. An ungrateful part of me groaned, but it didn't make it past my lips. I should appreciate the hell out of Liam for taking the time to dig through his resources and figure out what would help me most.

"Ready when you are," I said brightly and picked up my ever-present shoulder bag before gathering the books into my arms.

The men got up and joined me, snaring stacks of scrolls before they crossed the room. "This won't take long," Liam told me. His spell built around us and I absorbed the tantalizing feel of his magic. Just before teleport magic swept us away, I heard Stacia's voice in my mind, struggling with telepathy.

Not that we didn't use mind speech to talk with Death, but using it among ourselves was foreign. Her words were garbled enough, I couldn't understand her. *"Wait a moment before you try again,"* I sent back. *"I'm en route."*

I didn't say to where in case someone was listening in.

"What was that?" Liam broke the flow of his power before finalizing his travel spell.

"Stacia is trying to reach me. It's all right. Whatever it is will hold until we get to Scotland."

He nodded curtly and kindled his teleport casting.

I hoped to hell I'd been right, that Stacia's fumbling attempts at telepathy hadn't been a call for help. When I reached for her in a few minutes, surely she'd still be there. It would be horrible luck if something evil intervened and she'd moved beyond my reach.

Think positive, I cautioned myself.

Nothing good ever came from imagining the worst.

CHAPTER EIGHT, LIAM

I'd expected Stacia to communicate with Cait, but not quite so soon. Barely an hour had passed since she left Prague. My gut told me something had happened. Perhaps the spirit mob had decided any Reaper would do? But that would only happen if the Vampires piloting them had chosen a different strategy.

Made a certain amount of sense.

Cait was clearly onto their current bait tactic. They still wanted to snare her, but perhaps their latest gambit would be indirect. As in, we've got your friends. If you want them back...

Vamps excelled at playing dirty, but I didn't voice my concerns. Cait was a master at projecting a can-do attitude, but I'd noticed frayed spots in her aura. Being under almost constant attack from Vamps was taking a definite toll. I wanted to whisk her away to a place she'd be safe for a while.

Except no place like that existed on Earth. Not for her. So

long as she was here, the dead could find her. Both those genuinely in need of her magic and the faux dead sicced on her by their Vamp masters.

Would Death and the other deities still be willing to help?

I didn't see why not, but since I didn't understand their motivations in the first place, I was far from certain. Padhraic's idea to invite as many as would come to a meeting was solid. We'd find out quickly enough if any were still on board. We might throw a gathering and end up looking at a room full of Sidhe after the gods snubbed our invitation.

The walls of the Scourie Castle formed around us. I'd known this transit would be quick, and it was. I'd aimed for the main chamber since it was the cheeriest spot in the otherwise damp and unappealing structure. Perhaps fifteen meters square, it was mostly bare beyond a fire crackling in an enormous floor-to-ceiling hearth at the far end of the room.

Cait still clutched her armful of books, and she turned in a full circle taking in rusty suits of armor and an assortment of wall tapestries that hung in tatters.

"What happened to the furniture?" she asked.

"No one has lived here in hundreds of years," I told her. "After we left, I assume local residents took what they wanted."

"Have you been sleeping on the floor?"

Padhraic made a snorting sound. "I have. Can't speak for anyone else."

She walked close to the fire while muttering, "Chilly in here."

"I'll let everyone know we've returned," Padhraic said.

"Hold up," I told him and ran the past couple of days through my mind. My last communication with the other Sidhe had been when they restored Padhraic's full power and agreed he could accompany me.

Padhraic furled his brows, waiting.

"That stone Krin gave you, has it, um, done anything?"

"Nay. It might have been cut glass for all the trouble it's been." He withdrew the oblong crystal from a pocket. "I'd almost forgotten about it. Why did you ask?"

"Probably because I'd forgotten about it as well. Aye, let everyone know we've returned. If the council could convene an all-Sidhe meeting soon, we can get things going and at least pick a direction.

"On it," Padhraic said and loped out of the room.

What I didn't give voice to was that the Sidhe voting to wage war on Earth-bound Vampires was scarcely a foregone conclusion. Many of us probably viewed our problem as solved. The Leanan had been Sidhe once upon a time. It placed them firmly in our court, but we'd done battle and sent them packing.

I could just see my kinsmen dusting their hands together and quietly shunting the other Vamps off for some other magical camp to deal with. They'd allowed Padhraic to accompany me to the States, but my guess was it had been a field test of his newfound allegiance to us.

Whoever had been monitoring him through the crystal must have passed him with high marks. Convinced we could trust him, the other Sidhe wouldn't feel a pressing need to go after the rest of the Vampire crew.

If the consensus ran counter to taking on the Vampires and the dark gods, no one would be the least bit interested in inviting deities into our midst.

"That's odd." Cait had set her stack of books on the floor in front of the fireplace.

"What's odd?" I focused my attention on her. The twin vertical lines she got between her eyes when she was worried were out in force.

"Stacia. I can't reach her. Been trying ever since we got here. Damn it." She fisted a hand and punched the air. "I was afraid something like this would happen, and—"

A blast of familiar magic swooshed through the room. I didn't have to turn around to know Death was here.

"Oh you were, huh?" Death shouted and stalked toward Cait until she stood nose to nose with her.

Cait regarded Death from beneath lowered brows. "If you're about to launch into a blame-casting session, shelve it."

"Those other Reapers are in big trouble." Death was still shouting. "Because of you. You couldn't keep your fat mouth shut about all that extra magic, could you?"

Cait shifted her shoulder bag to one side and crossed her arms under her breasts. "Stacia came to me."

"So?" Death arched a silver brow.

"She wanted to know what was going on."

"You could have talked about your Vampire woes and called it even."

I thought Death would stop there, but she went right on rolling.

"Instead, you taught her to teleport. You told her how to

access her additional magic, and the minute she got back to Prague, she couldn't wait to spread the news."

"You never were particularly good at getting to the point," Cait growled. "What kind of trouble is she in? And if she's in desperate straits, why the hell are you here and not helping her?"

"I have a funny habit of not bailing people out who tripped over their own stupidity."

So far, I'd been silent. This didn't appear to be a venue for me to smile warmly and welcome Death to Scourie Castle. I settled for, "Good to see you again."

She rolled her eerie eyes. "Bullcrap. Lying doesn't become you."

"Perhaps not, but I'm not quite ready to totally dispense with civility."

Cait slitted her green eyes. "When you got here, you said Reapers, plural, were in trouble. How many and where?"

"I suppose you're going to ride to the rescue?" Death smirked.

"Hell yeah, I am. You're not doing shit to help them." Cait shook her head. "For Christ's fucking sake. These are your minions. Your people. How can you stand by and let them sink?"

"Easily. I established rules. So long as my *underlings*"—she stressed the word—"played by them, I was more than willing to protect you from the big bad world. No more." She settled her hands on her hips, elbows akimbo. "I'm done."

"Where are the Reapers who ran into difficulties?" I asked. Fairly certain Death would be immune to my magic, I wove a small compulsion spell into my question anyway.

"Now what's the fun in that?" She turned the ever-changing collage of her eyes my way. "Maybe you'll find them in time. Maybe you won't."

Cait rocked from foot to foot. No longer crossed over her body, her arms swung by her sides, hands curled into fists. "Why'd you show up here?"

"To make certain you knew the unpleasant results of your meddling." Death lowered her head until she was at eye level with Cait. "You do realize the jig is up. One Reaper —you—might have been able to keep the hidden magic a secret, but now half a dozen of you know about it."

"You should thank me." Cait skinned her lips back from her teeth. "I was doing your job. One you should have taken care of when all of us were in Reaper school."

"Something must be amiss with your hearing. Or your memory. I told you I already tried spinning it that way. Didn't work well."

"You told me," I spoke up. "Cait wasn't there at the time."

Death flapped a hand at me and returned her attention to Cait. "There are many things you do not understand, child. I had a system in place, one that ensured enough of the dead would cross the veil to maintain a balance point."

"Where do all the Vampire kills come in?" Cait shot back. "The ghosts sauntering around on the other side of the veil as if they own the place. No one seems to be claiming them for Hell, and they sure as fuck aren't going to the good side of the beyond."

"Language, child."

"Like I give a shit. You didn't answer my question."

I repressed an urge to step between them. This wasn't

about me, but it was tough to stand by while Death ran roughshod over Cait.

She's holding her own, I reminded myself. Much as I wanted her to need me, she was capable of fighting her own battles.

"Many aspects are out of kilter," Death ground out. "Your actions have made things worse."

I shelved my vow to stay out of it. "Perhaps they're worse now," I cut in smoothly, "but betimes things must grow worse before they can improve. The Vampire problem has been brewing for a long while. It predates when you assigned them to Cait. At least the Leanan aren't in the picture any longer."

"So far, I haven't seen where it's bought us anything," Death said.

"We only fought that battle a month ago," Cait protested. "Nothing is instant." She clasped her hands together. "Please. Where are the other Reapers? I'm going to go after them, and it would help me so much if I didn't waste days or weeks locating them."

"Help is a two-way street, child, and—"

"I am not your child," Cait shrieked. "If you're not going to help, leave."

"What? No offers of tea? Breaking bread with my Sidhe allies?" Death showed me a mouthful of teeth.

I lined my words up carefully. "The Sidhe are your allies, as we are supporters of all deities. The magical world is small, and we have to stick together."

"Listen to him," Death hissed at Cait. "You don't see the Sidhe knifing each other in the back."

I coughed and cleared my throat before I said, "The Leanan did precisely that."

"Aye, and look how they ended up. Trapped in a pit."

I held my hands up, palms out in a show of surrender. "The Sidhe are about to convene a meeting. We will determine if it's in our best interest to continue to fight Vampires, the dark mages, and Humans Rule. It is possible we won't agree on our next steps."

"What?" Cait yelped. "I figured at least that part of things was a done deal. How could your people decide to drop the ball now?"

"Easily. The Leanan were clearly our problem." I stopped there. Depending on how you slanted the mirror, the other evil manifestations I'd listed might fall into our wheelhouse.

Or not.

I was in an uncomfortable position. Much as I wanted to reassure Cait she could count on the full force of the Sidhe standing behind her crusade to annihilate the remaining Vampires, I wouldn't lie to her. Death had been instrumental in assisting us with the Leanan. I owed her for stepping in on our behalf and persuading the other gods to aid our cause.

Both women were glaring at me. I inclined my head Death's way. "You are most welcome to remain. If things proceed as I hope, one of the offshoots of our council meeting will be invitations to deities such as yourself."

Magic bubbled around Cait. A fledgling teleport spell. I didn't have to ask where she was headed. Off to hunt for the missing Reapers. "If you wait a bit, I'll come with you," I told her.

Anger sheeted from Cait, but underneath it, I also read

hurt. My disclosure about my kinsmen must have cut deep. "Would you have wanted me to lie to you?" I asked. She'd know what I was referring to.

"Never. Better to know where I stand." She tossed her head back, and her black hair spilled over her shoulders. "Depending on what I find, I might not be back. It's clear to me Reapers have to stick together since we can't count on anyone else."

The barbed comment was aimed at Death. And at me. Before I could apologize for my kin, tell her how important she was to me, her spell took off, and she was gone. It was the second time I'd been left standing next to Death in the wake of Cait's teleport spell.

"Planning to chase after her again?" Death inquired archly. "Or have you figured out she can take care of herself?"

"You make independence sound like a curse," I muttered.

"In some instances, it is."

I swung to face her. "Why'd you choose Cait?"

"For Vampire duty?" At my nod, she went on. "She's bright, capable, internally motivated, and she doesn't like to lose."

I frowned. "Surely, that description matches more than one of your Reapers."

"It does. Cait has always had a driven side, though. More so than any of the others. Jake was an experiment. He was the first Reaper with an exclusive assignment. It didn't go well. Vampires proliferated under his not-so-watchful eyes."

She hesitated for a moment. "Maxwell was another disappointment. A worse one than Jake, truth be told."

"I would think so, since he sold out to Vampires. I still haven't figured out what was in it for him."

"Neither have I." She pressed her lips into a thin line. "Except they left him alone. I also have yet to catch up with him. He's still out there."

"Any chance of him reuniting with his body?"

"None. I burned it. Normally, I bury my Reapers, but I was afraid the Vampires would have some way of reanimating him."

Death seemed more receptive than she'd been when she stormed in here. Should I give voice to the one thought uppermost in my mind? "You might not exactly want to hear this—" I began.

"Out with it, and then I'll be on my way," she broke in. "If your kinsmen put out a call to us, I may return. Depends on the will of the others. Many of my associates have wanted to rid Earth of the dark mages for a long while." She eyed me. "That's your angle. Not Vampires. Vampires won't buy you much."

"Thank you for the advice." I tried for a smile but probably only managed a rueful expression. "Your Reapers are loyal, but you stand at a crossroads. One where you can gather the reins and teach them about their additional magic while you maintain at least minimal control of your acolytes."

"I've considered and discarded that approach." Her tone was stiff, formal.

"It's the only one open to you. You were absolutely correct when you told Cait the cat was out of the bag. You can't stuff it back inside. Even if you started over with a new crop of Reapers, the old ones aren't going anywhere. Eventually, they'll reveal your secrets."

"No good choices," she agreed. "First, I must see how far the poison spreads, and then—"

"But the Reapers won't view it as poison. Additional magic is a gift. You could be their hero and teach them how to wield it, and..." I ran out of words. Mostly because they were bouncing off her as if she were a brick wall.

"You started this, Sidhe," she hissed in a low voice. "Where I come from, the one who instigates a problem is the one to fix it."

I nodded. "I offered you a solution."

"Find another."

I made a grab for my temper. "I don't work for you."

"Good thing. I demand absolute allegiance."

Breath puffed from my mouth, creating clouds in the chilly air. The fire wasn't doing anything to warm the cavernous room. Allegiance, much like respect, had to be earned, but I didn't go there.

"This isn't about allegiance," I said. "It's about an obstacle that began when Vampires spiraled out of control. Fueled by magic from the dark mages, they're the true problem. Mortals played right into their hands with the ill-conceived Humans Rule movement."

I stood straighter and added, "We're fighting a war on three fronts."

"Maybe," Death tossed out.

"Aye. 'Tis far from a foregone conclusion. The Sidhe are known for avoiding conflicts. Some of us will advise a return to the era when we remained hidden from human eyes."

"Not possible," Death said.

"I agree, but I'm only one vote. I'm going to check in with some of the council. Once I get a sense of what comes next, I'm going to try to find Cait."

"Why?"

"How can you ask that? Don't you believe she might be in over her head?"

"No. She has a quick mind. She'll figure things out."

Before I could ask how she could be so certain, she was gone. So much for her sticking around to see which way the Sidhe winds would blow. But then, she'd already told me she was leaving.

"Krin!" I raised my mind voice.

"In the kitchen. It's the only warm room in the castle."

I strode out of the main chamber, down hallways and half a set of risers to the set of rooms comprising the castle kitchen. Back when the structure had been built, kitchens had butteries, other rooms for food preparation, and yet others that contained ovens.

Krin sat in front of a cookstove, his feet propped on its edge. A dozen other Sidhe milled about, taking advantage of the stove's warmth. Padhraic perched on the edge of a table, head buried in one of the scrolls we'd brought from Malin.

"When's the meeting?" I asked.

"Tonight over supper," Krin told me.

"I'll be there."

"Why do I get the feeling you're heading out again?" Krin slitted his dark eyes. The crystal he'd tasked Padhraic with hanging onto lay across one palm, pulsing with a warm greenish glow.

"Cait's gone after some Reapers who are in trouble," I said. "I'm going to help her."

"Isn't that Death's job?" Dena asked, followed by, "Didn't I just sense her here?"

"Yes to both," I replied, "except Cait doesn't exactly work for Death any longer. And Death refused to lift a finger to help the other Reapers."

"How are either of those things possible?" Dena moved closer to me. A white robe swung with the motion of her hips.

"Cait quit." I didn't see any reason to go into details. Labeling Death as an overbearing bitch wouldn't exactly be something the rest of the Sidhe didn't already know.

"Does she get to do that?" Dena shook her head, clearly bewildered.

"I have no idea, but she did, and now Death has washed her hands of any responsibility." I also decided not to mention she'd placed the blame squarely on me for her Reaper's defection from the fold.

"All right. It explains Cait, but why would Death deny aid to her other minions?" Dena pressed.

"The short version is Cait told another Reaper about their hidden magic. Presumably, the Reaper passed the information on, and—"

Dena held up a hand, fingers splayed. "I understand. Death has a problem. Insurrection in her ranks. What's she going to do about it?"

"I have no idea."

Padhraic looked up from the scroll. "Want my company, mate?"

“Aye, it would be most welcome.”

Krin got to his feet and started toward Padhraic, crystal extended. Before he reached the other man, he must have changed his mind because he dropped the bit of quartz into his pocket.

“We’ll be back for the all-Sidhe meeting,” I told everyone. “Hopefully with a few Reapers in tow.”

“They’re not part of us,” Krin reminded me.

Dena patted my arm. “If Reapers are with you, we’ll find a spot for them to wait.”

“Thank you.” I hurried out of the kitchens before I said something I regretted, like we had enough problems without resorting to the false superiority we’ve always clung to. The belief we were somehow a cut above other magic wielders.

The last thing we needed was infighting.

Padhraic joined me. “Any idea where we’re going?” he asked.

“Aye. We’ll begin with Prague. It’s where Cait left Stacia.”

“Do you actually believe we can make much progress in a handful of hours?”

I didn’t answer. No matter how gargantuan a task it was, I would find Cait and extricate her and the other Reapers from whatever kind of fresh hell had captured them.

“You don’t have to come,” I said stiffly.

“Don’t be a dick, Liam. I wouldn’t have offered if I didn’t want to help. I know you love her.”

His spell billowed around us. Literally moments later, we’d traded the dank halls of Scourie Castle for Prague’s cobblestoned streets in the old section of town. We slipped between two buildings, and Padhraic dismantled the warding he'd wrapped us in.

"Your magic has made a good recovery," I told him.

He smiled, and it warmed his eyes. "Aye. I didn't realize how much I'd missed it. Sidhe power is clean. Being able to summon magic and not feel like I dipped my body in a trough of slime is a gift." He paused for a moment. "Thank you."

I clapped him on the back. "No need for more thanks. Let's get this project off the blocks." I sent magic spinning outward as I sought the particular feel of Reaper magic.

It bounced back at me immediately. Maybe this wouldn't take as long as I'd feared.

"'Twas almost too easy," Padhraic muttered.

He was right. We had to proceed with caution, or we might fall into the same trap that had snared the Reapers. "If they're somewhere beyond the gates," I said, "we don't have the magic to open them."

"We'll figure something out. Come on." Padhraic set off at a lope with me next to him.

CHAPTER NINE, CAIT

Death made me so angry I couldn't see straight. But I expected it from her. What I hadn't anticipated was Liam's admission the Sidhe might not pick up the mantle again. That they might exit stage left now that the Leanan had been dealt with.

My sense of honor was outraged, but then I'd never been a Sidhe. Clearly, they played by different guidelines. From my perspective, no one got to decide they were better than anyone else, and that their status earned them a pass. If the Sidhe walked away from this problem, they weren't any better than Humans Rule.

The incipient war against evil was everyone's problem. Even mortals since they ran the greatest risk of ending up collateral damage. Not because magic was inherently bad, but because they were so fragile.

A dull ache pounded in my chest. I wanted Liam to be on my side, but I feared he'd choose his Sidhe kin over me any day. Probably his bluntness was his way of warning me not to expect too much from them.

Or from him.

"Buck up," I muttered. "Hard to lose something I never had."

Truth in my words seared me, made my heart hurt worse. I'd get over Liam. I had to. I had work to do, and having half my brain spinning in circles over a man who'd never be mine was a recipe for disaster.

Why would I even still want him after what he'd admitted? I shouldn't, but letting go of the tender hopes I'd had for us—for him and me—would take time.

Because I'd just been there, I aimed for the thicket where I'd last seen Stacia. It's piquant greenery circled me with little effort on my part. Tracking her energy from here should be straightforward. I chased Liam out of my thoughts. My magic was still new enough, it required all my attention. Mixing air and earth, I built a tracking spell and cast a wide arc.

Reaper power beckoned from a spot perhaps a mile away, but it didn't belong to Stacia. I screwed my face into a mask of concentration. What should I do? Find the Reaper I could sense and talk with him—or her?

My gut told me it would eat up time I didn't have. I might have written off Stacia's garbled efforts at mind speech if Death hadn't shown up and announced pointblank that Reapers were in deep shit.

Because of me.

She had to mean Stacia, which also meant I had to be quick about things.

Maybe being closer would help with telepathy, so I employed mind speech and called Stacia's name. After half a dozen repetitions with no response, I gave up on that approach.

An idea barreled into my head, one so obvious and so simple I kicked myself for not coming up with it sooner. Part of my Reaper magic coerces the dead to do my bidding. Eh, maybe coerce is too strong a term. I can encourage them to move in a particular direction, but it's a lot like herding cats.

Once mortals get over the fact they're no longer alive, the ones who are reluctant to cross over dive into an unholy fascination with other ghosts.

Who's here? Who isn't?

Some ghosts, like Maxwell, hang around because they're ashamed. They want to at least try to atone for their sins before they leave. Like I told him, it won't make any difference. Whoever keeps score doesn't give extra credit for posthumous efforts. His fate was sealed the moment the Harpy stole his soul.

Other shades—mostly mortals who'd had their lives cut out from under them by accidents or disease at a relatively young age—weren't ready for the finality of crossing beneath the gateway. I've never tried to marshal them to do my bidding, but there's no reason why my magic couldn't be bent in that direction.

Raising magic to force them to cross is forbidden—except for Vampires—but I had something else entirely in mind.

Ghosts have an affinity for Reapers. If Stacia and her Reaper friends were trapped in the nether regions by the same Vampire minions who'd tried to capture me, I'd find out about it quick enough.

I altered the focus of my magic. If what I tried didn't work, I could always chase down the Reaper I'd sensed and find out what he knew. My eyesight shifted to the half-light of the realm of the dead. It's not so much a physical change as a psychic one. The thicket shaded to gray before it vanished; shades came into view. Interesting I hadn't been able to see them until now. Granted, they were quite a ways distant, but still...

My sickle appeared out of nowhere, balanced over one of my shoulders. What the hell? I blinked at it, surprised by its arrival because I hadn't seen it in years. Why would it chose to materialize now?

Curious and confused, I wrapped my fingers around its handle to stabilize it; the instrument pulsed warmly as if greeting an old friend.

The scythe is linked to the realm of the dead, but I've always considered it a cheap prop. Something to make me look the part, rather than an element of my Reaper birthright. I'd asked Death once where it went when I returned to Earth, but she never answered me.

Before the Vampire minions figured out I'd returned for a rematch, I loosed ribbons of enticing magic. My heather-and-wildflower scent intensified, and two ghosts, a man and a woman, sashayed toward me. Their days of doing anything as prosaic as walking were long past. Clothing from a bygone era hung off them in tatters. Clearly, these were ghosts with tenure.

"Have you seen other Reapers?" I asked, taking care to

keep the part of me that wanted to open a gateway under wraps. Reaping is as natural as breathing, and holding myself back from allowing a portal to jump to life wasn't easy.

Always before, cracking my grave vision and creating a gateway went hand in hand. It was surprisingly difficult to separate the two.

"Aye, we have," the woman told me. Red hair that must have once been luxuriant spilled around her in a faded cascade. Bone showed through spots in her chin and cheeks.

"They didn't try to Reap us, either," the man added in an archaic language I hadn't heard in centuries. Bald as a pinball, his skull shone through places flesh had long since fallen away.

Neither shade made any effort to get close enough to use me as a portal. I felt rather than saw other spirits closing from behind. Maybe my magical senses were growing sharper, but they had a different feel from the two floating a couple of feet away.

It was tough to be certain, but my money was on the incoming group being Vampire spawn.

Before the new crop got close enough to become a management problem, I wove what I hoped would be an irresistible spell. "Come on," I urged. "Help me find the other Reapers. They're my friends."

Spell in hand, I threaded it around the two who'd spoken with me. Others melted out of dirt and shadow, clearly drawn by my magic. So far, this was working better than I'd hoped.

"She wants the Reapers," the man told the other shades.

Raising bony fingers, he pointed toward my right, and I motioned him to lead the way. He took off faster than I'd anticipated with the other ghosts bunched behind and within him. Body boundaries aren't an issue for the dead. They passed through each other as the second cadre of spirits chased after us.

The woman sidled next to me. "They're evil, those ones." She jerked her chin over one shoulder.

"I know," I told her. "Vampires made them."

"Ha. Killed them, you mean, and then chewed holes in their souls. They couldn't pass over if they wanted to." She lowered her breathy voice. "No soul. No passage."

I wanted to smile. Her tone had suggested she was imparting a state secret to me. Reapers know these things, but the Vamp victims I'd pushed through the portal had enough in the way of a soul left to qualify for transport.

It was too good an entry to pass up, so I asked, "Why are you and the others still here? You have souls. I feel them."

"We have our reasons. Different for each of us."

"Well, if you ever change your mind—" I began.

"We know," she cut me off and whirled, spectral features drawn into a hissing snarl.

The Vampire minions were on us. I'd felt them getting closer and closer. "They can't hurt us." I meant to be reassuring, but the ghost woman snarled louder.

The clump of dead ahead of me seemed happy enough to do my bidding without a magical assist, so I switched things up. Where before I'd used air and earth, I added as much water to the mix as I could muster.

Vamps hated water.

Would the antipathy extend to their minions? I was about to find out.

I twisted to face a glut of shades. Shit. How many mortals had Vampires killed, anyway? I'd always assumed they either turned their prey or kept them alive for long enough to feed from for months, if not years.

Power flowed from my fingertips. It stopped the Vampires' ghost army in their tracks. Whew. Good call on my part.

"Kill them!" my ghost sidekick screeched.

"Nice try. They're already dead," I told her and focused on the seething mass of spirits pushing against the perimeter of my magic. There were a lot of them. Hundreds. Eventually, they'd break through.

Before it happened, I'd maximize my advantage. "What have you done with my friends?" I shouted.

"You'll never find them," a shade shouted back.

"They'll wander forever in our halls," another said with a snide intonation.

"Halls?" I mocked the speaker. "What in the unholy hell are you calling halls? This area"—I swung an arm wide—"is a liminal space, a boundary between the world where you ate and breathed and made love and Death's realm."

I didn't bother listing out Hades and Arawn and all the other deities who watched over the dead.

"You might not have noticed, but you're stuck here," I went on. "Forever if you chose not to pass over."

"They can't." The woman next to me sounded vindicated. As if their limbo state were a curse.

"Reaper!" floated to me. Clearly, my phalanx of guides had noticed I wasn't keeping up.

"Be there in a moment," I called and returned my attention to the seething horde. It was growing by the minute. Damn it. Next thing, a Vamp would stroll through. Or one of the dark mages.

That thought galvanized me into action. I had to find the other Reapers. Sparring with Vampire victims wasn't why I was here. I sent a rolling jolt of magic into the center of the glut of shades and then turned and ran toward where the other ghosts were leading me.

Remember what I said about shades being a curious lot? Not much is left for them to do, and they remind me of an old woman who lives at the end of a busy street peering through her window shades. Very little escapes her.

The same is true of loose spirits.

I trusted the ghosts knew precisely where Stacia and the other Reapers were, and they didn't disappoint me. My magic wouldn't hold the Vampire-slain at bay for long, but at least they weren't right on my heels anymore.

"You did good," my ghostly sidekick crowed. "You should come here more often."

"My task is to help you cross over," I said.

"Stop right there. I don't want to. Pah. I was hoping you were different." She edged into the group of ghosts ahead and to the sides of us, moving through bodies as she went.

I nodded to myself. She'd made a life for herself, and she probably never would cross the veil. I respected her decision, but too many like her spelled trouble for everyone else.

"Reaper!"

I hurried toward the summons, pushing through shades when going around them didn't work. By the time I located the man in archaic clothing, he was pointing at a crumbling earthen wall. I blinked a few times. No walls existed in this domain.

Where had this one come from? At least ten feet high, it extended as far as I could see.

"The other Reapers are on the far side," he told me.

"How do you know?" I asked.

"We saw them forced through," he said, accompanied by a chorus of "ayes," and, "We did, indeed."

I reshaped the same type of seeking spell I'd used from the thicket. Sure enough, Reaper emanations pinged back at me. My next shot out of the box was telepathy. *"Stacia. Can you hear me?"*

Nothing.

"Do you know what's on the other side of the wall?" I asked the shades. They stared back at me, not offering anything useful.

Either they were frightened, or they didn't know. Did shades experience emotions? My guess was they did. If Maxwell could be ashamed and resolute, there was no reason this bunch couldn't be fearful.

I walked a few feet in both directions and established I couldn't walk around the wall. Maybe I could climb over it, but it wouldn't be easy. I'd have to carve steps in the dirt, and they'd probably fall in.

Could I teleport through it?

Nope. I needed to visualize a destination, and I had no idea what was on the far side. While I paced and considered options, the shades faded away. The good ones, anyway. It was only a matter of time before the nasty-ass Vampire prey broke loose.

I kept coming back to the barrier. Had I moved to some corridor that wasn't part of Earth, but wasn't within the realm of the dead, either? Not that I'd spent all that much time in the nether world. I was usually only here long enough to craft a portal and shut it once the dead passed over.

I had to do something.

But what?

Telepathy wasn't doing it, so I shouted Stacia's name. It didn't do any more good than my attempts at mind speech.

Finally, because I didn't have a better idea, I swung the sickle off my shoulder and began cutting small ledges in the dirt. Utilitarian, the unadorned metal tool stood nearly as tall as me with a handle that didn't look as if it could heft the weight of the blade, yet it always did. Sparks flew when the pick contacted the earthen wall, and I felt a shock of power as the blade loosed its ability.

Good thing both my boots were still firmly planted on the ground. Not that I've had much occasion to wield my sickle as a cutting tool, but I'd never suspected it held power all its own.

Just one more thing Death neglected to mention.

I'd made it to about the halfway point chopping steps when the putrid feel of the Vamps' pet shades made my skin crawl. I eyeballed the series of footholds, but I didn't stop to think too hard before I dug my blade in and used it like an axe to help me climb. I would run out of steps long before I hit the top, but I'd be close enough to see over it and throw myself down the other side.

Maybe.

I was making a shit ton of assumptions. Like the other side looked the same as this one. I was in a magical realm. The other side could have a hundred foot drop into a moat with sea serpents or dragons or the Minotaur.

Yeah. Good thing I didn't just pole vault over the top and hope for the best. I still felt Reaper power pulsing from the other side. At least they weren't dead, but they sure weren't doing much to help themselves escape, either.

Had they been drugged?

Clonked over the head?

Ensorcelled?

The latter option was probably closer to the truth. Crap. If they'd been bound by magic, would I know enough to free them?

I was close enough to touch the top with my fingertips. I'd run out of footholds a wee bit sooner than I'd hoped, but this was good enough. I curled my fingers over the top, kicked a few more steps. They weren't very secure, but I didn't need them to be.

When I glanced back at my scythe, it floated up to me. If my situation hadn't been so desperate, I'd have laughed. Who would have guessed the damned thing was sentient. It was certainly linked to my magic, and...

I had one of those "aha" moments. My magic was stronger, or I was finally aware of it. Regardless, the sickle's new moves had to be reflective of my own magical state.

Glad I figured that out.

Panting from effort, I pulled myself up until my forearms rested on top of the wall. My shoulders were screaming in protest. I told them to stand the fuck down. At first, I couldn't see anything but a gray mist that obscured the other side.

Victorious screeches told me the Vampire minions had not only reached me. They were crowding against the wall. What would happen if I tossed the sickle into their midst? Would it cheerfully lop off heads? Arms? Herd the mass of undead bastards into Purgatory?

Heh. First I'd have to kick a gateway open.

"Dream on," I muttered and experimented with my vision. Grave sight wasn't cutting it, so I switched to my psychic view. It was a good choice. The mist dropped away.

Something that looked a lot like canyonlands in the western U.S. spread before me. Deep fissures and jagged cliffs. One of my footholds crumbled. Before I could kick my boot in and get a better grip, the other one failed too, leaving me hanging from my arms.

Crap. Shit. Fuck.

I jammed both toes in hard. One held. Barely. My panting had ceded to harsh gasps as I did my level best to suck in enough oxygen to keep going. If my heart beat any harder, I might go into cardiac arrest.

"Work smarter, not harder," I ground out and sent magic in front of my boot toes. My footholds deepened enough to take the horrible pressure off my biceps and shoulders. If I got out of this, I made myself a promise to spend more time at a gym.

Any workouts would be an improvement for my current non-schedule.

I dialed my vision back to mostly the harsh gray world of the dead.

Below me, shades were working on swarming up the wall. Their incorporeal status didn't lend itself to anything as physical as climbing, but they were busy forming a bridge of sorts where some crawled on top of others. It was kind of a quicksand affair because they sank through, but they were intrepid.

They just kept on trying. My arms were shaking. My shoulders were on fire.

I'd seen enough to convince myself the Reapers on the other side weren't in any immediate danger. Not so long as the Vamp minions remained separated from them.

What had the one shade told me? He'd seen the other Reapers pushed through this wall. Clearly, the Vampires' ghost army didn't have the wherewithal to manage something like that. So it must have been one of the dark gods. I didn't think it was possible, but my heartbeat edged up another notch.

There was only one of me. If I jumped down on the other side and started hunting for the Reapers, it would take a while to locate all of them. Even with magic. And once I did, who the fuck knew what I'd find.

They could be ensorcelled so deeply, unraveling the enchantment proved beyond me.

Uh-uh. I shook a mental finger at myself. *No negative thoughts.*

I'd cross the Reaper bridge when I got to it. For now, I had to do something about the growing mass of undead undulating below me like a bad imitation of a restless ocean.

The sickle hummed, almost as if it was urging me to snatch it up and kick some Vampire-minion ass. Once I opened a portal, I could force them through.

Some of them.

I wasn't as strong as Death, but I was more than a match for a passel of dead things.

So long as nothing else showed up.

"Don't think about it," I told myself. If I knew anything about the bastards leering up at me, I'd only have to dispatch a dozen or so before the others ran like hell for safer ground.

"How does that strategy strike you?" I aimed my words at the sickle.

It hummed louder. Even more than knowing it had understood me, the knowledge I wasn't alone any longer gave me courage. Twisting air into a cushion to make my next move possible, I let go of the ledge, grabbed the sickle, and jumped squarely into the mob of shades.

The whooping sound had to be coming from me. And my sickle.

Who would have guessed it could turn into such a staunch ally? Hell, who would have guessed a lot of things?

And then I quit thinking about anything but swinging my scythe and building a gateway. I had to make this work. Half a dozen Reapers were counting on me. No one else knew where they were.

Except Death, of course. And clearly, she didn't give a fuck.

CHAPTER TEN, LIAM

The Reaper trail led us into a deep thicket toward the back of a small park. I could sense both Stacia and Cait here, but Cait's energy signature was far more recent. Off in the distance, still more Reaper vibrations beckoned. I didn't recognize who they belonged to, though.

"What do you think?" Padhraic asked.

"Cait was here, and not all that long ago," I replied and cobbled a tracking spell specific to her together. Probably should have done that the moment we landed in Prague.

The air around us developed a liquid aspect that told me we were exchanging Earth for another plane, likely the realm of the dead. I hoped to hell Cait hadn't passed beyond the gateway, a place Sidhe magic couldn't follow.

The glistening ether that had begun to form snapped shut, replaced by the thicket.

"What the hell?" I growled, not used to having my castings reverse themselves.

“We have company.” Padhraic rocked back on his heels and turned to face the verdant archway we’d walked through.

I’d been so focused on my spell, I hadn’t noticed the distinctive smell of the dark mages. Not precisely rotten like Vamps, the dark gods oozed an unpleasant reek kind of like moldy bread or rotten onions.

“You’re so easy to locate, it’s ridiculous,” D’Chel crowed as he walked briskly toward us. A faux smile displayed acres of straight, white teeth. Tall and striking, he was dressed like a college professor in tweed slacks and an ivory cable-knit sweater. Black hair swirled around him, and his copper eyes glowed with satisfaction.

The bastard. He had us exactly where he wanted us, but not for long.

“We were just leaving,” I said. “Whatever this is, make it snappy.”

“What’s the hurry, pal?” Somehow he added a few more teeth to his phony grin.

He obviously needed us to remain right where we were. We could teleport, but he’d been right about me being easy to find. He’d had a taste of my blood. Meant he could track me anywhere.

“We are not friends,” I growled. “Or even associates.”

“Aye, we don’t owe you any explanations.” Padhraic stood tall, pushing his shoulders back.

“You.” D’Chel’s smile turned into a sneer. “Traitor to your kind.”

Padhraic cracked a crooked smile. “Sorry, but it’s tough to

take your assessment of me to heart. Pot. Kettle. And all that rot."

The only reason he was talking with D'Chel was to create a diversion. So far, there were two of us and only one dark mage—unless D'Chel was working his own diversion tactic and running out the clock until his nefarious buddies showed up. If I remembered right, he and Perrikus were friends, but the others hated one another. Majestron Zelia might be Perrikus' mother, but I don't believe there was much love lost between them. From her side of things, she viewed Perrikus more as a possession than anything else.

Padhraic and D'Chel were still trading barbs. Earth magic is where Sidhe live. I couldn't hide from D'Chel, but maybe I could immobilize him, keep him from shifting forms and slithering out from under my trap for long enough to find Cait.

And the other Reapers. I felt certain she wouldn't leave without them.

The dirt beneath my feet rippled, eager to do my bidding. It heartened me, and I opened my mind to the Earth-linked parts of my power, trying to be subtle enough not to alert D'Chel.

How I'd get from what I was doing to snaring the dark god wasn't totally clear, but I'd figure something out. Every minute that passed chafed. I'd wasted plenty of time at Scourie Castle after Cait left. D'Chel must know something I didn't. It was why he was here and not badgering Cait and the other Reapers.

My spell produced a tight weave that dropped over D'Chel's head. "Thanks for keeping him busy," I shouted at

Padhraic and worked fast to anchor the magical mesh to the willing ground. Padhraic helped, and we slathered layers of Earth-bound power over the dark mage. He bellowed, shrieked, and squawked as he ran through a variety of forms.

I'd warned the ground to be vigilant, to form an airtight seal, something bombproof enough even an insect couldn't crawl through. Good thing because D'Chel's current form looked a lot like a cockroach.

How fitting.

"It's enough," Padhraic said. "Let's get out of here."

Nothing would ever be enough to hold D'Chel for very long, but I'd take what I could get.

I grabbed the point and sent power after Cait's trail. A lot of power. I ran wide open, determined to break through whatever separated us from her. The thicket vanished along with D'Chel's outraged cries. From the sound of things, he'd morphed into a big cat. Maybe a mountain lion.

It didn't matter. Prague's wet greenery shifted into grays and browns as the entry point to the realm of the dead stretched before us. I couldn't see much at first until I switched to a psychic view. Then things cleared up.

"Christ! What a bloody mess," Padhraic shouted. "No wonder D'Chel tried to keep us occupied."

A crumbling field filled with shades stretched around us. I couldn't see them as clearly as a Reaper might, but their sheer numbers shocked me. A gateway pulsed about twenty meters away with Cait framed beneath its lintel. Light streamed from her, and she looked like an old world goddess as she swung a silver-gray scythe as tall as she was. Black hair billowed around her shoulders, and her eyes glittered like angry emeralds.

She was heartbreakingly gorgeous, but I hadn't come all this way to be thunderstruck by her beauty. I'd come to help. Not that it appeared she needed any.

Guess Death knew her better than I did.

I'd never realized Reapers actually had sickles. This one glowed with an inner brilliance as it cleaved through dead body parts. Cait booted arms and legs and heads through the portal. Once enough of a ghost had passed over, the remainder of him followed.

With a cry, I launched myself into the fray. Padhraic had already reached Cait's side. "How can we help?" he shouted.

Her gaze snapped up, settling first on him and then on me, and her mouth split into a vicious smile. "Push them through," she shouted back. "As many as you can."

One at a time would take forever, so I fashioned the sluggish air of wherever we were into a slingshot. This wasn't exactly one of the many corridors spanning Earth. More like a parallel world. One that served as a gateway for the dead.

Padhraic joined me, weaving his magic in with mine until we had a device that swept beneath piles of shades and punted them through the gateway. Cait moved to one side to offer us the widest possible opening.

It didn't take long. We were only on our third batch of shades when the others melted away. One minute they were clawing at Cait—while staying clear of her sickle—the next, we were all that remained on the field.

"Thanks," she called to us. "Usually, I'd tell you I didn't need any help, but I'm glad to see you. I underestimated the tenacity of those fuckers." Hefting her sickle one more time, she swung it until the pick buried itself in dirt. The gateway winked out of existence as rapidly as the shades had decamped.

"Are the others here?" I asked.

"Yes. This way," she said and took off at a lope.

Padhraic and I flanked her. So far, we'd gotten lucky. When D'Chel wormed himself out of our trap, he'd be furious. Out for vengeance. I wanted to be gone before that happened. He could locate me anywhere, but I'd rather face him in Scourie Castle than where we were.

"Been expecting one of the dark gods to show up," Cait said around panting breaths.

"You have good instincts," I told her. "We'd have been here sooner, but D'Chel waylaid us in that thicket in the park."

"Damn it. What happened to him?" She twisted her head from side to side, clearly expecting him to pop up like a kewpie doll in a shooting gallery.

"We snared him in a spell, but it won't last forever," Padhraic answered her.

Cait stopped in front of an unnatural barrier. It fairly screamed dark magic, and my bet was enchantment held it together. "We have to get to the other side," she said. "I climbed to the top and looked over. It's a snake pit over there. Not literally, but finding Stacia and the others won't be easy."

I glanced at the wall again. "You climbed that?"

A snort rippled through her. "Yeah. Wasn't easy."

"We can take it down," Padhraic said.

"I thought the same," I muttered. Our power was still melded, so I focused it on the wicked weave of magic that seemed to be holding the illusion in place.

"Ward yourself," I shouted. Too late for me and Padhraic to take my most excellent advice, so we ducked, arms shielding our heads as rocks and dirt blew every which way, filling the air with a choking layer of dust and grit.

Like most magical constructs, this one cleared quickly, leaving a few hummocks of dirt and piles of rocks. Cait sprinted around them, intent on finding the trapped Reapers. Her sickle was clutched beneath one arm, but I suspected it would have stuck with her even if she wasn't hanging onto it.

Magical accoutrements were like that, especially those keyed to a person's energy.

"I don't get it," she called over one shoulder. "This sector doesn't look anything like it did. No rock walls. No canyons."

"Those must have been part of the illusion," I called back. "The one we shot holes in."

Padhraic stumbled to his feet. I did the same. "You all right, mate?"

"Aye. You?" At my nod, he laughed. "Next time, we build a ward first, eh?"

I shrugged. "It would have slowed things down. Hard to argue with success." I ran after Cait. Padhraic flanked me.

"Stacia!" Cait shouted, followed by a visible bolt of Reaper magic.

"Over here," a chorus of voices replied. The Reapers sounded dazed, but at least they were with it enough to answer.

Excellent. Meant we wouldn't have to waste time and magic figuring out where they were. Or what had them in thrall. By the time Padhraic and I caught up, Cait was in the middle of a group of half a dozen Reapers. All looked more than a little ragged around the edges.

"You know Stacia," Cait said. "This is Abby." She pointed at a short woman garbed in long skirts with pale blonde hair cut close to her head and deep-blue eyes.

Padhraic inclined his head. "I'm Padhraic, and that's Liam."

"We'll take care of introductions and catch up back in Scourie," I said. Before anyone lodged a protest at my rather peremptory announcement, I'd already started crafting a group teleport spell.

"Why not Prague?" Abby asked.

"It's not safe," Cait answered. "One of the dark gods is trapped there."

"Who are they?" a male Reaper asked, followed by, "Why is your sickle glowing?"

Cait shrugged. "I have no idea. It's never acted like this before today. In truth, it's been absent for a while. I figure it returned because I finally claimed the full spectrum of my power. Your other question is harder. Until recently, I thought the dark mages were caricatures from Marvel Comics."

"Hurry," Padhraic urged.

Nostrils flaring, I scented the air and smelled what had tipped him off. If D'Chel hadn't gotten loose, he'd alerted more of the dark mages. The decaying onion smell of the dark gods was fast approaching.

I tossed my mostly finished journey spell over everyone and kindled its magic. The half-light of the netherworld faded, replaced by darkness. I expected a bevy of outraged protests to follow us, but either the dark mages weren't into screeching their discontent, or we'd escaped before they'd had a chance to voice their fury.

"What happened to you?" Cait was asking Stacia.

When I looked for her scythe, it wasn't there any longer. Fascinating. It must be linked to the realm of the dead, maybe to the gateway. I'd have to ask.

Stacia still wore the same plain tan slacks, faded-red stretchy shirt, and a black hooded pullover. Exhaling in a breathy rush, she said, "I'd no sooner gathered the others and begun telling them about our missing magic—and what we could do about retrieving it—when these two men walked right through my door. As in literally through it—without bothering to open it first."

"Did one have black hair and the other auburn?" I asked.

"Aye, both were so beautiful, I was certain they had to be Vampires," Abby said. Wrapping her arms around herself, she shuddered.

"Things grew murky after that," Stacia added. "I have no idea how we got from my room to the place you found us."

A low whistle escaped before I could do anything to hold it back. The scope of the spell that had created the barrier—and the illusion Cait had seen on its other side—while holding seven Reapers hostage was impressive.

And chilling.

We were up against major evil, and the Sidhe hadn't yet decided if we'd fight at all. Would what I'd just witnessed make a difference? Probably not. Reapers weren't Sidhe, but it was only a matter of time before evil that pervasive found its way to us.

With a start, I understood. It already had.

Vampires and the dark gods were why we'd had to leave Malin.

All that was left was to convince the other Sidhe we couldn't sit this one out, like we'd sat out so many other conflicts because someone like Hollis, my old Sidhe warlord, had decreed they had nothing to do with us.

"Liam." Padhraic elbowed me, and I returned my attention to my spell, fine-tuning it to drop us in Scourie Castle's great room. Might not have been the best choice because of its almost total lack of chairs, but I herded our small group nearer the fireplace.

"I'll get us some tea and biscuits," Padhraic said and hustled out of the room.

Stacia threw her arms around Cait. It took a moment before Cait hugged her back and lost the shocked expression that had etched into her features.

"Thank you so much," she said. "I tried to reach you with telepathy right after those men broke in, but I had no idea if I got through."

"It's all right. Truly it is. But we need to teach you how to use all that previously concealed power." Cait let go of Stacia. Turning, she nodded at the other Reapers. "Welcome."

"Thank you," rose from everyone's throats.

"Not trying to intrude on your reunion," I said, "but on behalf of the Sidhe, I'd like to extend my welcome as well.

You're in Scourie Castle. We're in the northwestern part of the Scottish Highlands, and you're welcome to remain as long as you'd like. The castle is large, and most of it unused."

A man with brown braids stepped forward and held out a hand. Tattered jeans encased his long legs, and he wore a tan button-down shirt with a gray wool jacket over it. "I'm Pavel. And I don't mean to sound like an ingrate, but why would the Sidhe help us? Our people have never been close."

I resisted rolling my eyes. "Aye, on account of my people being a bunch of stiff-necked jerks who were convinced we were better than other magic wielders."

"In this instance," Abby said, "they were correct. Reapers have always been at the butt end of the magical totem pole."

"Because we were kept in the dark about our magical potential," Cait reminded her.

"The reason I'm extending Sidhe hospitality," I broke in, "is because I'm who revealed Cait's magic to her. Death is far from pleased with me, but that's beyond the point. The important part is I feel responsible for ensuring all of you understand your power well enough not to get into trouble using it."

Cait smiled at me, and I wanted to hug her.

Pavel nailed Cait with his dark eyes. "Stacia told us you stood up to Death. That you told her you were done. Is that accurate?"

Cait nodded slowly. "Obviously, I'm not done Reaping. It's part of our makeup, of who we are. But I'm through reporting to Death."

He frowned and drew his brows together. "So what does that mean? You're freelancing now?"

"I guess so," she replied. "I'll still Reap, but it will be on my terms."

"We could all do that." Excitement coursed beneath Abby's words.

"You've been reading my thoughts," Pavel told her.

My gaze roved around the group. Their enthusiasm touched me. In some ways, they reminded me of peasants who'd thrown off a feudal overlord.

Cait held up a hand. "According to Stacia, Death was providing housing for you. Maybe food. She won't keep doing that if you defy her."

"Give us credit for a few smarts." Stacia sounded hurt.

"I'll give you all the credit in the world," Cait said. "I just wanted to make certain you were aware there'd be tradeoffs. They weren't a big deal for me since I've been taking care of myself since I left Reaper school."

Abby's mouth rounded into an O. "What? Death never helped you?"

"Help comes in many guises," Cait clarified. "After she foisted Vampires off onto me, she showed up plenty to help me fight them."

"Speaking of Vampires," Pavel said, "what happened to Jake?"

"Death barricaded him into Hell—along with the Vampires," Cait told him.

"Mmph. I told him he'd have to something besides sit on his arse," Abby mumbled.

"Am I the only Reaper who followed the rules about not fraternizing?" Cait asked.

"Probably." Stacia flashed a warm smile.

Her next words surprised me.

"I'm going to work with Cait from now on," Stacia said. "She can teach us about our magic. How about the rest of you?"

"Hold on." Cait's gaze fell on each Reaper in turn. "I'm not looking to replace Death. I don't want minions or acolytes."

"Who said anything about a chain of command?" Stacia positioned her head straighter. "Working with someone presumes joint decision-making."

"Sounds good to me. I'm in," Pavel exclaimed.

"Me too," sounded from Abby and the other four Reapers.

"Perfect." Stacia grinned. "We can split up Reaping duties and make plans for how we'll feed and house ourselves after the Sidhes' hospitality runs its course."

"How can you be sure about this?" Cait demanded. "I haven't seen any of you in hundreds of years."

"If you disappoint us, we'll select a new teacher," Stacia said. "It's called democracy. I picked it up from hanging around humans."

Right on cue, as if she'd been lurking in the wings, Death chose that moment to pop through a gold-edged portal. She'd traded her hunting leathers for a black robe sashed in crimson. A golden scythe balanced across her shoulder blades.

"Lovely to see you all in one spot," she said in glacial

tones and clapped her hands smartly together. "Back to work, everyone. Souls are piling up out there."

I kept a close eye on the Reapers. It was one thing to talk of rebellion, quite another to launch one. Part of me fully expected the six Reapers to fall back into line. Cait wouldn't, but she might have been cut from a different cloth.

After exchanging glances with the other Reapers, Stacia approached Death, stopping about a meter away. "We all quit. We'll still Reap, but we don't report to you any longer."

"Is that so?" Death asked in clear, ringing tones.

"Aye," Pavel answered her. "We've chosen Cait as our adviser, but the mantle could shift depending on how things go."

Death drew herself tall. I'd been a fool the day I'd thought she looked like a college ingenue. Nothing as ancient and imposing as the goddess standing before me could be anything but supremely powerful.

"You don't get to quit. You don't get to select who you report to. It's not how I designed the system." Death clapped her hands once more. "Nice chat, now get back to work. All of you."

Tension radiated through the room, so thick it was palpable.

"My choice needn't be yours," Cait said, sounding worried.

I didn't blame her. Who knew what Death would do in the face of an open insurrection.

"We've made our choice," Stacia said.

I thought she'd stop there, but she kept on talking. "You treat us like children. Your favorite name for us is even child.

Well, guess what? None of us have been children for a very long time."

"Your point?"

"I can't speak for the others," Stacia said, "but I'm done. I'm furious you withheld critical information about our magic from us. If Jake had known what he could do, maybe he wouldn't have been so flummoxed when you assigned Vampires to him. And yes, he did talk with me about it. He was in so far over his head, he was drowning.

"You didn't help him. Eventually, he gave up, just kind of folded in on himself and waited for the ax to fall."

"He's no concern of yours. What about the rest of you?" Death settled her eerie eyes on each of the other Reapers in turn.

One by one, they echoed Stacia's sentiments. Anger simmered around Death until the air developed a reddish cast. When she extended her arms in front of her, fingers extended, I stepped between her and the Reapers. "You will not harm them."

"Butt out, Sidhe. This is not your affair."

"I'm making it my affair."

Padhraic chose that moment to come back into the chamber carrying a tray laden with cups and a large teapot.

Death flicked her fingertips his way, and the tray flew out of his hands. Crockery sailed every direction, clattering to the ground and breaking on impact.

I was already facing Death. It was ill-advised, but I snarled, "Leave. You are no longer welcome in these halls."

"Really, Sidhe? On the brink of war you should cherish your allies, not alienate them." Before I had a chance to respond, she was gone. The blast of power behind her egress almost drove me to my knees.

"It's all right. I can get more tea," Padhraic said.

"This isn't about tea," I told him and everyone else. "It's about respect. I don't care how angry Death was, no one acts like that in someone else's house." And then I remembered the antique wall hanging she'd shredded in my flat in Malin.

"There is it in a nutshell," Cait said. "Death has never respected any of us."

Amid a backdrop of conversation among the Reapers, I helped Padhraic pick up the broken mugs. Together, we piled them atop the tray and went back to the kitchen for another go.

"Death was right about one thing," Padhraic said.

I nodded. "Don't remind me. My temper just cut us off from our strongest allies."

"Maybe," Padhraic murmured. "Depends how the other deities view her. They won't appreciate you disrespecting her, but perhaps they've never approved of how she runs her ship."

"The worst part," I mused as we brewed tea and grabbed more biscuits for the Reapers, "will be telling Krin and Dena and everyone about this."

"Like as not they already know." Padhraic snorted.

"What's that supposed to mean?" I slitted a look his way.

"You're the same Liam you've always been," he retorted. "Open mouth, insert foot. After a few millennia, no one is expecting that to change. Why should it?"

"Because at some point I should have grown old enough

to know better?" I slapped a hand down on the counter. "What I did may mean it's truly not in our best interest to—"

"Quit second-guessing yourself. Death was out of line before you ordered her out of the castle."

"Aye, but being right doesn't buy me much."

"Eh, stop worrying. Since you're here, grab another tray, and let's hope for better luck this time around."

I couldn't reel the clock back, couldn't undo my fit of pique, so I sorted a tray from a stack of them and piled more mugs onto it. I've always been good at playing the ball where it lies. Other than one time recently, the gods and goddesses have never helped us. I was being naïve to view their assistance as a fish-or-cut-bait event.

We'd figure things out. We always have. Perhaps our insularity wasn't as much of a curse as I'd always believed it to be.

CHAPTER ELEVEN, CAIT

It's painful for me to admit this, but I've never been quite so glad to see anyone as I was when Liam and Padraic dropped out of nowhere into the center of my fight with the Vampires' stooges. I'd dispatched so many I'd lost count, but they hadn't given up. I could have been imagining it, but it seemed like for every one I booted through the gateway, five more showed up.

Because ghosts merge into one another, it's as hopeless as counting amoeba. Besides, what did it matter if there were a hundred or a thousand. I'd taken a stand and backing down wasn't an option. This was only step one. The other Reapers were still on the far side of that bizarre barrier. I had to send the shades packing before I could tackle the tangle of cliffs and gullies I'd glimpsed when I'd scaled the wall.

The more I thought about the barrier, the less I liked it, but at least I'd seen the other side. Meant I could teleport rather than clambering over the damned thing. Turned out I didn't have to. The Sidhe recognized some twisted spell holding everything together. Once they dismantled it, the wall literally blew up.

Things went fast after that. I'd barely determined which Reapers were part of Stacia's group when we popped out in Scotland at Scourie Castle. I swear, Death must have been doing her spy routine. The point at which she chose to show herself was simply too much of a coincidence not to be planned.

She always did have a flair for the dramatic.

Or maybe she figured she'd heard enough? She was as angry as I've ever seen her. Usually, she's chilly but controlled. When Liam planted himself squarely between her and the Reapers, I didn't know what to expect. Before I could move to his side in a display of solidarity, Padhraic showed up with tea things, and all hell broke loose.

That was when Liam ordered Death to leave.

I was proud of him—and horrified too. What chance would we have against the dark mages without Death's help? She'd pointed that out to him before vanishing in a swirl of heated magic. Power so strong it nearly knocked Liam over.

Speaking of magic, I hadn't anticipated the other Reapers would care one way or the other about Death lying to us regarding the extent of our power. Eh, that's not quite accurate. Sure, they'd care, but I never guessed they'd be bothered enough to stake their own claim for independence.

They had far more to lose than I did, but when I made certain to clarify that, they seemed hurt I hadn't viewed them in a more favorable light. As something better than whores who only hung about because Death paid the bills.

Big surprise my social skills left a lot to be desired. I'd mostly only had mortals to practice on.

The whole thing merged into a confused jumble after that.

Would I have been so contrary if Death had taken better care of me? Probably not For one thing, I wouldn't have had to work.

Work was what had made me independent.

Finding something I loved as much as Reaping made an enormous difference in who I was, in my attitude. If I hadn't discovered myself behind the yoke in a cockpit, I might never have had the guts to stand up to Death. It had felt damned good to finally to tell her to fuck off, but it left an empty place inside me that would take years to heal. Much like a secondary mother, Death had shaped all of us Reapers into who she wanted us to be.

Walking away was essential, but that didn't mean it was easy. Or the proper path for everyone.

Once Liam and Padhraic went after more tea, balancing a tray of broken crockery between them, I sank to a crouch in front of the hearth and studied the small group of Reapers.

"If any of you want to go home and collect your things, you probably should get moving," I told them.

"Not a good idea." Abby shook her head. "I'm older than the rest of you, and Death isn't done. She may never be, which means we'll need to develop ways to keep her out of our minds."

"How do you propose to do that?" Stacia asked.

She'd stolen the thoughts out of my head. If there was a

way for me to clip the apron strings, I'd never come close to discovering it.

"I have no idea," Abby replied, "but it's something we need to work on. And sooner rather than later."

Abby was one of the original Reapers. I'd forgotten that. "Death told me Reapers knew the full scope of their power at first, but it didn't go well. Was that true?" I settled my gaze on Abby, waiting.

She frowned. "I don't know. It's possible she erased our memories. She'd almost have had to. Either that or do away with the first batch of Reapers."

"What exactly did you mean by Death not being done?" Stacia asked.

"She has a system in place," Abby answered. "One that requires all of us."

"Actually, more than all of us," I cut in. "We're always shorthanded. But if she makes more Reapers, it will take them a while to grow up, plus there's no guarantee they won't find out about their magic."

"By the time we're done, everyone will know," Pavel growled. "I still can't believe Death went to such draconian lengths to control us."

"Believe it," I muttered. "I'm not sure about this next assumption," I added, "but Death must know more about the Vampire threat than she's letting on. There's a reason she assigned them first to Jake, and then to me."

"But that means the problem has been building for a while," Abby said. "It's been well over a hundred years since Jake was handed that task."

"If she knew about the Vamps, does it mean she also understood their link with the dark gods?" Pavel asked.

I shrugged. "Hard to say, except there's a whole lot we'll never know. She was damned quick coming up with help when we captured the Leanan Sidhe. So quick, my guess is she and the other gods have had more than one discussion about the problem."

"Will they still help us?" Stacia furled russet brows.

"Another question I can't answer," I replied, "but at this point, I suspect the answer is no once Death gets through telling them what a bunch of miscreants we are."

The books I'd brought from Malin were right where I'd left them. I straightened and walked close enough to pat the top of the stack. "Liam picked these out for me to help train my magic."

"Let's split them up and get started," Stacia said. "We can each read something and teach one another."

"No time to waste," Abby agreed. A corner of her mouth twisted into a wry expression. "Maybe some of this will come back to me. Unless Death was just trying to make herself look good when she claimed we started out whole."

We'd just divvied up the reading material and settled on the floor in front of the fireplace when Liam and Padhraic walked back into the room. They carried two trays this time, and set them close to us. Once Liam's hands were free, he flicked his fingers at the fire, and it blazed a little brighter.

I glanced at him. "Magical?"

He made a snorting noise. "Aye. Not much in the way of wood left here. Between structures and fuel, the forests vanished long since."

I'd known that at one point, but after living amidst the lush timber in the Pacific Northwest, I'd forgotten how bare the UK was outside of special governmentally protected groves.

I scooted to the trays and poured mugs of tea for everyone. Sweet rolls redolent with cinnamon and nutmeg smelled divine. They reminded me how hungry I was.

For a time, we read and ate. After I'd inhaled a second sweet bun, Liam tapped my shoulder and beckoned me to follow him. The room grew noticeably colder as we crossed its width and entered a hallway.

"Not going to be good enough if you want a private conversation," I told him. "Reapers have sharp ears."

He smiled, and my heart did its little flip-flop thing. I longed to tell him how stunning he was, how much I ached for him, but it wasn't why he'd dragged me out here. Besides, we had bigger problems than me lusting after him.

Lots bigger problems.

"How about this?" The scents of sandalwood and fresh wet greenery surrounded us as he draped a sound shield into place.

"That will work," I said. "I might be able to drill through it, but only because I've had a head start using my new magic." I waited, curious what he had to say that required privacy.

"How are they doing?" he asked.

I thought about his question. "I don't think it's sunk in yet," I said. "Right now, it's all a grand adventure, but none of them have ever gone hungry or been cold because they had to sleep outside or in a falling-down hovel with holes in the roof. Or no roof at all. Why?"

"Will they fight if it comes to it?"

"I believe so." I chewed my lower lip. "A bigger question is how to bar Death from our minds. Abby was one of the original Reaper batch, and she's convinced Death will continue to hound us until we capitulate or find a way to keep her out of our heads."

Liam set his mouth is a tight line. "I fear it's worse than that. Pushing you back under her thumb won't help at all unless she erases your knowledge of the additional magic." Breath swooshed from him. "That particular bit of enchantment lacks...specificity. She might eradicate your memory of the last ten years—or fifty—and not give a fuck."

"Mmph. Not exactly good news, but not unexpected, either." I smiled crookedly. "Between the two of us, we've done a fair job of turning her into an enemy."

"I gave her an option. A damned good one." Liam shook his head. "She spit on it."

"Well?" I spun one hand in a circle. "What was it?"

"To suck it up and teach her Reapers about their power. She could have maintained at least a semblance of control. Couched it in terms something like these were desperate times, and her acolytes had need of their magic."

"She wouldn't have gone for it because it wasn't her idea," I said remembering many suggestions I'd floated, all of which she'd shot down.

"Regardless, she selected a path that's bound to blow up in her face. Once all of you have mastered telepathy, I assume you'll reach out to other Reapers, and in turn, they'll talk with their associates."

"Probably, but the process will take a while. Death could be a real pain in the rear in the meantime. The more Reapers who ditch her, the worse things will get. When is the Sidhe meeting?"

"Soon, but I wanted a moment with you first." He cupped the side of my face. His palm was warm, and I leaned into his touch, ashamed by how much I craved it.

"You were amazing today."

Pleasure at the compliment heated my face—and my heart. "I did what I had to."

"Nay. You reached far above that." He ran his thumb along my jaw, soft and tentative.

"You're giving me too much credit. Death told us about Reapers being in trouble. She was clearly planning to let them sink."

"Of course she was," Liam muttered. "It would have saved her the trouble of erasing their memories of however much Stacia told them before the rug got pulled out from under her disclosure."

I settled a hand over his, never wanting him to stop touching me.

Whoa. Dangerous ground.

"While the Sidhe are meeting," Liam said, "feel free to help yourselves to whatever you find in the kitchens. And prepare the Reapers with some basic defensive maneuvers."

"I'll teach them how to build a ward," I said. "We can already do that, but it's not part of our normal repertoire."

"Padhraic has already begun instructing them in the

different types of shielding. He and I talked about it before I invited you out here. The oldest of the books, the one with the cracked tan binding, might have ways of barring Death from your minds. It's worth a look."

"You're worried."

He wrapped his other hand around my shoulder. "Aye, about many things. I'd list them, but sometimes it's best to deal with whatever crops up and not get diverted by what hasn't happened yet."

I closed the inches between us and inhaled his clean, magical scent. I wanted him to kiss me. Who knew when we'd be alone again? And then I remembered my admonition not to get lost in my attraction for him.

Maybe someday, but not right now.

"You're so lovely," he murmured just before he settled his mouth over mine. Different from our first kiss, this time his lips were tentative. Probably even more than me, he understood the full weight of what we faced.

None of it was going anywhere, though. I could take a five-minute break from everything and enjoy the man pressed against me.

I wrapped my arms around him and opened every cell in my body to his kiss. He made a delicious male sound deep in his throat, part purr, part growl, and splayed a hand across my back. Heat from his palm sank through my clothes, searing me. He nibbled my lips, bit them, sucked them. I traded off deep kisses with little butterfly ones as the exotic scent of his magic thickened around us. Heavy on sandalwood and musk, it was heady, and I inhaled like a starving woman.

Where my breasts were crushed against his chest, my nipples pebbled into hard little marbles, sending jolts of pleasure cascading through me. His cock rose in a column and pressed into my belly. I ached to reach between us and curl my fingers around his hot length, but if I did, we'd end up just going for it right here.

Not the best idea.

I'm not exactly a romantic at heart, but Liam and I could do better than the chilly flagstone floor.

He threaded his hands through my unbound hair, cradling my head as he trailed kisses across my cheeks. His mouth ended up resting on my forehead. Both of us were breathing hard. Desire so pervasive I could almost see it swirled between us.

"All I meant to do was kiss you." His voice held a harsh rasp.

"All you did was kiss me," I teased. "I'd say mission accomplished."

"Oh, but I want to do so much more." He tucked my head into the hollow between his neck and collarbones.

"Maybe. Someday," I ventured.

"More than maybe." Liam sounded fierce. He wound his fingers through my hair again and moved back enough to gaze into my eyes. "We will find a way, Cait."

I wanted him to desire me with an intensity akin to my own, but evidence he did scared me to my bones. What if I couldn't hold up my end of a relationship? I'd never been able to before. Other than telling Death to pound sand, nothing had changed, and—"

"Ssht." He smoothed his thumbs over my cheekbones. "I

know your thoughts, and it will be all right. Believe in yourself. And in us. We'll figure this out. I haven't exactly been nominated for any husband of the year awards."

The corners of my mouth twitched. "That's because you've never been married."

He lifted his shoulders slightly. "See? I rest my case." He butted his hips into my belly. His cock was even harder than it had been while we were kissing. "I want your body, but it's your heart and soul and mind I'm falling in love with. You're courageous, principled. You don't hesitate about doing the right thing."

My face had moved from warm to on fire. I squirmed against his grip on my head, but he didn't let go. "You're giving me too much credit. I haven't done anything special."

"Let me be the judge of that. I've seen people with a whole lot more magic than you turn their backs on simpler tasks than the one you dove into headfirst earlier." He kissed my forehead again. "I have to go, or I'll be late. I'll find you when the meeting is over. If you follow this corridor and take the third door on the left down some stairs, you'll find the kitchens. Help yourself to whatever strikes your fancy. Everyone else too."

I nodded. "Thanks."

"No need." He let go of me, and the places his body had been touching mine felt hollow, abandoned.

"Yeah, there is. You believe in me, even when I find it hard to believe in myself."

He laughed, rich, deep, and warm. "What are friends for?"

"I have no idea. I haven't had very many."

"Makes two of us. See you soon."

The magical mist that had surrounded us dissipated. I stood quietly and watched him walk away. Only after I couldn't see him any longer did I turn and retrace my steps into the castle's main chamber. I didn't cross paths with Padhraic, so maybe he'd taken a different route. Or teleported.

"Anything we need to know about?" Stacia glanced up from a book that was open across her lap.

"Not yet. The Sidhe haven't decided their next steps."

"Padhraic said that." Abby nodded. "He's also a most excellent teacher. He showed us four types of wards and had us practice."

"It will take a little doing," Stacia said, "but we have the basics down."

"Everything is certainly different," Pavel murmured. "So much more to think about."

I scanned the group. Lilly had a book that matched Liam's description. Dark curls hit her at shoulder level, and she had smooth ebony skin. Dressed similarly to Stacia, she wore tan slacks and a blue plaid shirt topped by a fuzzy black jacket.

I squatted next to her and tapped the book. "Liam says maybe there's something in this one that will help us keep Death out of our heads."

"If there is, I haven't found it," Lilly said, "but then I wasn't exactly looking for it, either."

"May I?"

She nodded and pushed the book toward me. "Of course."

I rolled onto my butt and set the book in front of me, taking care to keep it closed. I had no idea if I could coax it into giving up its secrets, but I'd sure as hell try. After a bit of experimentation, I settled on mostly earth mixed with air and asked the book to show us the path to our independence.

No one was more surprised than me when the cover thwacked out of the way, and the pages began to riffle as if a stiff breeze had just swept through the room.

I kept magic flowing until the pages came to rest. The tome was penned in what looked like Sumerian cuneiform. Good thing Reapers are all linguists at heart. I was old, but not so long-lived I remembered when people actually spoke that language.

"Well?" Stacia scooted closer, reading over one of my shoulders.

"Too soon to tell," I murmured. I didn't want to raise false hope, but the fact that the book had responded to my urging was encouraging. Assuming I'd stumbled on the correct spell. For all I knew, the crooked lines in front of me were instructions on how to slaughter a goat or raise a demon to heckle an enemy.

CHAPTER TWELVE, LIAM

Dinner was long since over. Relative quiet during the meal had provided an opportunity for me to relive the feel of Cait in my arms, her mouth against mine. I'd taken a chance and told her how I felt about her. Maybe not much of a chance, but for someone like me, who'd always kept my emotions under a million layers of studied indifference, it was a giant step.

It might have been shameless, but I'd helped myself to her thoughts, seen her confusion—and her desire. Sex would be the easy part for both of us. The commitment side of things would be harder. We were both strong-willed, and she'd have to believe I wouldn't make a bid to control her.

Easy to say. Harder to do. Sidhe are born believing we have an absolute right to run the universe. That part of me wasn't going to go away, but I'd have to be damned careful not to direct it Cait's way. Also, Sidhe rarely paired off. We never talked about it, but all of us understood eternity was a very long time to keep love alive. So we settled for affairs: fun with no strings and often outside our kinship circles.

None of the Sidhe in the dining room had permanent mates. Up until I'd met Cait, I'd been perfectly satisfied with the status quo. Something about her made me long for more, and I knew I'd never be content with the occasional fling again. I'd wanted to tell her all of that, but it would have to wait until we had more than a few stolen moments.

I returned my full attention to the Sidhe ranged around the chamber. Our discussion had mostly run down. As I'd expected, we'd split into two factions with slightly more than half of us on the "we have to do something about this" side of the fence.

"How about this?" I projected the question with magic to slice through myriad conversations in progress. We'd chosen to remain in the dining room since the Reapers were in the space we'd normally have used. Not that anywhere in Scourie Castle was warm and cozy, but the dining area was half the size of the castle's primary chamber with a much lower ceiling.

Rows of tables and benches had once filled the space. Many had rotted, and we'd fed them to various fireplaces scattered throughout the castle. The remaining furniture had been dragged close to a coved hearth that took up one corner of the room.

I felt the weight of many sets of Sidhe eyes and kept talking. "For those of you who don't view Earth-bound Vampires as our problem, how about if you gather as much intel as you can dig up on Humans Rule? Their organization is a threat to everyone with magic, and the more we know about their weaknesses, the better equipped we'll be to take them down."

Krin made his way to my side. "I've been thinking about that very thing," he said and turned his attention toward the assembled Sidhe. "I believe the time for us keeping to ourselves is drawing to a close. Back in Malin, some of you were protesting because others with magic weren't jumping in to help. They've been just as insular as we have."

"Nay," a man called from one of the back tables. "The suggestion was for witches and Druids and Fae to actually do something. I didn't care what or how."

"How are you anticipating that would work?" I asked. "If each type of magic-wielder is doing their own thing without any coordination, we'll have chaos. Duplication on some fronts and nothing on others."

"Might be better than what we have now," the man argued.

"Back to my Humans Rule suggestion," I said. "Any volunteers to take on that project?"

"What would we be doing, exactly?" a woman with straight steel-gray hair asked.

"They're using magic," I said flatly. "Not all of them, and certainly not in any overt fashion, but Cait and I discovered some of them dabbling in power either Vampires or the dark mages had gifted them with."

"The Leanan were guilty too," Padhraic tossed out.

"When we find them using power, shall we kill them?" The same woman sounded more enthusiastic, her dark eyes glittering with anticipation.

"Griselda!" Krin's tone held censure. "'Tis no longer how

we operate. We would set things up so their kin caught them red-handed."

"Not nearly as interesting," Griselda muttered. "Or as satisfying."

"You wouldn't even be pitting them against each other," I cautioned. "Not yet. We have to amass a body of evidence before we start revealing the extent of the slippage. I don't want to alert the dark gods we're onto that portion of their plan until our proof is overwhelming."

"Any idea what their overarching strategy is?" someone else asked.

"What they've always wanted," I replied. "Absolute control."

"But why now?" Dena stood off to one side. "That's the part I'm having trouble with."

I didn't have any answers. Nor did I have a clue who the six dark mages might have joined forces with. That last bothered me. I like to know who my enemies are.

"For now," I said, "those of us who fancy a good brawl or two will remain. The rest of you can leave. If you do a bit of sleuthing into Humans Rule, be discreet. Flaunting magic in their faces will be sure to get them riled up. They'll use it as fodder for membership drives, and then we'll have still more of them to dispatch."

Benches squealed as some Sidhe pushed themselves away from the tables, got up, and walked out of the room. I did a surreptitious nose count. Only twelve of us left, a far lower percentage than I'd expected. As I waited for things to quiet down, I spoke with Krin.

"Thoughts?" I kept my voice low.

"We have to go after the dark gods. And whoever might be masterminding their operation."

It was the same conclusion I'd come to. How we'd accomplish it was the stumbling block, and it was a damned big one. We couldn't kill them. Capturing them might buy us a smattering of time, but they'd escape, and then we'd be back to square one.

"So you believe they're not working alone?" I asked Krin.

He shrugged. "Probably not. Eventually we'll draw out whoever is behind this."

I envisioned rolling a boulder over and unearthing a monster with tentacles and horns, but I kept it to myself. Seer ability has never been in my wheelhouse, so my mental imagery probably sprang from uncertainty.

Despite all the unknowns, I was squarely behind the push to raise our banner and go to war. What if it was the wrong decision? One that drove my kinsmen into the *Dreaming* or away from Earth entirely?

"Have you seen anything in your glass or your pool?" I directed the query to Dena.

She shook her head. "I was waiting until after we met to scry what I could about our future. If I employ that type of power too often, it weakens and becomes less accurate."

"Thank you." I turned to the group. Confession time had arrived. Nothing for it but to tell them what had happened with Death. Since I'd rehearsed what I needed to say, I synopsized the gist of the exchange in very few words.

Once I was done, Krin said, "Not the most politically astute move, but I understand why you did it."

"Death outdid haughty and patronizing, even for a deity.

I didn't blame the Reapers for standing up to her," Padhraic said.

"The gods haven't exactly been front and center helping us," Dena pointed out.

"They kept the dark mages out of the way while we dealt with the Leanan," a man called.

"Aye, true enough," Dena replied. "When was the last time before that incident where you recall them assisting us? In anything."

"Good point," the man said. "Never."

As they were talking, an idea took shape. "Padhraic and I have spoken about inviting the gods here, but I have a better idea. What would you think about launching a few delegations to seek out some key gods? That way, we'd be going to them, and not running the risk of having them snub our invitation."

"It beats taking Death's word about no one being willing to help us," Krin said, followed by, "Which gods?"

"I'm not sure we have to choose," I said slowly. "Finding any of them will pose a problem. They all know one another, so we'll talk with whomever we locate. They'll pass the word to others."

"Aye, but what word will they be passing?" Krin asked. "It would help if we knew for certain they'd be on our side."

"It probably won't be a clean sweep," I told everyone, "but some deities may decide this is important enough to break their longstanding aversion to dealing with anyone outside their pantheons."

"If Death is right, and they all thumb their noses at us, what are our options?" Griselda spoke up.

"We don't really have any," I admitted. "We have no way of corralling the dark mages without some assistance." I paused for a moment, organizing my thoughts. "If they refuse, we'll have to focus on the Vampires and Humans Rule. Maybe if we make a big enough dent in both organizations, the dark gods will give up and go home."

"Where do the Reapers stand in all this?" Dena focused her dark gaze on me. "Other than Cait, this isn't really their fight."

"They'll back Cait," I told her.

"How can you be so sure?" another Sidhe asked and waved a hand toward the back of the dining room. "Some of us didn't hang around."

"They're grateful to Cait. Not only did she set herself up as the fall girl by defying Death and revealing their hidden power, she also risked herself to pull them out of the realm of the dead."

"How does our power marry with theirs?" another Sidhe asked.

"It's strangely complementary," I answered. "When Cait and I work together, the product is stronger than our individual efforts."

"They caught on quickly when I taught them several types of wards," Padhraic said.

I nodded, pleased Padhraic was solidly in the Reapers' court. "Reapers aside, we need to know what we have to work with. Maybe we'd be better off if several of us hunted for the gods individually, rather than forming delegations. We could leave now and report back tomorrow morning."

"I'll go," Krin said.

"Me too," Dena agreed.

I wanted to tell her to remain behind so she could try to divine what lay ahead, but she didn't report to me. The closest thing we'd had to a commander had been Hollis, and he was dead.

"I'd like to help," Padhraic spoke up, "but it might be best if I went with Liam."

"Cait will want to come with me," I told him.

"In this case, three probably isn't a crowd," he replied. "The dark mages regard me as a turncoat. It might bode well for how others view me."

Krin looked from Padhraic to me and shrugged. "Your decision."

Several other Sidhe volunteered. We agreed to reconvene as soon as all of us were back.

I walked from of the room, pleased with our progress. I wouldn't have been surprised if everyone had opted out, but they hadn't. Padhraic caught up with me. "Let me know when we're set to leave."

"It won't be long," I told him.

"I'll be ready. No matter what happens, it feels good to wield clean magic again."

I clapped him on the back, remembering how narrowly he'd avoided the same fate as the other Leanan: being tossed into a magical pit. "Did we make a mistake not saving any of the others?"

"Probably not. I was always an outlier, and I'd learned to keep my mouth shut. See you in a few." He took off up a nearby stairwell.

Cait would be waiting to hear what had transpired. I

hoped she and the other Reapers had gotten some rest, but when I strode into the castle's primary chamber, they'd paired off and were practicing magical maneuvers. Power shimmered around them, turning the air silvery with violet streamers. Scourie Castle was magical in its own right, and clearly it had welcomed the Reapers into what had always been a Sidhe stronghold.

Perhaps it knew more than any of us, or had a longer memory.

Scents redolent of heather and wildflowers wafted my way. No wonder the dead were drawn to Reapers. Their scent was soothing and enticing by turns. I hung back watching as Cait and her kinsfolk dipped and swayed, clearly entranced by their new power.

I still didn't understand why Death would have concealed all that ability. Surely, her cover story about it creating a management problem couldn't be the only reason. Had she worried her minions would surpass her ability? Seeing them blend magic and work together, I could easily envision a scenario where Death would have had to move from an autocracy to a more democratic leadership style.

It would have been hard for her. She was one of the original deities, no doubt dating to the beginnings of everything. In the era when she was forged, a strict line of command was in play. Power was intoxicating, and she'd chosen not to change with the times.

I didn't agree with her methods, but I understood them. She was the only goddess who oversaw an actual work crew, and it was in everyone's interest for Reapers to blend in. The more magical they were, the harder it would be for humans to trust them.

The Humans Rule movement had begun almost as soon as magic emerged from the shadows. At first, it was only a few frightened bigots, but over the years it had developed into a groundswell of outrage. Nothing like fear and hatred to drive a mob mentality.

I moved beyond the darkened alcove where I'd been standing and walked purposefully toward the fireplace end of the chamber. I've always had a tendency to get lost in philosophical musings because I like to understand how things work, but I could indulge in mental meanderings later.

Cait twirled and headed for me. "What happened?"

The others Reapers stopped midstride, and everyone crowded toward me. Their transcendent expressions shaded to determination—and concern.

"Most of the Sidhe recognized the dark mages and Vampires as our problem. A few will focus on ferreting out dirt on Humans Rule. The rest of us developed a two-pronged approach."

I glanced from one Reaper to the next, pleased I had their undivided attention. They clearly didn't view Vampires as only Cait's problem.

"We have to determine if at least some of the gods and goddesses will help since we lack adequate weapons to deal with the dark mages," I continued. "If Death is wrong about them holding back, we will go after Perrikus and his crew first."

"And if she's correct?" Cait asked.

"Then we will focus on Vampires and Humans Rule, working on the theory if we make a big enough hole in their ranks, the dark gods will give up and return to wherever they came from.

"Several of us are leaving to outline our problem to the deities—assuming we can locate any of them. We will regroup in the morning and finalize our strategy predicated on what we find out."

"I'm coming with you," Cait said.

"I figured you'd say that," I told her. "Padhraic will be part of our group too."

"We'll help," Stacia said.

"Aye," Abby seconded. "We can cull through the realm of the dead. Maybe we'll turn up Hades or Arawn. I've run into them a time or two."

Cait narrowed her eyes. "They're Death's best buddies. Do you think it's wise to rattle their cages?"

Abby tilted her head to one side, forehead furrowed as she considered Cait's question. "We only have Death's word about being friends with them. Can you imagine her being friends with anyone?"

"Maybe not." A corner of Cait's mouth twitched into half of a wry grin. "Friendship presumes doing things for each other, not sucking up all the glory for yourself."

I thought back to D'Chel taunting Death about being too busy fucking to leave Hell. "It's possible Hades or Arawn could be her lovers, so I'd tread carefully."

"Pfft." Abby flapped her hands my way. "Those rumors have been floating around forever. Hades and Arawn are so wrapped up in each other, they'd never notice Death if she whipped her robes off and paraded naked through Hell."

Surprise ratcheted through me. Not that I hang about lusting after gossip, but I'd never heard that juicy tidbit before. I silently wished them well. Tending the dead had to be a thankless task, and if they'd found solace in one another, more power to them.

"Before I forget," I said, "did that one sourcebook have anything useful about shielding your minds and your location from Death?"

"Maybe," Stacia replied carefully. "It's cuneiform, so interpreting it was difficult."

"Our take was that perhaps each of us has something like an implant. A magical beacon Death placed within us before our birth," Pavel added. "The thing we couldn't figure out was if removing it would also remove our Reaping ability."

"We were hoping the Sidhe could sort it out," Abby said.

"We might be able to. It obviously requires deeper study," I told her, determined to take a look at the lore book once I had a free moment. I hadn't liked Pavel's comment. It inferred everything about Reaping might be tangled into a magical Gordian knot. They were tricky to deal with. Pulling on one cord often tripped something, and then the whole mess exploded in your face.

"We should get moving," Cait said.

"We pretty much have teleporting figured out," Stacia told me. "We'll return, hopefully with good news."

Cait turned to her. "Remember the part about holding onto the image of your destination. It won't want to remain center stage, and if it doesn't, you'll pop out wherever you happen to be."

"We'll be fine," Pavel told her. "No mistakes we can't recover from."

There actually were a lot of mistakes that would take time to dig out from under. "You'll be in pairs, right?" I asked. Nods ran through the group. "Excellent, then you can watch over each other. We all used some variant of the buddy system when we were coming into our powers."

"So we'll meet back here?" Stacia asked.

"Aye. The Sidhe will be here too, so everyone can hear everything at the same time." I wasn't certain if my fellows would agree with my decision to plop everyone into the same room, but too bad if they didn't.

Allies were allies. The Reapers were putting themselves on the line, and they were deserving of our respect. Keeping them segregated from the primary decision-making body was ridiculous. I'd have to remind the Sidhe that Reapers weren't exactly immortal, although the full spectrum of their power might shift that equation in their favor.

The Reapers were breaking into dyads. Cait asked, "Where's Padhraic? And where will we go first?"

"Padhraic is waiting to hear from me. I'm not sure quite where we should look first. This isn't the olden times when gods walked the Earth openly."

"I have a few ideas."

"Are you going to share them?" I set a course through the castle toward its main doors. We could leave from the courtyard. I also raised my mind voice to let Padhraic know where to meet us.

"Of course. You've talked about the *Dreaming*. Would it be a reasonable place to start? Even if there aren't any deities there, maybe some of the folk who are would know their whereabouts."

The wooden doors banded with hammered iron swooshed open, and we walked through into a damp, drizzly night. Ice coated almost every surface, and I instinctively drew magic to warm us. Padhraic trotted down the steps after us and tossed a coat at me, and another at Cait.

"Thought we might need these," he said.

"Thanks." Cait slid her arms into the fluffy white jacket and zipped it.

I did the same. "Cait suggested we start in the *Dreaming*."

"It's a decent idea. If it doesn't pan out, we can begin a systematic search through some of the closer corridors circling earth."

"My spell," I said and summoned the magic that would move us into the *Dreaming*. I hadn't been there since ascertaining the Leanan had escaped, and we wouldn't remain long. The place sapped your energy to do much more than, well, dream. Hence, its name.

CHAPTER THIRTEEN, CAIT

A Few Hours Earlier

After the pages from the ancient tome in front of me quit riffling, I blew out a breath I hadn't been aware I was holding and started to decipher the symbols. Stacia helped a lot. So did Abby. "Well," she said after we'd been at it for better than an hour, "that's downright creepy."

"You think?" Stacia sounded rattled.

"Are you certain we didn't make a mistake interpreting the runes?" I was relieved I hadn't unearthed a shopping list or a recipe but was unnerved by what was spread before us.

How could a few pages penned in what looked like animal blood change everything?

"All of us saw the same thing," Lilly said. "I mean, we translated the symbols a bit differently, but the bottom line didn't change."

"So the bitch marked us," Pavel growled. "No wonder she

knows where we are all the time. I say we unmark ourselves."

"Not so fast." I turned my head and locked gazes with him. "What if we lose our Reaping ability right along with the psychic signposts that reveal where we are?"

"Don't forget the pathway into our minds," Abby said bitterly. "It's tangled up with everything else."

"How could we lose our Reaper magic?" Pavel drew his brows into a tight line.

I shrugged. "We don't know enough to go mucking around in any of this. All we know is Death did something to each of us before we were born. If she did more than one thing, we're probably all right. But what if she mixed everything together? If that's the case, I can see us losing everything in one fell swoop. She won't be able to find us any longer, but we'll be busted back to being mortals."

Pavel growled in frustration. "She'll never tell us the truth."

"No," Abby seconded. "Why would she?"

"Maybe the Sidhe can sort it out," I ventured and tapped the cracked vellum pages that lay open on the floor. "They might be able to instigate some kind of psychic search to dissect the supernatural beacons we all got saddled with."

"We can ask," Stacia said and shuddered. "I'm with Abby. This whole thing is downright disturbing. All these years I've labored under the illusion I was more or less a free agent, but what I've been is a puppet. One with zero privacy."

"We'll get it taken care of." I tried my best to sound reassuring. I wasn't at all certain how important Death's ID tokens were when balanced against Vampires, dark gods, and Humans Rule. We'd have to tackle Death spying on us at some point, but it might not happen for a while.

"Let's get back to practicing," I suggested. "We were doing pretty well with wards. Let's give teleporting a go, and then we can work on defensive maneuvers."

We were still hard at work when Liam returned. Given the short amount of time we'd been at it, I was encouraged by how well we worked together. Everyone was generous with magic and suggestions. Together, we'd navigated our way through a few thorny spots without having to hunt for answers in the lore books.

Soon, Liam and I were heading for the courtyard where we'd meet Padhraic and go to the *Dreaming* in search of a hopefully receptive god or goddess. Compared with Death, they had to be easier to deal with.

Maybe. Best not to make any assumptions.

I hadn't thought about how much colder it would be outside, so I was grateful Padhraic had the foresight to bring jackets. After I'd zipped the coat up to my chin, I smiled. "Thanks, and I'm glad your Sidhe magic is fully back online."

"Makes two of us." He nodded at me just before Liam's casting formed a portal that glowed with a shimmery white light.

Quite a while back, Liam had mentioned the *Dreaming* required a particular incantation to enter. "Do Sidhe control access?" I asked as he gestured me to walk through the gateway.

"For the most part," he replied, "although some other magic wielders can penetrate the protections around it."

The moment I crossed beneath the lintel, everything changed. It wasn't cold anymore, and the air smelled sweet and clean. It held undertones of Sidhe magic, but ever so much more. One moment, I smelled freshly mowed hayfields, the next baking bread. Chocolate chip cookies bombarded me next, and I realized the *Dreaming* had somehow identified all my favorite scents.

I knew without looking around that the gateway had shut. "Do you suppose Death can still find me in here?" I asked.

Liam nodded. "Not any point in building something like whatever she marked you with, if it couldn't pierce Earth's boundaries."

"Building what?" Padhraic asked.

"It appears Death marked each of her Reapers," I said. "It's why she knows precisely where we are every minute. And what we're thinking. Basically, it's why we can't hide anything from her." The more I talked, the angrier I got.

The *Dreaming* must have sensed my fury because waves of soothing magic surrounded me, dulling the edge of my discontent.

"But that's terrible," Padhraic said. "Surely there's a work around."

"There wasn't one when you were a Leanan," Liam pointed out. "Ridding you of your Vampire nature took heaps of Sidhe magic."

"Aye, but this is different..." he began.

"Not so different as all that," Liam cut him off.

I stopped walking and batted at the warm, soothing air determined to envelop me. I wanted to hang onto my edge, not have it blunted by the *Dreaming*. "It is different," I protested while I still had the wherewithal to form thoughts. "None of the Reapers want to be shackled to Death in that way. Wasn't the transition to Leanan more...voluntary?"

"Aye and nay," Padhraic said. "Our original transition, absolutely. By the time the dark mages came along, we'd been imprisoned for a long while. They made a lot of promises. It was only after we indicated interest we discovered what we'd have to do to access the pretty world they'd promised us. By then, we'd smashed enough bridges, going back wasn't exactly an option."

"Breaking out of your jail didn't endear you to the rest of us," Liam muttered. "Granted we were slipshod, and it took a while before we discovered your absence."

"Once you did, it was only a matter of time before you came after us," Padhraic said. "We knew it would happen eventually, but we were free. Most of us saw it as an improvement—even if it wouldn't last forever."

"Which was precisely what the dark gods were banking on," Liam countered. "Damn it. They played you."

"'Fraid I have to agree," Padhraic said. "Back before the other Sidhe tired of our bloodsucking ways and imprisoned us, it was just us and the Earth-bound Vamps and bloodlust. The dark mages added a whole other layer of evil to our natures, one that became more apparent as the years passed."

I pressed my fingers against my temples. Holding onto a train of thought had turned into a pitched battle. "Gah. I don't like it here."

Liam hooked a hand under my elbow. "The magic of this

place senses your unhappiness and is doing its best to soothe your worries."

"Mind control," I blurted. "This is worse than what Death dishes out. At least she doesn't force us to feel a certain way."

"Not sure it's worse," Padhraic said. "Merely different. Both instances chip away at your agency, your strength."

"We can discuss the Reapers' problem with Death later." Liam eyed both of us. "'Tisn't why we're here." He addressed his next words to me. "This will go easier if you don't fight the *Dreaming*. It only seems like you'll be lost forever if you don't launch a counterattack,. The only reason the magic that powers this place is being so persistent is because you're pushing back."

"Got it." I sucked in a breath. I'd been panting shallowly, convinced if I breathed deeply, I'd be lost. I trusted Liam. He wouldn't lie to me about something this important.

We started forward. Once we moved past the mists surrounding the gateway, we were in a forest on a cunning path that wound among majestic trees. I've always loved walking in the woods, and my panic at having my free will snatched away began to subside.

Either the *Dreaming* had gotten its claws into me, or it had lightened up because I'd stopped panicking. Maybe some of both.

"Pretty here," I murmured.

"Och, lass, we all experience it differently," Padhraic told me. "I'm in New Zealand on the South Island on one of my favorite beaches."

I swallowed hard, my alarm from earlier clamoring for

recognition. "How can you find anything relaxing here?" I demanded.

"We trust the *Dreaming*," Liam told me. "Sidhe built it in concert with some of the Celtic gods because immortal beings need a respite from time to time."

"All of us understand the consequences of remaining too long," Padhraic said.

"Which was why the lot of you breaking out of here was so unexpected," Liam muttered.

"We never would have were it not for Perrikus, Adva, and D'Chel. They were most persuasive, and they levied power that counteracted the inertia from our long tenure."

Liam nodded sharply. "It reminds me we never talked with you about your escape."

"I'd be glad to fill in whatever the Sidhe council wishes to know," Padhraic replied formally.

If I was in a forest, and Padhraic was on a beach, I wondered what Liam wandered through, but it didn't matter. A flash of magic made me squint my eyes. When it cleared, my sickle was in my right hand.

"Wow! I've never had it show up anywhere except the realm of the dead." I glanced about but didn't sense anything dead or dying. Not here.

"The *Dreaming* detected your magic wasn't complete," Liam said. "It fixed the problem for you."

I considered what he'd said. "Does this mean if a Reaper spent a short amount of time here, they'd be able to easily reclaim the full spectrum of their power?"

"Depends," Padhraic said.

"Only if they were open to it," Liam cut in. "The

Dreaming senses what you need and amplifies it. If a Reaper didn't want to access their additional power, the *Dreaming* might have the opposite effect and bury it deeper."

"Interesting," I murmured and inhaled the evergreen scent surrounding me. "How long before we get to where we're going?"

"I don't know," Liam said. "We will keep walking until the *Dreaming* deems we've walked far enough."

I failed to appreciate how building a place like this could ever have been considered a good idea. I was doing better at shielding my antipathy, though—and the *Dreaming* had backed off its full-scale attack on my aversion to its pandering. Wrapping my fingers more firmly around the scythe's handle, I cleared my mind of anything the *Dreaming* could latch onto.

With no warning, the forest dropped away, and a large clearing stretched before us. "Now we wait," Liam said.

"Not for too long," Padhraic murmured and began to walk the perimeter of the clearing. "Four transits," he said.

"I'll keep track," Liam told him.

I watched while Padhraic paced. Once he'd called out, "One," Liam grabbed a pointed rock and dug a short trench in the dirt. Crap. It wasn't possible to both walk and keep track at the same time?

I focused on my scythe. I'd always viewed it as kind of a theatrical assist, something to soothe humans and make us fit the Grim Reaper image. I hadn't actually appreciated it had power of its own until my last Vampire battle. At least I didn't chafe against how many things Death had kept from us.

I no longer cared. The only important thing was getting out from beneath her thumb. Apparently telling her I quit hadn't been much more than a gesture. She knew full well she could still keep tabs on me.

Padhraic was partway through his third transit of the clearing when a man strode toward us. He seemed to come out of nowhere, but the rules of physics didn't apply in places like this.

Long, dark hair framed his sharp-boned face. It hung loose in front, but the back portion was braided close against his skull. Dozens of braids trailed down his back. He was taller than Liam and broad-shouldered. Leather garments embellished with red-and-blue dye clung to his frame. Boots laced to just below his knees. A war axe swung from a sheath by his side, and a broadsword was attached to his back by a scabbard with thongs that wrapped around his body. Still more weapons draped from cunningly crafted bits of rawhide. His face held the same ageless quality that marked the gods.

I knew Liam well enough to understand he masked surprise when he bowed low and murmured, "Cathbad. 'Tis a rare pleasure to see you again."

I rustled through my memory banks. If it was the same Cathbad, this had to be a Druidic seer who'd lived better than a thousand years ago.

"The pleasure is mine, Sidhe." Cathbad inclined his head. "What seek ye?"

"Do ye come as an emissary of the Celts?" Liam asked. He'd switched to an old form of Gaelic to match Cathbad's choice of language.

"Aye, they sensed your presence and sent me to determine what boon ye seek."

Padhraic made his way to us and went to one knee. "Ye honor me with your presence."

Cathbad nodded. "Good to see ye've found your way back from darkness."

"I doona deserve forgiveness," Padhraic murmured, "yet it is welcome." He rose but kept his gaze on the ground.

Cathbad turned his attention on me and raised his dark brows. "Reaper, eh? We've not had many of your kind here. No dead to cull."

I didn't understand what was driving me, but I curtseyed as a sign of respect.

"We do seek assistance with a problem," Liam said. "After the dark mages freed the Leanan Sidhe from their prison deep within the *Dreaming*, they made certain our Vampires joined forces with the Earth-bound variety. It took many hundreds of years, but the energies keeping magic pure have slewed sideways."

Cathbad frowned. "The Leanan Sidhe appear to be imprisoned once again."

"They are," Padhraic said. "All except for me. I've renounced my association, and the other Sidhe reshaped my magic."

Liam rocked from foot to foot, clearly uncomfortable with what he was about to divulge. "Our magic is no match for the dark mages," he murmured. "The boon we seek is help returning them to wherever they were before they decided freeing the Sidhe Vampires would be great sport."

"I see the problem," Cathbad said. "If my masters are not

willing to deal with the dark ones, they will pass the word along to the other pantheons. Someone will contact you." He hesitated, his dark eyes never leaving Liam's face. "Do ye have an alternative plan?"

"Aye. We will do what we can to chop holes in the Vampires' ranks. Another problem is a group of mortals who've taken it upon themselves to proclaim magic is the root of all evil."

"Word of them has filtered to us." Cathbad nodded. "'Tis far from the first time our kind has fallen under suspicion because of our talents."

"But they're frauds," I spoke up. "We caught some of them using magic. Not well, mind you. But for mortals to dabble in magic at all is forbidden."

"Interesting." Cathbad's dark brows shot up. "Of course ye'll expose them."

"We are in the process of gathering enough information so what we do is effective," Liam replied. "The world has changed, and we need irrefutable evidence."

"Who is teaching them?" Cathbad growled.

"The Leanan had a hand in it," Padhraic said. "As did the other type of Vampire. Occasionally, they'd receive an infusion of power from one of the dark mages, but it was as likely to drive them mad as not, so mortals avoided them."

"Mortals who wield power all eventually lose their minds," Liam muttered. "Perhaps it's for the best."

"Perrikus and D'Chel had an eye for the ladies," Cathbad said. "And Majestron Zelia is like a black widow spider."

I took a step backward. "Awk. Do you mean she has sex with men and then murders them?"

"'Tis precisely what I meant to impart." Cathbad narrowed his eyes. "Have all of you grown so blunt?"

I looked away and was aware of my face growing warm. Good thing I'd said sex rather than fuck. "Sorry, I didn't mean to offend you."

"I ken as much," he replied in a softer tone. "I will take my leave."

"I hope our paths cross again," Liam said.

"They are bound to, sooner or later." Cathbad almost smiled.

When he turned to walk away from us, he began to sing in a clean, pure baritone that tugged at my heart and my soul. If the song had words, I couldn't make them out, but the music was transcendent. It made me long for a younger world, for simpler times when mortals gathered around fires and had no idea what was happening a few miles away.

I was still lost in longing when Liam touched my shoulder. "We should depart."

I shook myself to clear my thoughts, but wisps of the song tantalized me. "What just happened?"

"He's the most famous of the bards," Padhraic said, "and now you know why. No one who's ever heard his music emerges unchanged."

"'Tis said it brings out the truth within each of us," Liam said. "I'm deeply honored he chose to gift us with a song. Not many outside the gods have heard him sing."

I shut my eyes for a moment, not wanting to let go of the enchanted spot my mind and heart had turned into. When I opened them, I asked, "If his music taps truth, would it also urge evil to show itself?"

Liam nodded. "According to lore, he's drawn wickedness from the worst of magic wielders and turned it against them."

"What a shame he can't fight on our side," I said.

"He already has, lass," Padhraic told me. "The gods may have suggested he show himself to us, but he is not bound by their edicts."

"But he called them master," I pointed out.

"Aye, but he answers to no one," Liam said. "He never has, although he threw in his lot with the Celts around the time of the Crusades."

Magic burbled around Padhraic, and a portal edged in blue opened in front of us. I stared at it, and then at the men. "We don't have to return to our starting point?"

"The Dreaming has an infinite number of entrances and exits," Padhraic said. "When you step through, you'll be back in Scourie Castle."

I chuckled.

"What's so funny?" Liam asked.

"Never thought I'd be anxious to get back there. It's not exactly the coziest spot."

He looked at my scythe. When I followed the line of his gaze, I noticed it was glowing. "Intriguing," he said. "Your magical accoutrement is soaking up the feel of the *Dreaming*. I might be mistaken, but I bet you could open a portal without our assistance."

"How? The sickle will vanish as soon as I step through."

"I think not, but shall we find out?" he invited.

Always one to take up a challenge, I walked through Padhraic's gateway and into the courtyard of Scourie Castle.

Dawn was just breaking, adding a pearlescent pink edge to Scotland's perpetually gray skies. True to Liam's prediction, my sickle was still with me.

"It appears you were right," I told him. "Don't let it go to your head."

He snorted laughter. "No worries on that front. I'm wrong so often it keeps me humble."

"We did a good night's work," Padhraic said. "Let's see what everyone else accomplished."

"Aye, and we'll determine our next steps from there." Liam hooked a hand beneath my arm, and together we trudged up the wet, slippery flagstones leading into the ancient Sidhe stronghold.

If I closed my eyes, I could still hear Cathbad's song running about in my head. I hoped I never lost the ethereal feeling the music had shaped within me. For the first time in my long life, I was beginning to view myself as more than someone who held gateways for the dead.

It felt as if I'd taken a big step up in the magical world, and I rather liked it.

CHAPTER FOURTEEN, LIAM

We were the first ones back. Cait scanned the empty room. "If it's not essential to wait here, how about we tackle the other problem?"

"Which one?" Padhraic asked and offered a crooked grin. "We have so many of them, it's hard to keep track."

"I'd like both of you to take a look at the lore book that describes how Death created her task force." Cait clarified.

I clapped her across the shoulders. "Good idea."

"Why thank you. On a more serious note, if we can't keep Death out of my head, there's not much point in my mini rebellion."

Something about her tone caught my attention, and I stared at her. "You're not considering recanting?"

Cait shrugged. "We can only fight on so many fronts. We have to prioritize the dark gods, Vamps, and Humans Rule, probably in that order. If the price for Death's assistance marshaling the other gods is me doing a little bowing and scraping, it might be worth it for now."

Where it sat balanced across one shoulder, her sickle took on a translucent aspect, almost as if it was ready to abandon its mistress. Was independence the price for its presence?

"I don't care for that idea," I muttered. "Neither does your scythe."

Cait glanced at the silver-gray length topped with its curved blade. "Everything appears to be interconnected."

"It's the way of magical accoutrements," Padhraic agreed, but his tone was solemn.

"I appreciate your motivation," I said to Cait, "but you were on the right track when you took a stand. Now isn't the time to back down."

"Wish I was as sure of that as you." She stood taller. "The whole point of me quitting was to establish myself as an independent entity. If Death can peek in on my location—and my thoughts—anytime the fancy strikes her, what I did falls into the empty gesture category."

"If all she did was observe—" Padhraic began.

Cate chopped a hand downward. "She wouldn't stop there, though. Why should she? She wants me to fail. She needs to prove a point, which is that Reapers are powerless without her to guide us. While she might have done a slow burn if the only errant Reaper was me, the fact I seem to be leading a charge that's attracted other Reapers is certain to make her dig in with both feet."

Breath whistled from between Cait's teeth. "Which circles back to my original point. The one where we can't afford to attract even one more hostile element. If Death is sabotaging our efforts, it could well make the difference between success and failure with the dark mages."

I doubled up a fist and drove it into a nearby wall. My knuckles stung, but not enough to distract me. It's rare that I get truly angry, as in out-of-control furious, but if Death had been here, I'd have smashed that same fist through her face. Not that she'd have stood still while I punched her, but I'd love to wipe the trademark supercilious grin off her face. The one proclaiming she knew more than any of the rest of us.

"Let's take a look at the lore book," I growled, hoping it held something more definitive than I suspected it did.

Cait led the way to the room where the Reapers had been practicing. The magic-infused fire had burned down to a bed of winking coals. I flicked enough power its way to get it to flare up. It would never warm the room, but seeing flames offered an illusion the cavernous space was something other than a glorified deep freeze.

Padhraic and I moved the book closer to the hearth and settled it on the floor between us. "Show us what you found, lass," Padhraic said.

"The book is still open to that section," Cait replied. "It's on the left-hand side, partway down. Only a few lines, really." She shook her head. "Not that I've ever labored under the illusion I was particularly important, but whoever penned that tome barely gave Reapers a second thought."

"The question of the hour is if anything can be done about the magical beacons without disturbing the rest of the Reapers' magic, right?" Padhraic furled his dark brows.

Cait nodded. “Yeah. Not much point in excising the marker if we lose everything else along with it.”

I scanned the half page, and then started over at the top. The runic language was far from specific, substituting symbols for words. I felt the weight of Cait’s gaze on me, hopeful but not expecting too much.

“We need to find another sourcebook,” Padhraic said flatly.

I nodded. “Aye, one that has more in the way of detail.” I snapped my fingers. “I know just the scroll that might contain what we seek.”

“Where is it?” Cait asked.

“Back in Malin. Where else? Not in my collection, but part of the main Sidhe library.”

Alarm flared in her widened eyes, and she slapped her forehead with an open palm. “I am so flipping dumb. I shouldn’t have asked. Not out loud, anyway.”

Before she said anything else, I hastily drew a teleport spell together. If Death had been listening in, she’d have picked up on the location, but she might have trouble getting past the wards of the building the Sidhe had used for a common area. Even if they didn’t stymie her, she still had to locate the scroll I had in mind.

Unless she simply torched the whole library.

The idea filled me with fury, but she hadn’t batted an eye before she’d destroyed an irreplaceable wall hanging in my home. From her side of things, Reapers had declared war on her, and any retaliation was fair play. She had one ace in the hole—her link to Reapers. If we were successful disarming it, word would spread. Soon, her army would dwindle to a mere handful of diehard minions.

She had an option, but when I'd floated the idea of her leading a band of the willing—rather than the coerced—she'd discarded it out of hand. Too bad for her. Cooperative recruits always fought with their hearts. Her job would have been simpler, and the Reapers would have been far more content.

"Do you want me to come along?" Padhraic was asking.

My attention snapped back to him and Cait, and I considered his question. "Maybe not. Death knows I have a link to Cait, but it might be advantageous if she doesn't assume every Sidhe is an enemy."

"Aye, we don't need her any more paranoid than she already is," Padhraic murmured.

"No shit," Cait mumbled under her breath.

"I'll let everyone know you'll return soon," Padhraic said, "assuming anyone shows up to tell."

"Thanks." My casting hit terminal velocity, and I whisked us to Malin.

Because I was aiming for a Sidhe realm, my magic was deadly accurate, and we ended up not just in the building that had once served as a courthouse but in the upstairs room we'd converted to a library.

"Wow!" Cait turned in a circle, taking in the floor-to-ceiling shelves jampacked with source materials. The library represented a collection we'd begun millennia before, adding to it as new items came available.

While she was ogling our collection, I sent seeking magic spinning outward and build as bombproof a ward and sound shield as I could manage around the library. I didn't sense Death, but neither did I want to say her name out loud.

Or telepathically.

"Where do we begin?" Cait asked.

Rather than answering, I hustled to a corner and reached upward. Several scrolls heeded my summons and floated into my waiting hands. I set them on a scarred table that ran the length of the room. As old as the building it sat within, the table had been crafted back in the days before all the trees in the UK had been cut down.

Rather shortsighted in retrospect, but it had taken a long while before conservation measures had addressed replanting efforts. I gave two scrolls to Cait and bent over the two I'd kept. Time was critical, so I let magic do the heavy lifting, gratified when the dusty lengths of vellum unrolled and re-rolled, exposing what I'd requested.

I hoped.

We'd been at it for maybe half an hour when a sharply drawn breath from Cait brought my head up. "Did you find something?"

"Yeah."

I couldn't interpret her tone, so I walked to where she sat and read over her shoulder. Unlike the cuneiform scroll, this one was written in an old form of Latin. After scanning the panel, I muttered, "Too dangerous. We have to keep looking."

Twisting her chair around, she turned until she faced me. "Dangerous, yes, but doable. Continuing to search is just wasting time."

"Your opinion, not mine," I said, tightlipped, determined

not to reveal how alarmed I was at the prospect of her losing not just her magic, but possibly her life.

"But it says right here"—she pointed—"that all you have to do is rearrange this one part in my magical center. It's not all that different from what the Sidhe did to Padhraic."

I opened my mouth and then shut it. I'd nearly blurted our backs had been up against the wall. We had to strip Padhraic of his Vampire nature, or he could never rejoin the Sidhe ranks. We'd come close to destroying him in the process, but he was tough.

"Well?" Cait persisted. "From a mechanical point of view, it looked the same to me. Not that I was present when you worked on Padhraic, but he said you reshaped his magical center, and—"

I held up both hands. "You're correct. The intervention is similar, but the risks are enormous. This isn't merely a matter of stripping you of your magic along with the beacon that makes you visible to Death."

"I trust you." She focused emerald eyes on me. The expression on her face, fierce and hopeful, smote me.

"More than I trust myself, except it can't be just me. A dozen Sidhe took part in Padhraic's alteration." I knelt in front of her to be at eye level rather than looking down. "How about this? We give our search another half hour. If we don't find anything more promising, less risky, we'll return to Scourie Castle where I will discuss this solution with Krin and Dena."

Cait drew her dark brows together, creating twin vertical lines between them. "Discuss, eh? What if they won't help us?"

"How about if we don't jump to negative conclusions?"

"You're right, of course. I agree to another half hour of reading." Cait's voice held an unusually formal note.

It was as close to a concession as I was likely to receive. Straightening, I returned to the scroll I'd been perusing. A grandfather clock sitting in one corner ticked off the minutes so loudly, I nearly sent magic to silence its mechanism. Finished with one scroll, I started on the next.

Everything I read was in agreement on several points. Death selected Reapers when they were still within their mother's wombs. Once she'd settled on a likely candidate, she slipped a magical cocktail into their developing souls that would eventually form into a magical center. The cocktail had multiple elements. One, naturally, was the magic that made them irresistible to the dead. Another was a full complement of magical ability to support Reaping. That was the segment Death had selectively hidden from her minions. They did need some of that power, but far from all of it. The final element enabled her to track her Reapers' locations. Because each component had begun as an independent bit of power, there was no reason they couldn't be separated out.

On a theoretical level.

I feared the three portions hadn't remained separate, that they'd twined together in ways that would make it difficult—if not impossible—to separate without harming the Reaper. If Cait was unlucky, and things went south, she could end up insane or a vegetable or dead. Of the three, the latter was actually preferable, and I would not be the instrument of her demise.

I loved her, and I'd rather live with Death peeking over our shoulders than risk not having Cait at all. But this wasn't exactly my choice. Playing fast and loose with my own magic was one thing, but Cait had the final say over the status of her own.

"Geez," Cait muttered. "This is unsettling."

"What?" I looked up.

"Death may have selected us prior to our birth, but not every developing baby took to the implanted magic. Some ended up stillborn. How the hell did she square up killing innocent children?"

"I'm not sure she would even view herself as responsible." I shrugged. "Why would she?"

"How can you say that? Sort of a win some, lose some attitude?"

"Aye," I replied. "Something like that. On a related topic, who raised you? This"—I tapped the scroll—"seems to imply it wasn't your natural parents."

Cait nodded slowly. "I don't recall much before I was maybe four or so, but as soon as the dead found me, my childhood ended. The villagers revered Reapers back in those days, so they took turns hosting me, moving me from house to house."

The clock might have ticked even louder, perhaps to jolt me back to why we were here. I wouldn't have put it past the old thing. Like every item that spent much time in the Sidhes' realm, it held its own magic.

"We've hit the half-hour point, and I haven't located a different mechanism to separate you from Death," I said. "In truth, everything I've read points to the procedure we found earlier being the only one."

"It's past time for us to return," she agreed. "This is what I mean about splitting our attention too many ways. We should be back in Scourie, plotting our war against the dark mages."

"Which presumes we'll have divine assistance from some quarter."

"Yeah, I get that," Cait said. "If we don't, we'll focus on Vamps. Now that I have all my magic, I won't have to resort to elaborate tricks to move Vampires past the veil. I'll be able to suck them through the gateway just like Death. I'm nowhere near as strong as her, but if the other Reapers help —and they will—we should be able to make a pretty decent dent in their numbers."

"Always good to have a plan B," I murmured and got up from the table, tucking the scroll containing basic instructions beneath my arm. I'd memorized them, but the other Sidhe would want to lay eyes on the source document before consenting to help.

Cait splayed her hands on the table and pushed to her feet. "Should we put the scrolls away?" she asked.

"Nay. They'll find their way back to the shelves. Sometimes they enjoy a brief stint not jammed next to all the other books."

Cait grinned. "Listening to you, I almost believe they're sentient."

"They are. So's everything within most of the Sidhe buildings, and—" My head whipped around seconds before Cait's did.

"Damn it," she muttered. "This is why freedom's just a fancier word for stuck."

"In your case," I told her, "freedom is apparently meaningless."

Even quick journey spells took a few moments to pull together. I couldn't move us out of here before Death popped in. Besides, I'd be damned if I'd leave the goddess alone in the Sidhe library. Who knew what she might dig up. To be on the safe side, I returned the scroll beneath my arm to its high shelf.

Sure enough, Death shimmered into being a meter away. This time, she hadn't bothered with a portal. No robes this trip, either. Or leather. Instead, she'd donned a long white skirt covered with runes I hadn't seen in centuries. Designed to augment her power, they were probably what made it possible for her to defeat the wards on this room—and the building itself, which held its own protections.

A rose-and-teal shawl was draped around her shoulders, covering a white silk blouse. The only item of clothing she'd stuck with were her high-heeled boots.

"Aye?" I quirked an eyebrow her way. "To what do we owe the pleasure?"

She made a snorting noise. "You know damn good and well why I'm here." Death crossed her arms beneath her breasts and addressed her next words to Cait. "You cannot let the Sidhe chop up your magical center. It will be the death of you."

Cait blew out a noisy breath. "The thing about believing people"—she glared at Death—"is they have to have told you the truth on other occasions. You, my dear, have blown your credibility not once but many times. Why should I trust you now?"

I was proud of her. She wasn't angry, just matter-of-fact. With everything Death had pulled, Cait wouldn't have been out of line screaming in her face and telling her to fuck off.

"I didn't have to go to the trouble of warning you." Death shook a finger under Cait's nose. "It may have escaped you, but I'm not just short your services. You've seduced half a dozen others, and they're rampaging through Hell stirring up shit."

It might not make much difference, but I wrapped wards around my mind. That the cadre of Reapers had made it through a gateway and into Hell proper was good news indeed.

"They can't be 'rampaging,'" Cait was saying. "They can't remain there long."

"That was with your old magic," Death corrected her. "The uncovered portions contain protections."

"Have you rethought our conversation?" I asked, ignoring the fact Death hadn't exactly included me in the discussion.

She shot a pained look my way. "Why would I do something like that? Quiet, Sidhe. I didn't come all this way to talk with you."

I clamped my jaws tight. My first instinct was to order her out of the stronghold, but curiosity won out. I started to ask a question, but Cait beat me to it.

"Why am I so damned important to you?" She straightened her back, standing tall. "Why can't you just give up and go away and let me live my life?"

It was a reasonable question, and I expected a rational

answer. That's the thing about expectations, though. They have a way of blowing up in front of you.

Death swung both arms to the sides and lowered her gray brows until they formed a single, thick line. Cait held her ground, but uneasiness sheeted from her, changing her aura from its usual multihued glory to a muted gray.

"This is not about you," Death shouted. The collage of imagery moved faster across her eyes. "This is about me. Do you hear? Me. I was tasked with a job so long ago, Earth had barely cooled after detaching from the sun. Over time, I experimented, honing methods that were efficient and effective. I will not stand by and allow a single Reaper to lay waste to millennia of effort."

Her voice had risen until I shielded my ears with a layer of magic.

"Me?" Cait screeched, incredulous. "You're blaming me for the Vampire problem? You've come unglued."

"Show some respect," Death hissed.

"Yeah, I will when you do." Cait had swapped uneasiness for anger, the gray of her aura shading to crimson.

"We were dealing with the Vampire problem." Death tilted her chin.

"Like hell you were," I tossed out, tired of being quiet. "We had to leave Malin because Vampires killed so many mortals. Humans Rule is having a heyday attracting new members because of the Vampire problem you have under such stellar control."

"I told you to shut up," Death snarled, showing me a mouthful of teeth. She'd lost any semblance of appearing human. Ageless. Ancient. Ferocious. Imposing. She turned to face me. "Leave now."

"Um. This is my realm. You're the visitor here. Besides, I'm not leaving Cait." I kept my voice low, reasonable. No reason to antagonize her further.

Before Death could levy the power crackling from her fingertips against me, Cait stepped between us. "Why are you really here?"

"I told you, child. You never did listen well."

"I listen fine," Cait retorted. "What you said makes no sense. You view me as a problem. I'm out running amok, teaching other Reapers about the power you hid from us. Seems to me, if you truly believed the Sidhe would kill me by severing my ties to you, you'd just let it happen.

"Instead, here you are, pretending to care."

Cait blew out a breath. "I repeat. Why are you really here?"

"Misguided though it might be, I do care about you," Death said silkily. So silkily I heard the lie even absent magic.

"Not going to work." Cait shook her head and glanced my way. "Time for us to leave."

"I haven't released you," Death announced in a gravelly voice.

Cait thumped her in the chest with an index finger. "I don't work for you any longer. I can't do much about you spying on me and knowing where I am. Not yet, anyway, but you cannot force me to your bidding any longer."

"Don't test me."

"I believe I just did."

My gaze moved from one woman to the other and back again. Neither seemed inclined to yield, and this had shifted to a contest of who was going to blink first.

"Fine." Death tossed her head until silver hair danced around her shoulders. "Remember, you made these rules. I'm just playing along."

A psychic boom rolled through the room, obscuring my vision with a gray mist. When it cleared, Death was gone, along with the scythe. Cait lay on the floor moaning softly. I made a dive for her and cradled her against my chest. I should have scanned her first, checked for damage, but holding her was more important.

"Ssht. It's all right," I crooned.

Her eyes flickered open, and she struggled against my grip, eyes round with fear.

"Cait." I tried again. "She's gone. It will be all right. We can return to Scourie. I'll have Dena take a good look at you, and—" I'd meant my words to be reassuring, but she struggled harder.

"Who are you?" Cait yelped. "I'm not going anywhere with you. You're hurting me. Let me go."

What I did next was more reaction than logic. We didn't have time for me to convince Cait Death had done something to ensorcel her. Damn it. I hoped the problem was simple, that Death hadn't gone in and wiped out everything about Cait that made her who she was.

She thrashed back and forth, teeth snapping as she tried to bite me. I barked a word to knock her out. It worked. With my comatose love still firmly in my arms, I retrieved the scroll I'd been focused on when Death showed up and teleported to Scourie Castle.

"Whatever this is," I told Cait, "we'll figure it out." She couldn't hear me, but I needed to say the words anyway. Tears rolled past her closed lids and down her cheeks.

I've never felt so helpless, or so frightened.

The castle great room formed around us. Raising my mind voice, I called Dena and Padhraic and Krin while deepening my sleeping spell. If Cait woke now, she'd be scared, confused, and furious. We had to determine what Death had done to her first.

Then we'd correct it.

Maybe, if we were very fortunate, Cait wouldn't remember any of this. Once we got past it, I vowed to take whatever steps we had to. Before I'd viewed severing Cait's ties with Death as optional, if it turned into too much trouble—or proved too big a risk. No more. Death popping in at will had moved from inconvenient to unacceptable.

"What happened?" Dena raced into the room.

"Not sure. Death paid us a visit while we were in Malin, and—"

Dena placed a hand on Cait's forehead. Power flared, and she muttered curses in Gaelic.

When I couldn't stand not knowing, I said, "Tell me."

"Bring her to my workshop," Dena said. "We'll lose her if I take the time to explain this to you."

Her blunt words were like a mule kick to my midsection. Scroll tucked beneath my arm and Cait in my arms, I took off at a dead run. Dena was a talented healer along with her psychic ability, and even she had said it might be too late.

Believe I exhorted. Faith was the key to magic, so I wiped doubt from my mind. Krin and Padhraic were already there when I laid Cait tenderly on Dena's worktable.

"Withdraw your spell," Dena told me tersely.

"She isn't in a good place," I said.

Dena leveled her liquid dark gaze on me. "I can't work through your casting. If you don't withdraw it, she'll die."

I reeled in my spell as fast as I could.

Cait began to scream. Long, anguished howls that tore at my heart. Dena reeled off a set of orders, but I couldn't focus on any of them. Cait's agony superseded my ability to think.

"Liam!" Dena's tone could have carved stone. "If you don't heed my instructions, you may as well leave."

"Sorry. Tell me what you need." Determined to do everything in my power to save the woman I loved, I pushed everything else aside. My pain. My fury. My despair. One thing was certain. If Cait died, I would hound Death through this world and every other until I found her. And then I would raise every weapon at my disposal to annihilate the bitch who'd caused this.

Revenge had a settling effect. It always does, and I followed Dena's commands as she battled to reattach the magic Death had wrested from Cait's soul.

CHAPTER FIFTEEN, CAIT

The last thing I remember was Death saying something about me making rules, and then everything went black. When I came back into myself, I floated in a void. Nothing to look at. No sounds. If there'd been water, I'd have thought I somehow ended up in one of the Samadhi tanks that were popular toward the tail end of the twentieth century.

In the vague reaches of my mind, I thought I should be worried, fighting whatever this transition was. Instead, peace filled me. Knowledge that the struggle was over, and this would be my forever future.

"No!" Who said that? Had the sound come from me?

Unlikely. I'd found happiness. Bliss. I could ignore words. They no longer applied to me.

Me.

Momentary panic set in. Who was I? Why couldn't I remember even something as simple as my own name?

Had I ever even had a name?

Most people did. Was I an outlier? Had names not mattered in my universe?

I became aware of hands on my back. Who did they belong to? Were my eyes closed? Was that why everything was dark?

It took a long while, and a ridiculous amount of effort to pry my eyes open. Light flooded my corneas and revealed a stranger staring at me with the oddest expression on his face. He looked worried, but terror raced through me kicking my heartbeat up as I fought to free myself.

No matter who he was, I didn't know him, and he shouldn't be hanging onto me. I told him to let me go. He didn't. I writhed and fought and lashed my body back and forth, but it didn't make any difference.

Maybe I wasn't fighting all that hard. My carcass felt alien, like it belonged to someone else. There was this unpleasant latency between what I wanted to do and it actually happening. I tried to bite him, but then I fell back into darkness.

Not the pleasant void where nothing mattered anymore. This place only felt empty, but iridescent ropes bound me. They pulsed, meaning to soothe, but it only upset me more.

Except this time, my body refused my commands. No matter what I told it to do, it flopped around like a landed fish. I had to think about that. About what a fish was and how they looked out of water. The image had come from somewhere.

Eyes wide open in this eerie place, I figured I was dying. This had to be how it happened. First your arms and legs quit working. Last thing to go was the mind. No. Last thing to go was smell.

How did I know that?

How did I know anything?

My cheeks grew damp with tears. I tried to lift a hand to brush them away but wasn't able to. It made me feel small, powerless. I wanted to find a hole, crawl inside, and never come out, but the ropes held me prisoner. Something altered in my non-environment. Tendrils of light replaced the darkness. The ropes fell away. I should have been delighted.

I was free, but I still couldn't move. It hadn't been the ropes after all.

Screams filled my ears. I wanted whoever was screeching to stop, but then I understood those tormented howls were coming from me.

I tried to stem them, but they kept coming, bursting from my open mouth of their own accord.

What was wrong with me? If I was dying, I needed to get on with it. Go out with dignity, not like a ninny. The world would be better off without me. Hell, I couldn't remember who I was, what I'd done.

Maybe I'd never done anything. Maybe I was a ghost. Once upon a time, I may have known something about ghosts. The word battered against memories that refused to unfold.

Something sharp as knives and hot as fire cut into me. Stabbed me over and over in a row down my chest. The rich, copper tang of blood filled my nostrils. It took a moment before I understood it was my blood.

Shit. I hadn't been dying fast enough. Someone, the

shadowy someones bending over me, wanted to do me in. *Fine. Hurry. Don't torture me. Get it over with.* I tried to push words over the squeals of agony, but they refused to emerge. I wanted to tell them where my heart was.

To drive one of those burning stake things through my heart so I could be gone for good. A tiny, buried part of me yelped, told me I was better than that. Stronger than that, but I didn't care anymore. Not about being stoic. Certainly not about being strong.

Someone shrieked, "Now." For once, it wasn't me. The air around me got shiny, liquid. Air didn't look like this. Ever. Why could I see something that normally wasn't visible?

Panic thickened my throat, made it impossible to keep screaming. But it was also harder to breathe. I fought and fought. Drowning shouldn't take this long, and then I understood I wasn't drowning. Terror was making it hard to breathe.

Wait. I wanted to die. Right? I'd been longing for death, for an end to everything. Until the word marched across my mind, and then the last thing I wanted was to face my demise. Something was very wrong here, but I couldn't puzzle through what it was. Why would I be afraid of death.

It's more than a word. More than an end to everything, a quiet little voice informed me. *Death is a person, and all this is her fault.*

I tried to shake my head, might have managed a teensy movement. How could death be anything other than the cessation of life? I was losing it to think death was alive.

If I'd been able to laugh, I would have. The whole thing

was absurd. Here at the end of everything, I was playing word games. Death was a concept, not a person.

You're wrong. The same voice was back. I ignored it. Random neurons must be firing willy-nilly throughout my dying brain.

The indistinct forms leaning over me came back into half focus. At least they'd quit stabbing me, and the flow of blood down my chest and belly had slowed. Excellent. Death had to be near if I was running out of blood. My spirit cringed. Something about the word, *death*, was more than unpleasant. It scared the bejesus out of me.

Last time I'd worked my way through that problem, someone tried to make me believe I'd somehow met Death. Must have been Halloween where a ghoul masquerading as Death got my attention.

The same voice that had said, "Now," with authority was talking again. I tried to pick up words, strained to understand. All those people grouped around me had a plan. They had to, or they'd have left me to my misery.

Left me to die.

Words reverberated through my head. A hand closed around my upper arm, a face—familiar yet not—hovered right above my head. "Be brave a wee bit longer. This will hurt, but it will be the end of it."

I did my best to nod that I understood. The death I'd longed for was finally almost here. My body was broken. My spirit not far behind. How did someone who didn't know who they were deserve life?

Pain crashed over me. The hot knives from earlier were

nothing compared with now. I was being boiled alive, flesh carved from bone. My blood splashed onto the floor, replaced by more blood in an endless rinse, repeat cycle.

Even my hair hurt, and my teeth. Screams tumbled from my mouth. Tortured howls because the agony was so exquisite, so brilliantly unbearable, I had no choice. In the midst of the fresh torment, knowledge spilled through me. My name was Cait Carrick. I was a Reaper. I flew airplanes.

Death had tried to end me in the Sidhe library in Malin, Ireland by ripping my magical center out of my soul.

Fuck.

What good was my recently returned brain? No one could hurt this much and survive. I managed bursts of words between screams. Primitive words, but identifying myself was worth fighting for.

"I'm Cait," I wheezed. "Cait Carrick. Tell Liam sorry. Love him."

"Damn it, Cait. Fight this. I will not lose you," a man's cracked and broken voice growled from somewhere behind me. I did my best to turn my head to see who'd spoken, but my vision was occluded by haze.

"Liam?" I croaked.

"Yes, love, it's me. Don't abandon hope. Not after everything you've gone through."

"Keep it flowing," the "now" voice ordered. "We've almost got this."

Another wave of pain cascaded through me. Not as bad as before, but enough to steal my breath and my wits and capture all my attention. At least I remembered about breathing through pain. I sucked air to the bottom of lungs that were suddenly functioning again. Maybe they always had been.

A blazing desire to live filled me, racing from the soles of my feet over the top of my head. With it, the pain ebbed, and my vision cleared.

Against hope and reason, I was going to survive. After being convinced I was on my way out, the knowledge I'd been wrong was intoxicating.

I thrashed weakly. "Let me sit."

"Not so quick. I'll make you a nourishing tea," the "now" voice said.

I squinted. "Dena?"

The Sidhe with beautiful ebony skin and clear dark eyes smiled. "Aye, lass, and a few anxious moments ye gave us all." Her white robes were spattered with blood. My blood.

"You'll have to tell me," I gasped, "but in a little bit."

She patted my upper arm. "We'll make time whenever you're ready. I was speaking Gaelic, and you understood me. Appears your memory is on its way to being restored. Thank all the gods and goddesses for their wisdom and mercy."

"They may have guided your hand"—Liam came into view—"but without your tenacity, we'd have lost Cait."

The murmur of voices caught my attention, and I understood many Sidhe had labored to save me. Liam had moved next to me and laced his fingers in with mine. His silent presence was solid, reassuring. Krin was here and Padhraic and some of the Reapers too.

Dena squeezed my arm. "Your magic is whole again—minus the tentacle linking you to Death."

Relief punched me in the gut. "No more spying?"

"Aye. No more spying, and now I'm going to brew you tea to speed your recovery."

"Already done." Krin handed a steaming mug to Dena.

She set it aside, and someone placed pillows under my shoulders to prop me up. My head spun a little, but the dizziness didn't last.

Liam let go of my hand and retrieved the tea, holding it to my mouth.

"I can manage the cup," I protested.

"'Tis rare for me to wait on anyone," he said with a flicker of his old humor. "Indulge me."

I blew on the tea and took a tentative swallow. "Ewww." I made a face. "What's in this? Rotten snails?"

"Och, she guessed my secret ingredient," Dena quipped.

"I actually prefer rotten clams," Krin said with a deadpan expression.

I tried to smile. I'd never have guessed the Sidhe made a habit of joking amongst one another, but they were now. The first taste hadn't made me puke, so I swallowed more of the tea. Despite its bitter, acrid taste, I sensed magic in the brew, enchantment to counteract what I'd been through.

Stacia, Abby, Lilly, and Pavel surged around the surface I lay on. A long table judging from its height. "We were so worried about you," Stacia said.

"And furious with Death." Abby's voice was harsh and bitter.

"How could she have done this to one of her own?" Lilly shook her head.

"Means none of us are safe from her." Pavel aimed his

next words at Dena. "Can you cut our ties to Death like you did with Cait?"

Dena nodded slowly. "Aye, and with far less fanfare. I know what I'm doing now, and you're not hovering at the edge of ruin."

I drained the mug. Liam took it from me and set it aside. "All right." I looked from face to face. "My last memory was Death reaching inside me. What she did wasn't painful. I went into kind of a floating stasis."

"You want to know what happened between then and now?" Liam's deep voice rumbled.

"Yeah, so I can put this behind me, and we can get back to what's important." I shook my head. "All this energy. All this magic should have been aimed at the dark gods, at the Vampires. And Humans Rule. Damn Death and her fucked up agenda to rule the world."

"Nay, lass, only her Reapers," Padhraic said, "although it might amount to much the same thing."

"I'll be brief," Liam said. "Death departed in a cloud of magic so strong it knocked me off balance. When it cleared, your scythe was gone along with Death, and you were sprawled on the floor. I picked you up, held you tight."

"Yes, go on," I urged after he'd stopped.

He looked away from me. "You, um, came to, but you didn't know me. You fought me. I'm not comfortable with what I did, but I spelled you back to sleep to transport you here. I had no idea what was wrong, but I understood Death had robbed you of an elemental part of yourself. Time was critical. I couldn't risk having a conversation where you might have told me to piss up a rope, and—"

"It's fine," I cut in. "For Christ's sake, you saved me. You don't owe me any apologies because you might have trod on my sensibilities."

"The moment I saw you," Dena said, "and heard Liam's account, I realized Death had tried to excise the entirety of your magic. Good thing for you she was angry and did a sloppy job. The magic from Cathbad's song helped too. Death wasn't counting on it in her slash-and-burn equation. Liam got you here in time for me to patch you back up. The good news part for the other Reapers is I have a decent understanding of how Death constructed the implants."

"Whenever you have the time and the magic," Stacia said in formal tones, "we would very much appreciate your skills."

The last two Reapers had been hovering near the doorway. Zed and Davin bowed before Dena. "Please accept our thanks as well for saving Cait," Zed said. He and Davin were twins with cropped red hair and brilliant blue eyes. Dressed in tan pants and plain gray jackets, they might have selected ordinary garb to draw attention away from their twin status.

"We've been worried ever since we heard what Death did to Jake," Davin said.

"We'd welcome a permanent solution to our long association with Death. She never used to be this way," Zed added.

I considered his assessment. It was right on target. Death had always been haughty and patronizing, but her pathological need to control every aspect of her Reapers' lives had shot off the charts these past few years.

Dena's gaze moved from one twin to the other. She shook her head. "'Tis only one of you who is marked by the beacon. You"—she pointed at Zed—"have always been free, but my guess is you're always together."

"Son of a bitch," Davin said.

"At least now we know why she told us we had to work together," Zed muttered.

"No shit. I used to think we were lucky to be the only Reapers who were paired with someone else." Davin narrowed his eyes to slits.

"Can I get off the table now?" I asked.

"I believe so." Dena touched my forehead with two fingers, and I felt more of her magic, warm and healing, pour into me.

"Where would you like to go?" Liam asked.

It was stupid and selfish, but I wanted to go home. To my houseboat and my bed and my things. "How soon before we have a war council?" I asked.

"Probably won't happen until tomorrow," Krin said.

Tomorrow wasn't very far away. I didn't feel right asking Liam to burn through two major teleport spells on the heels of the power he'd lavished on saving me.

It reminded me of something I hadn't done. "Thank all of you so much." I sat straighter and crossed my legs beneath me. Dried blood flaked off my clothing. "I can still sense magical residue all around me from your healing. There's no way I can ever repay you, but—"

"No need, lass. Victory is its own reward," Krin said.

"Are you hungry?" Liam asked.

"Yeah, I am, but I want to clean up first." I reached for

him, and he helped me to my feet. “When you asked where I wanted to go, my first thought was home, but it’s not practical. How about your flat in Malin?”

“Good choice,” he said and grinned. “One of us keeps a well-stocked cold box.”

“We’ll see you back here in a few hours,” Krin told us.

“I scarcely blame them for not wanting to hang about here.” Dena rolled her dark eyes. “Scourie Castle is many things, but cozy isn’t among them.”

“Before you go,” Stacia said, “we bring decent news from Hell.”

My ears perked up. Good news was always welcome. “You found Hades?” I asked.

“Him and Arawn both,” Abby said. “They remembered a couple of us, and at least heard us out about our dark mage problem.”

“Aye,” Pavel added. “We told them Death was on a rampage about us breaking free of our contract labor status, and—”

“More like indentured servant status,” Lilly broke in.

“The important part,” Pavel continued, “was what they said afterward. Something akin to they’d been expecting a Reaper rebellion for years.”

“Might have been nice for them to encourage us,” Stacia muttered, “before things got this bad.”

“You can tell everyone tomorrow,” Krin said. “We will gather in the main room at fifteen hundred.”

“Thank you for including us,” Stacia said. She gave me a quick hug and left the room. The other Reapers followed suit, and I embraced each of them, touched by how much we could support each other. Who would have guessed? After our enforced isolation, it was a miracle we did much more than give each other a serious side eye.

"What time is it now?" I asked Liam.

"We have about twenty-four hours," he told me. "Not nearly enough time to feed you and get you into clean clothes and see you get some rest."

I liked him clucking over me, but I'd have died before I admitted it. "You have blood all over you too," I observed.

Rather than answering me, the scent of his magic, heavy on sandalwood and damp greenery, rose around us. When it cleared, we were in his living room in Malin. Not my home, but close enough.

His fair hair had come loose from its customary binding and fell around his shoulders, adding to his otherworldly beauty. His hazel eyes glittered violet in the muted light of the room. He faced me and cupped my face in both his hands. Emotions—relief, desire, tenderness—played over his expressive features before he crashed his mouth over mine.

All my promises to maintain distance crumbled. I'd said I loved him. It had slipped past my lips when I was certain I was dying. If I could admit needing him, longing for him, when I believed it was my last chance to let him know how important he was to me, why was it so hard for me to let my walls down now?

His lips were warm and insistent. Enticing enough, I wrapped my arms around him and shunted my doubts aside. He loved me. He'd proven it by his actions. Except he didn't have to prove anything. Not to me.

I had a lot to absorb about this whole love thing, but I kicked the floodgates open, more than willing to learn.

CHAPTER SIXTEEN, LIAM

I probably should have trotted upstairs and drawn a hot bath for Cait, but she looked so beautiful and so vulnerable and so fierce once I'd transported us to my flat, I kissed her. I admit, I didn't try very hard to force reason to the forefront. I was tired of shoving my emotions to a back seat, and the truth was I couldn't stand the distance between us any longer, couldn't bear not having her as close as she could be.

I hungered for her with an insatiable need that ran far deeper than our bodies. Our souls were entwined. She was mine. My destiny. And I was hers. She'd said she loved me, but it had been a deathbed confession. I'd been shackled to her mind and her magic throughout Dena's long cure, pouring power into her to keep her life force from departing.

I'd done my best to respect her privacy, but I couldn't escape her certainty she was dying. It had been stenciled into every breath.

Death had done a number on Cait. One I'd never forgive her for. If it hadn't been for Dena's intuitive knack with healing—and Sidhes and Reapers digging deep into their magical reservoirs—we'd have lost her. In the end, Cathbad's residual magic might have been what saved Cait. Remnants of his music must have sensed she was under attack because I'd located them wound protectively around what was left of her shredded magical core.

When my mouth covered Cait's she'd hesitated long enough I almost drew back, but then she closed her arms around me and returned my kiss. Yearning flowed from her, something she'd always kept dammed up. I threaded my fingers into her hair and held her head, our lips still crushed together.

She licked at the seam between my lips, and I opened my mouth to her tongue. We teased each other, trading deep kisses with bites and suckles. Time stuttered to a halt. The only thing that mattered was our bodies pressed together, cementing our commitment in ways that didn't require words.

Her hands played across my back, grabbing hold of my hair and pushing it aside. Between us, her nipples formed peaks that pressed against my chest, and my cock swelled into a column against her belly. She nipped my lower lip. I nipped back. Next, she swiped her tongue across my cheek and buried it in in my ear before returning to my mouth.

I trailed kisses down her throat to the hollow between her collarbones and back up. Our breathing quickened. The scent of dried blood still clung to us. What was I thinking? If we were about the make love, I wanted to wash the stench of her near death away first.

I raised my lips from hers. “Cait. Darling. I love you.”

She smiled crookedly, her mouth swollen from our kisses. “I love you too. Don’t know why it was so hard for me to admit, maybe because it means—”

“It can mean whatever we want it to,” I cut in.

“We write our own rules? I like that.” Her grin broadened, and I offered silent thanks to Danu that Cait’s beautiful smile hadn’t been snuffed out forever.

She’d been watching me closely. “Did I die?”

I nodded. “More than once, but you had enough magic left to counteract it, and your spirit refused to budge.”

“Because I know too much. Shades who travel too far from their bodies don’t fare well.”

I still held her head between my hands. “Let’s go upstairs. Two can fit in that tub.”

A soft laugh bubbled past Cait’s lips. “And you know this how?”

“It doesn’t matter. You’re my future. Nothing in the past threatens any of that.”

“Better watch it, Warwick. You’re saying all the right words.”

“I mean every one of them. Come on.” Untangling our bodies, I took her hand and, together, we mounted the steep staircase. I hated to let go of her for even long enough to get the tub filling and toss sweet herbs into it. While water flowed into the oversized clawfoot tub, I turned to her and lowered the zipper on her jacket.

Bits of blood floated to the floor, but we could toss

everything into the washer later. She pushed my coat off my shoulders and undid the buttons on my vest. Our clothing piled up on the floor. The outline of her high, firm breasts was visible through the thin fabric of her top. I filled my hands with them, reveling in the feel of taut nipples that betrayed her heat and her need.

Moaning softly, she leaned into me before making a grab for her shirt and tugging it over her head. Breath clotted in my throat. Seeing her breasts with a layer of cloth over them hadn't prepared me for how incredible they'd be naked. Sitting proudly on a sculpted ribcage with their cherry-colored nipples, they begged to be touched.

Her fingers grappled with the buttons of my shirt. Before I lost all sense, I bent and turned off the taps. When I straightened, she ran her hands over my chest. Her touch sent ribbons of desire streaming through me. Stepping close, she pressed her breasts against my naked torso. The shock of skin-to-skin contact blew the top off my lust.

My breath hitched as I rode herd on my cock so it didn't come spontaneously.

"We have to get the rest of these clothes off," she said, her voice thick with heat and need.

I recognized the wisdom in fighting our way past our trousers and shoes, but I didn't want her to let go of me, ever. And then I remembered magic could help. "Abracadabra," I murmured as pants, underthings, and even shoes joined the stack of discarded clothing.

"Neat trick." Cait grinned at me.

"I could teach it to you."

"Later." She took a step back and raked me with her gaze.

"Wow. You are one incredible man. Even hunkier without clothes than with them on."

The compliment pleased me more than I could say. I'd never cared about being attractive to anyone before, but I cared now. "You're stunning," I managed, so aroused I didn't expect my tongue to work.

"Bet you say that—" she began, and then switched gears and said, "Thank you. I want to be pretty for you."

I lifted her over the side of the tub and lowered her into the fragrant, steaming water. Once she was settled, I climbed in and sat behind her so her back rested against my front. "Why'd you change your mind?"

"About responding to your compliment with a flip comment?" When I nodded, she went on, "I want this to be different. I want us to be different."

It was good enough for me. I reached for a bar of sandalwood soap and a cloth and washed blood off her face before running the soap and washrag over her shoulders and breasts and back and belly. All the wounds—psychic and physical—Dena had opened to better access to Cait's magical center had knitted closed with magic, leaving smooth, silken skin.

Touching Cait was a special kind of heaven. Her skin felt electric beneath my fingertips, igniting my arousal until the pressure of her spine against my erection was agonizing.

Without warning, she turned around and straddled me. It placed her sex right over my distended member, and she lowered herself slowly, tantalizingly, until I was encased in the wonder of her body. The slick heat of her vault felt unbelievable.

She leaned forward until her breasts were crushed against my chest. "We're not quite clean yet," she murmured, "but I couldn't wait any longer."

I moved my hands to her hips and lifted her until just the tip of me was inside before lowering her again. She tightened around me. I twitched my cock in tiny little circles and then lifted her again. Sensation flooded me, a global arousal that invaded every cell of my body. Her nipples hardened still more where they pressed into my chest.

She angled her head and kissed me. I jammed my tongue into her open mouth. If I'd had a third appendage, I'd have plumbed her ass. Filling all of Cait pleased me, delighted me, so I reached around and gripped her butt, teasing the tiny bud with a fingertip.

No longer waiting for me to lift and lower her, she thrust her hips and made a hot little sound that told me she had to be close. Tension in her nipples and pussy grew until it broke into rhythmic release as she crested. I rode through her climax, determined she'd come at least once more before I did.

When she pulled away from my body and got to her feet, I was confused. "Come back," I begged.

"Not going anywhere." She ran her tongue over her upper lip. "On your feet. Take me this way." She'd splayed her hands on a nearby wall to stabilize herself and shook her ass in my face. The cheeks separated and displayed an alluring display of spiky black curls.

"Damn it, woman. You have the finest ass I've ever seen."

"You can look all you want. Later."

Cock distended, balls aching, I didn't require a second

invitation. I surged to my feet and drove into her from behind. Once I was seated good and deep, I reached around and took a breast in one hand. The other burrowed between her legs where I rubbed her slick, swollen nub.

I couldn't hold back any longer, and I thrust into her sure and fast. Her clit shuddered beneath my touch, and her vault dissolved around me. This time, I gave up any pretense of control. Semen juddered from me in thick hot gouts. My heart thudded against my ribcage, and breath was elusive. With it all, I just kept on coming, drowning in pleasure.

We stood there shuddering and groaning for a long while. My errant appendage hadn't shown the least sign of retreating. If I'd asked him, he'd have told me he was good for an infinite number of rounds.

"Want to start over?" Cait asked after our breathing had slowed.

I twitched my cock where it was still buried in her body, and she laughed. "Not with sex. With clean water."

I was riding high on lust and love and the wonder of the woman in my arms. "Anything you want, love. Now and forever."

She pulled away from me and turned so we faced one another. "I do believe you meant that."

"Every word." I kissed her forehead. "How about this? I'll go downstairs and make us something to eat. I can dump our clothes in the washer and use the downstairs shower."

"I'll be down as soon as I wash the blood out of my hair."

I wrapped my arms around her. "I hate to let go of you for even that long."

She nuzzled my neck. "Necessary evil."

After more kisses, I reluctantly let her go. When she curved her fingers around my cock, it was either leave now or not at all. I gathered up our clothing and floated down the stairs. I didn't remember being this euphoric ever. Not even when I was learning magic as a child.

I had our clothes in the wash, myself clean, and dinner well underway when Cait walked into the kitchen swathed in one of my many robes. Her damp hair was beginning to form little ringlets around her face. "Can I help with anything?"

"Clothes might be ready for the dryer."

"Probably better than me mucking about in the kitchen. It's a damn good thing one of us knows how to cook. Oh yeah, my scythe is back. It's leaning against that old desk in the living room."

"Good. I've been worried about it."

"Why?" She angled her head to one side.

"It's part of your magic. Your real magic, not the partial bits Death allotted to you."

Cait made a face. "I don't want to talk about her, but I suppose we can't avoid it forever." She ducked under the curtain that kept my laundry area separate from the kitchen.

When she returned, I said, "We could avoid it forever, so long as she doesn't show up. Somehow, I don't see that happening. This thing with Reapers is bound to develop a life of its own."

"What do you mean?" she asked and picked up a plate I'd made for her.

Once we were settled at the table with our food and a bottle of wine I'd opened earlier to let it breathe a bit, I said,

"So far, we have seven Reapers who've thrown down the freedom gauntlet. Other Reapers will find out. They'll want the same thing. Most of them, anyway."

Cait closed her teeth over her lower lip. "Gah. She'll blame me."

I nodded. "She already does. Although, it's quite possible she believes you're dead."

"She'll find out quickly enough she failed," Cait pointed out. "And it will piss her off even more. She might not be able to track me with precision, but she knows where *Carrick Sky Sports* is—assuming I ever get back there. And my home. She knows where it's located too."

I'd actually thought about that. "We'll have to work on your defensive magic. I need to research this, but I believe the scythe would be effective as a weapon against her."

"Why would she have given them to us if that was true?" Cait raised her dark brows and started eating. "This is good. Everything you cook is amazing. I don't see how you do it, but I'm not complaining."

"Thank you. I like to cook. Far as the other goes, I don't think Death could keep Reapers separated from their sickles. Not entirely. She had things arranged so the instruments only showed up when you were Reaping, but that was an artifact of your partial magic. Once you claimed the full extent of your power, it included your tools."

"Interesting theory. Is there a way to corroborate it?" Cait took a sip from her wineglass.

"Sure. Now that I know which books and scrolls address Reapers, it should be simple enough to find." I waited until we were done eating to ask, "Can we talk about us for a moment?"

She smiled and nodded. "Of course."

But a shadow crossed her face as her skittish colt look resurfaced. It smote me that she didn't have more faith in me and was still ready to bolt at the slightest provocation. I reached for her hand; she hesitated before she gave it to me.

"We have a lot facing us," I began.

She nodded solemnly. "Yeah. We do. Maybe falling into one another's arms was premature."

Her statement was like a slap across my face. "Not what I was going to say at all." I tried for supportive, but I'm certain my tone held censure. Damn it. I jettisoned the rest of what I'd planned to outline about the upcoming battle and how I wanted to protect her so nothing like today happened again.

"What did you want to say?"

"I'm not sure it matters. Are you sorry about making love?"

"No. It was wonderful, but sex is easy. It's all the rest that's hard. Especially for people like us." She tilted her chin up. "I've met a whole lot of Sidhe. Are any of them married?"

"A few, but none at Scourie Castle."

"Same for Reapers, except there's no caveat. The simple answer is none. Some of us pair up with mortals. You can imagine how badly that goes. Nothing like watching the love of your life die while you keep going. Can't stomach that too many times, and—"

I got up and walked to her side of the table. "Come here," I invited.

She rose and asked, "Come where?"

I led the way to one of my sofas and sat, drawing her down beside me. Once she was settled, I returned for our partially full wineglasses and handed one to her while I took a seat cattycorner to hers. I wanted to look at her, and have her be able to keep her eyes on me. And her magic—if she chose.

"Let's start from the top," I said. "Today was so horrible I don't have words for it. I never want to be as scared or feel so helpless when it comes to saving you. What I'd hoped to accomplish back at the table was convincing you to remain by my side in the battles we have yet to face."

I blew out a breath and kept going. "I feel responsible for what happened to you earlier. I had no idea Death would react so viciously. If I'd been more on top of my game, she'd never have gotten her claws into you. I'd have warded you, kept you safe."

Cait scooted forward and laid a hand on my knee. "What happened to me earlier was my own damned fault. Me and my big mouth. I know Death well enough to understand her foul moods and ill temper, and I baited her just the same. I was angry, and when that happens, my common sense takes a hike."

"Regardless." I caught her gaze and held it. Her eyes were mossy with hints of gold in their centers. "I will do anything to avoid a repeat of today. There were hours when I had no idea what the outcome would be. If you'd died, you'd have taken a part of me with you."

She grimaced. "Aw geez. I'm sorry I jumped down your throat. I don't know why I assume the worst. It's an even ickier habit than my temper. When you said we needed to talk, I assumed you were about to launch into how we should keep our relationship secret because the other Sidhe wouldn't approve, and—"

"They may not. Some of them anyway," I cut in. "I don't care."

Her eyes sheened with unshed tears. "You shouldn't have to choose between your kinsmen and me."

"I won't have to. The ones who are critical of us won't be those who are close to me, certainly not the group who pulled out all the stops to save your life. But this isn't about the Sidhe. It's about us."

"Will we ever go back to Seattle?"

"If it's what you want, we'll give it our best shot." I wasn't sure about the next part, but I said it anyway. "You won't have to work anymore. Unless you want to, that is. I can make sure your airplanes have a hangar."

"I'll pull my weight. If I can't keep *Carrick Sky Sports* self-sustaining, I'll have to sell it."

"But that would break your heart," I protested.

"Probably, but we have a whole lot to get through before returning to my airplanes is even a possibility. What happens next?"

"We get some rest. You, especially. We have another meal, and then we go to the war council at Scourie Castle. By then we may have heard from some of the Celts."

"Hades and Arawn sounded promising too," Cait said.

I nodded. "Arawn is a Celt. We'll play the hand we're dealt." Placing my fingers over hers, I leveled my gaze at her. "Evil will not triumph. It never has, and it won't this time, either."

"How can you be so sure? I want what you said to be true, but dark forces have gained a hell of an advantage."

"Believe in us," I told her. "Not just in Cait and Liam as a couple, but in the scope of white magic, good magic. There are more of us than there are of our enemy, and we've always come out on top."

"It's true, but only after some pretty dark days."

"We're up to them. I have a hard time imagining any day worse than this one after I understood Death had tried to end you."

Her crooked smile was back. "And even it had a happy ending."

"Indeed." I drained my wine and then stood, drawing her to her feet. "Come upstairs. Let me spell you to sleep."

"Can we snuggle and talk first?"

Her prickly edges had fallen away. I draped an arm around her shoulders. "I'd love to snuggle and talk. I like it a whole lot better when you don't have one foot out the door."

She laughed. "Me too, but don't tell anyone. You'll ruin my badass image."

"Your guilty secret is safe with me."

We were both laughing as we trooped up the stairs. I'd learned something about Cait—and myself—tonight. If I'd grown angry in the face of her withdrawal, she'd have retreated further, and our fledgling trust in one another would have foundered.

A clunking from behind us alerted me the scythe was doggedly following us upstairs. Cait looked over one shoulder. "Damn. It's worse than a puppy." When she extended a hand, the sickle jumped into it.

"It's a lot like me," I told her. "We both want to keep you safe."

"I'm honored to have such stalwart protectors, and it's not a flip response. I truly mean it."

"I know you do." A savage need to keep her safe shook me to the very core of my being.

We reached the top landing, and I sent a wee bit of magic to turn back the covers. Cait balanced the scythe by its handle in one corner. Untying her robe, she dropped it over the end of the bed and crawled in. Her body was amazing. Even more perfect than I remembered it with her long legs, flared hips, flat stomach, and high tight ass. Muscle corded across her back and shoulders and down her arms, suggesting a sinuous strength.

My cock shot to attention, obvious through the silk robe even before I tossed it over a chair.

"Oooh, come to bed and bring him along." Cait batted her eyes my way.

"Couldn't keep him away if I tried," I joked and slid in next to her. A few adjustments and my mage light provided a soft blue illumination.

She trailed her fingers down my chest and stomach before curling into my arms and tossing a leg over my hip to open herself for me. "Are you sure?" Heat and need flooded me, but she needed rest.

"Quite sure." She wriggled until I slid into her and was lost in sensation coursing through me.

CHAPTER SEVENTEEN, CAIT

We made love before we fell asleep and again during the night, reaching for one another filled with blind need. I may have spun fantasies of him loving me, but judging from his urgency and the way he held me, touched me, he'd longed for the same thing.

Liam was a delight in bed with his lithe hard-muscled body, his shimmery golden skin, and his generous cock. Long, thick, and perpetually hard, he'd satisfy any woman's dreams. I still couldn't quite believe he was mine. Not only for the sex, but I was focusing on it because the rest of everything scared the crap out of me.

He might be saying all the right words now, but what would happen a year from now? Or fifty? Or a hundred? There were solid reasons the Sidhe so rarely paired up on a permanent basis. Why was Liam so certain I was the one for him, and we could make this work?

I wanted to ask, but maybe he didn't have answers. Love

was pure emotion. Often it didn't translate well into words. Besides, I was looking for airtight guarantees in a realm where there were none.

What it boiled down to was whether Liam was important enough for me to take a chance. I wasn't quite there yet. Almost, but could I bear opening my innermost self to him and having him walk away?

I reminded myself it was a two-way street. I might be the one to leave. The way things were looking, I was less committed, but it was only a show I was putting on. I would have been crushed if he'd made it clear we weren't more than comrades in arms with a few additional privileges tossed into the mix.

It might be a safer path.

Let things ride for a bit and see how well we got along out of bed...

Gah. What was wrong with me? I was acting like a simpering ninny going back and forth over something I either accepted. Or didn't. I'd led a pretty insulated life. It had benefits, and big disadvantages.

This was a lot like flying. I'd have to take some things on faith, reach for that golden ring—assuming I truly wanted it —and accept the consequences.

"You're awake." Liam rolled over and faced me, kindling a silvery mage light. "And your mind is busy."

I nodded. No point in denying my upsy-downsy thoughts since he could help himself to them whenever he wanted. "Just working through things."

"So long as I'm still part of your life at the end of your machinations, I'm good with it." He smiled, and my heart did its little flip-flop dance. Why was I so terrified of being happy?

Because it never lasts, one of my cynical inner voices supplied—in case I'd forgotten.

He cradled the back of my neck and murmured, "No one can promise anything will last forever, but if we take care of now, of today, we'll find ways to work things out."

"Did you do time with one of the Zen masters?"

His smile notched wider. "Nay. We Sidhe predate them by a good big bunch. Enjoy what we have, Cait. Lying next to each other, breathing one another in. Soon, we'll be in the midst of goddess only knows what. These will probably be the last few hours we have to ourselves for a long while."

I nodded. "Death hasn't given up. Sooner or later she'll figure out she didn't kill me."

His expression darkened, the smile forgotten. "I have a few things I plan to say to her."

"Um, like what?"

"I want to clarify where I stand, so she thinks twice before attacking you again. If you'd died, I'd have become her single worst nightmare. I wouldn't have rested until the other gods cut her off and she was cast out of every pantheon, forced to walk alone forever."

His reaction surprised me. Surely, I wasn't worth devoting years to retribution. "Revenge can be cold company," I murmured.

"Not in this case. I'd also have made certain every single Reaper was set free. Even the ambivalent ones." He drew me against him, tucked my head into the hollow of his shoulder. The beat of his heart was strong, steady, reassuring.

"We probably should get up," I said after a while.

"Do you want to?"

"Not really, but we must be due back in Scourie soon. I'm 90 percent recovered. Hard to justify staying away longer."

He nodded. I felt the motion against my head. "I'll make us breakfast, and then we'll leave."

"If you hadn't totally spoiled me with your lovemaking, the clincher is your culinary skills." After a final snuggle, I pulled out of his embrace.

"In that case, I'll make a point of whipping up special dishes. It helps to have someone to cook for besides myself."

He swung his legs over the side of the bed and got to his feet. I loved watching the flow of muscle and sinew as he moved. Lithe, elegant, his body was sheer perfection with its long limbs and graceful proportions.

"I could look at you forever," I told him.

He turned from where he'd plucked his robe off the floor. Fair hair spilled down his chest and shoulders, adding to his ethereal good looks. "I feel the same way about you."

My face warmed with pleasure at the compliment, and I stood as well. A glistening jolt of magic hovered over the bed, arranging the covers neatly. I muffled a snort. Perhaps I could make short work of my household drudgery with magic. The idea held a certain appeal.

Liam draped the robe I'd worn the previous evening around my shoulders, and I followed him downstairs. My pet scythe bumped down the stairs behind us. I settled it in a corner of the kitchen, hopefully near enough to me it wouldn't feel the need to relocate. While Liam busied himself in the kitchen, I retrieved our clothes and folded his.

Before I left the laundry alcove, I put mine on, noting most of the bloodstains were gone. Most, but not all. They served as a reminder of Death's treachery, and I wasn't in any hurry to eradicate them.

Liam and I chatted of this and that as we ate sausages and toast and drank a spicy, black tea he'd brewed for us.

"Do we have time for a quick visit to the village?" I asked.

"Sure. What are you looking for?" Liam had donned his freshly laundered garments in between finishing his breakfast and downing two cups of tea.

I frowned. "Not sure. I like things tidy, and I want to make certain I didn't miss any shades from the last Vampire rampage. Maxwell's gone, and I don't imagine Death reassigned another Reaper to this region. It's quite remote."

"Aye, I haven't forgotten about Maxwell. He's gone but not yet crossed over. You want to give him another opportunity."

"Him and others—if there are any."

Liam raked his unbound hair back from his face. "Remember last time shades tried to use you for a portal in Malin?"

"Yeah. How could I forget? I'll be careful."

"We need a foolproof method to sort true ghosts from the ones Vampires are using as bait to lure you."

I set my mouth in a tight line. Here it was. A downside to owing anybody anything. "I'm not going to quit Reaping because Vampires are out to get me."

He stood and walked until he stood next to me. Then he drew me to my feet. "No one said anything about you not

Reaping." He tipped my chin up with his index finger. "No one."

Shame sparred with defiance. I tried to look away but couldn't. "Sorry. I don't know why I'm so reactive."

"It's all right. You avoided falling into the last trap Vamps baited with shades. How did you recognize they were different?"

"It's not all right, though," I blurted. "I should trust you."

"You will. Give it time." He sounded so certain, he almost convinced me.

"To answer your question," I went on, "they have a different feel. It's not all that subtle. Even the other shades sense their evil."

"Good. I'll pay attention so I can sort it out too."

I hefted my scythe and started for the door. "I'll point it out, if we run into any Vampire minions. This shouldn't take long. And then we'll go to Scourie."

Liam pushed the door open, and together we hurried along cobblestone streets to the gateway separating the Sidhe realm from modern Malin. Before we were through the mists, I sensed shades. Lots of them. The dead are drawn to me, but the attraction is mutual.

Up until Death saddled me with Vampires, I actually loved my job.

"Even I feel the press of spirits," Liam said.

"I'm needed," I told him and walked briskly to the town park. It was quite early still; Kilkenny Green was devoid of mortals. Shades clustered thickly around me, clamoring for passage. I shifted to my grave vision, and the park changed, illuminated by the half light of the world of the dead.

My sickle glowed gray-silver, glittering like a signal fire might have in olden times.

Liam stood next to me. He could travel this far, but not beyond the gateway once I built it. "Where'd you all come from?" I asked, curious how fifty shades could have congregated in this tiny hamlet in Northern Ireland.

"There are no Reapers," an old man told me. Thick white hair fell to his stooped shoulders. From the looks of things, he'd died of natural causes and not been dead all that long.

"But why here?" I asked. "Why not move south where there are more people and presumably more like me?"

"We started there," a young blonde woman replied. Maybe sixteen, her skin was riddled with lesions. Death hadn't come easily to her. She'd suffered, perhaps for months, if not years.

"Aye. We met one another as we traveled," the old man said. "No reason not to join forces. Being dead is a lonely business when you can't cross the veil."

"I don't sense Vampire taint," Liam spoke into my mind.

I didn't, either. My Reaper part was clamoring to get moving with a gateway to offer these poor souls respite from an Earth they were no longer part of. The scent of heather and wildflowers intensified as I called a portal. My sickle vibrated gently where it pressed against my palm. One by one, the spirits passed through me.

Until no more remained.

I'd done a good turn here today, and I was humbly grateful my Reaping magic hadn't been wrested from me. I'd just begun to dismantle my gateway when I heard, "Wait!"

Hands still raised, I turned toward the voice. My eyes

widened as Maxwell glided out of shadows and floated to where I stood. "I'm ready," he said. "You were right about everything, and I owe you an apology."

I shook my head. "You owe me nothing."

"Hold up." Liam hooked a hand under my arm. "He reeks of Vampire."

"Of course I do," Maxwell said. "I was just in one of their lairs, trying for the hundredth time to convince them to stop feeding power to humans. It's not natural."

"Say that once more." Liam's words were curt.

I felt a jolt as a truth weave settled over Maxwell's ghostly form. He repeated his words, but I felt certain he'd been honest. Otherwise, he'd have bombarded us with excuses.

"It's good," Liam said, and his netting vanished in a flurry of motes of light.

Maxwell looked broken, forlorn. Before I opened my arms to allow him passage, I asked, "This Vampire lair. Where is it?"

"You have to stay away, Cait. They hate you."

"Yeah. I get that. But I still want to know."

He rattled off directions to crypts in an old castle on the outskirts of Dublin.

"I know where it is," Liam said.

"May I pass?" Maxwell asked formally. He knew the rules. Either I offered passage or turned him down.

I opened my arms, praying I'd made the right decision. He hadn't tried to shield his association with the Vamps, but had he crafted a tale with an eye to deceiving me?

I felt him as he became one with me on his way through the portal. That's how it works. Ghosts have to walk through me, or they'd never make it past the gates. My power protects them as they cross the liminal space, the transition between Earth and the realm of the dead.

His changeover wasn't quick. He told me again how sorry he was, and a few other things. I sensed his fear, but the only help I had to offer was what I was doing. There's a point in every ghost's transit where I have control again. Once he reached it, I persuaded him through and let the gateway close.

Kilkenny Green swam back into focus as I shuttered my grave vision. Liam wrapped an arm around me. "Are you all right? Your scythe shone brighter for Maxwell than the others."

I nodded. "That was hard. He was stuck. He had to leave. He knew it, but he didn't like what awaited him, so he clung to me as long as he could. Poor bastard."

"Why did he have to leave?"

"Death was after him. He told me she'd nearly caught him a few times."

Liam frowned, and we started walking back toward the Sidhe compound. "How would passing through her have been different?"

"There are others beyond the gateway. Those who serve as decisionmakers. At least Maxwell had a chance this way. Someone might take pity on him and not consign him to Hell. He believed Death would have just dumped him there."

"She probably would have." Mists closed over us as Liam led us into the ancient part of Malin. "Unless you want to go back inside, we can leave from here."

"It's silly," I said, "but my bag—the one I always carry—is still in the library. I don't especially ever want to see that room again, but—"

"You don't have to." Liam raised an arm. Power crackled from his fingertips. Moments later, my satchel flew through the air and landed at my feet. I shifted the scythe to one side and draped the bag over one shoulder.

"Nice trick."

"I can teach it to you. It's a simple seeking spell with an added boost from air magic."

"Maybe later. I'm ready to go."

Power burbled around Liam as he built a travel spell. He settled an arm around my back, and I leaned into him. Worry ate at me, but I wasn't ready to talk about it. Not yet. What in the hell had happened to all the Reapers in the UK? Those ghosts shouldn't have had to transit the British Isles to find passage.

I wrested my thoughts back to more pressing concerns. Like the Vampire lair. Handy to have a target. A group of us could take out the whole seethe. It wasn't the only one, but surely its loss would knock a hole in their ranks.

Malin's old buildings faded, replaced almost immediately by the dank smell of old stones and Scourie Castle. "That was fast, even for you," I told Liam as I waited for the mists of his travel spell to dissipate.

I blinked, and blinked again, certain my eyes were playing tricks on me, but then a chorus of, "Cait, Cait," rose all around me. My mouth fell open; I shut it fast and set my bag and scythe down.

"I'll be damned," Liam murmured as he scanned the

castle great room. A space that was packed with Reapers. Some carried scythes not unlike my own. Others didn't.

At least now I understood why the shades were piling up.

All the Reapers were calling out my name as they formed a circle around us. Stacia detached herself from one of the groups and ran to me, smiling broadly. "Isn't this grand?" She grabbed my hand. "It's not all of us, mind you. But more are coming every hour."

"What did you do?" I croaked.

"Well, all of us knew at least a few others. We got the word out. About Death almost killing you by ripping your magical center to shreds. And then we told them they could be free just like you and me and a whole bunch of the rest of us."

"How did everyone get here so fast? I was only gone for a day."

"We must have helped," Liam murmured. "This has the feel of Sidhe enchantment, and I'm thrilled my kinsmen saw the need to take a stand. It bodes well for our alliance."

"The Sidhe did help." Stacia's smile widened. "And are continuing to do so by clipping our bond to Death."

"Next group!" Dena's unmistakable voice rang from the far end of the room.

A group of Reapers hustled to her side, clearly eager to cut their ties with Death. Liam waved an arm in her direction.

"You're back," she cried. "Excellent. I could use the help. I've pressed everyone with a smidgeon of healing magic into service, and I'm still not keeping up."

"Go on," I told Liam. "I'll be fine."

Dena trotted to where we stood. "All these Reapers changes everything." Excitement thrummed beneath her words.

I wanted to share her enthusiasm, but the main alteration I could see was that Death's need for revenge would consume her. One Reaper was an acceptable loss. Half a dozen not so much, but it was looking as if every Reaper on Earth couldn't wait to make a bid for freedom.

Before I could even formulate a question, Dena kept talking. "Don't you see? Ridding the world of Vampires will become trivial with Reapers accessing their full magical ability. Once Vamps are out of the way, there won't be anyone to poison mortals with magic."

"Except the dark gods," Liam muttered.

"Pffft." Dena waved a hand in front of him. "They'll be so demoralized by the Vampire rout, they'll crawl back into the holes they came from. And as soon as their magic matures, Reapers will be able to accomplish the same thing I'm doing. We'll sort out who possesses healing ability, and I'll train them."

"Good to know we won't always be a drain on your resources," I told her.

Liam gave me a quick hug and hustled from the room with Dena and the next batch of Reapers. Wisps of conversation floated back to me. Liam's comments suggested he was worried the dark gods would be more persistent than Dena assumed.

I cupped my hands around my mouth and whistled to get everyone's attention. Once the room quieted, I said, "All this is wonderful, but shades are piling up out there. I just ushered maybe fifty through a gateway in Northern Ireland. They said they'd traversed the length of the British Isles hunting for a Reaper."

"Not good, but Death always assigned us," a man called.

A sigh rustled from me. We'd have to establish who wanted to work where, but only after we'd dealt with the current backlog.

"Can you make a quick trip to your old territories?" I asked. "Just to do some cleanup until we get things straightened out. I'm not trying to be pushy or anything, but we can't let the dead wander. For one thing, they'll be sitting ducks for Vamps to prey on."

"What do you mean?" the same man asked.

I offered up the condensed version of how Vamps coopted mortals they'd killed, turning them into a danger for Reapers. Before, it had only been me they'd targeted, but that could spread.

"But if they're already dead," Stacia asked, "how could the Vampires establish control?"

"I don't know, and I don't especially want to find out," I replied and scanned the assemblage. "How many of you are waiting for Dena?" About thirty hands shot up.

I nudged Stacia. "Get Abby and Lilly and Pavel and Zed and Davin. That will make seven of us. Let's split up everyone who has access to the full range of their magic and teach them to teleport."

She clapped her hands together. "Perfect." Raising her voice, she got cracking getting everyone organized. By the time she was done, we had seven groups of ten Reapers, one for each of us.

"This was Cait's idea," Stacia told everyone.

The chant of, "Cait, Cait," rose again.

"Quiet," I shouted. "Once you have teleporting down, you can return to your assigned territories and deal with the dead. Be alert, though."

"What should we be watching for?" Pavel asked.

"Any shades who smell even remotely like Vampires. Any who act oddly. You've all been at this long enough to notice if something is off." I took a breath. "If you make a mistake like I did, you'll know right away. Vampire minions feel different. It hurts when they pass through you. If that happens, cut the flow immediately. Shut the gateway. A single evil shade won't do you in. More than that, and you'll have to work to escape the realms of the dead."

"Got it," Pavel said. All around me, I saw heads nodding.

"We'll take care of the shades and then return," Davin said.

I worked with my group of Reapers until I was confident they could leave and return. They had a whole lot more in the way of instruction than I'd had, and they caught on fast. We'd all been using magic for a long time, and our familiarity was an asset.

The number of Reapers thinned out as they left to do their jobs. Some returned quickly and resumed chatting amongst themselves. Stacia and Pavel joined me. Abby and Lilly did as well. "We have a request," Stacia said, her tone oddly formal.

I arched a brow. "Yeah? What?"

"Well, we're used to having a leader. Until we get used to being on our own, would you help us out?"

I took a step back. "Death wasn't a leader. She was an autocratic dictator. You're not asking me to take her place, are you?"

"Oh fuck no," Abby said. "Not even close. But like today, we needed direction. You provided it."

"This wouldn't be forever," Pavel said. "Only until we've had a chance to establish some kind of structure." He looked at his feet. "Until you mentioned the dead, they were the last thing on my mind, and that's not right."

Stacia bobbed her head. "We all got so excited about breaking loose from Death, everything else just floated away."

"I don't care for the idea of exchanging one boss for another," I told them. "Maybe rather than just me, we could form a council, kind of like what the Sidhe have. It would have to be democratic, so Reapers would vote on who sat on it."

"I like that," Pavel said.

"Me too," Abby murmured.

"Once we're all back here, I'll let everyone know," Stacia said.

"So we can get the ball rolling," Abby added. "Best to get a jump on this now."

Reapers shuffled into the room, and Dena gathered up the next batch. It looked to me like she'd be done soon.

Assuming no more of us arrived. I'd often wondered how many Reapers there were. Nearly a hundred had been here when Liam and I first showed up.

A whooshing sound brought my head snapping around in time to catch my sickle as it made a beeline for where I stood. For some reason, it must have thought I required its magic. *Oh-oh. Not good.*

"Ssht," I told everyone about the same time their scythes flew toward them. "Not sure what's up, but something's out there."

We turned as a group in time to see Death blast through a gash in the ether. Robed in black with a scythe of her own, she landed on both feet and drew her lips back from her teeth in a snarl.

"Well, well, well. Handy you're all in the same spot."

I stepped forward, placing myself between her and the other Reapers. "This is far from all of us. What do you want?"

"Didn't have the decency to die, eh?"

"That's beyond the point." I battled fury that boiled through me and a consuming need to scratch Death's eyes out. "If you'd been a reasonable boss," I gritted, "none of this would have happened. Underlings only rebel when they're unhappy."

"Shut up," she growled. "Next time, I'll finish what I began."

"Ha! Lots of luck." My scythe took on a reddish glow, stark against its gray color.

The crowd of Reapers flowed around me creating a wall between me and Death. "You will not harm Cait," rose like a mantra, repeated again and again.

I stifled a groan. They were going to make things worse. I edged off to one side so I could still keep an eye on Death.

"Get back to work," Death shouted so loud it made my ears hurt.

"We don't answer to you any longer," Pavel said.

She flicked her fingers his way. He didn't even flinch. "We're free. You can't hurt us, not like you used to."

Death pushed her open palm Pavel's way with the same non-result. I saw a bolt of power bounce off him. Before Death could up the ante on her assault, a ululating cry rose from the back of the huge room. Feral, strident, it was a call to arms. My scythe vibrated in my hand, clearly loving the summons.

Liam bounded around the crowd of Reapers and planted himself in front of Death.

"We are about to have a long overdue talk," he announced.

"Think again, Sidhe," she hissed. "I don't have time for you."

"Nay, you think again," he countered.

Dena, Krin, Padhraic, and half a dozen other Sidhe shimmered into view next to Liam. "Got her," Padhraic said. "She won't be leaving until we release her."

"You can't detain me," Death screeched, writhing against something I couldn't see. "I'm a goddess."

"Then I suggest you start to act like one." Liam didn't raise his voice. His tone was clear and cold and determined.

I pushed around the crowd of Reapers until I stood by his side. He was in this up to his eyeballs because of me. The least I could do was stand tall and offer him my support.

It was what partners—and lovers—did.

CHAPTER EIGHTEEN, LIAM

"You've got this down to a fine art," I told Dena after the last Reaper to receive her ministrations had left with instructions to send the next batch our way.

She shrugged. "Cait was quite the testing ground. After repairing what Death did to her, the rest of this has been simple. And far quicker than I might have believed."

I nodded. "Magic wielders have a particular way of doing things."

"They do," Dena agreed. "And Death wasn't especially creative. She found a configuration that worked for her and repeated it. Once I figured it out, unraveling the beacon portion went fast."

I was just finishing with clearing up Dena's work area before the next group of Reapers arrived when I felt a disturbance. The castle may have been magical to begin with, but after millennia of hosting Sidhe, we'd imbued the very stones with a sentience that alerted us to the presence of our enemies.

"What was that?" Dena narrowed her eyes.

I sent power winging outward, and a string of Gaelic curses blasted from me. "Death is here," I said.

"Are you certain?" Dena asked.

"Aye. Quite. Round up Krin and Padhraic and a few others and meet me in the great room."

Dena hooked a hand under my arm. "Are you certain you're ready to confront her? She nearly killed the woman you love."

"Never readier," I growled.

"We can't end a god," Dena reminded me. "No matter how much you might want to."

"I plan to make it abundantly clear she will never lay a finger on Cait again. Or any of the other Reapers, either."

Dena cast a pointed look my way. "And that will buy you precisely nothing."

"I'll figure it out as I go," I told her and bolted from the room. I'd considered teleporting, but this was actually faster. Fury, white-hot and blinding, consumed me. I did need to get a handle on it, or I'd just come out swinging. And like as not, lose.

With the Sidhe's ancient battle cry ringing from me, I burst into the room and bounded to the spot where Death stood, surveying the Reapers like a determined bird of prey. In that moment, I understood she wasn't much different from the dark mages. She demanded absolute obedience in her service.

I made a grab for rationality and told her, “We are about to have a long overdue talk, you and I.”

“Think again, Sidhe,” she hissed. “I don’t have time for you.”

“Nay, you think again,” I retorted.

Dena, Krin, Padhraic, and half a dozen other Sidhe arrived. I saw power glistening from their upraised hands out of the corners of my eyes and recognized a binding spell.

“Got her,” Padhraic said. “She won’t be leaving until we release her.”

“You can’t detain me,” Death screeched, tossing her body from side to side as she strained against the Sidhe spell. “I’m a goddess.”

“Then I suggest you start to act like one.” I didn’t raise my voice. In the face of Death’s out-of-control fury, it was easier to locate a cold, clear place within myself. In no universe ever did I want to be anything like the imperious bitch hissing spittle and curses.

No reason to drag this out. She wasn’t worth draining Sidhe magic down to dregs. I took a few steps closer. “You nearly ended Cait, but you were sloppy. Thanks to you, we figured out how to undo the binding segment of your implant system. Any Reaper who asks will be freed.”

“You wouldn’t dare.” Fingers curled into claws, she ripped at the partially visible shielding. It bent but didn’t give.

“Too late,” Dena called from where she stood. “We already have. If you wish to direct your anger appropriately, I am the chief healer here. What you did to Cait Carrick sickened me. Clean kills are one thing, but you left her to suffer the torments of the damned."

"Ye doonae ken." Death had switched to a very old form of Gaelic. "She is mine to do with as I please. Mine! Do ye ken that? Every Reaper is. I made them, and I can unmake them as I deem fitting."

A long, keening howl of outrage filled the room. If Death had any chance of reestablishing order, she'd just blown it sky high.

"I warned you," I said, deciding to stick with English. "You could have rebuilt your ranks on a more democratic platform. If you'd been the one to unlock their concealed power, the Reapers would have lauded you."

The howls changed to boos. I even caught a few "nevers" and "not in this lifetimes."

"See?" I swung an arm to one side. "Too late. You've alienated your acolytes by treating them like they don't matter."

"They doonae."

"Validation stings, but thanks for being honest. It's especially refreshing after all the lies." Cait tossed her head back.

"Keep a decent tongue in your head."

"When did you know me to sugarcoat anything?" Cait retorted.

"Two more items," I said. "The first is stay away from Cait. She is my mate, or soon will be." I tacked the caveat on after hearing a startled gasp from Cait.

"Appears to be news to her," Death noted acidly.

Reapers had been wandering through carelessly

constructed neophyte portals ever since I'd entered the room. Clearly, they'd been practicing teleporting. The moment they saw Death, they either cringed or froze. Their reaction to their erstwhile boss made me angry—and sad.

I ignored Death's commentary. "You could still redeem yourself," I told the goddess.

She cast an incredulous look my way. "Save your breath, Sidhe. Redeem myself in whose estimation?"

"All of those who walk the right side of the magical street." I'd kicked the gates open, so I kept on talking. Nothing to lose. I was never going to make her favorite-person list at this point, nor did I want to.

"What will the other deities assume when they find out you tortured one of your Reapers? For that fact, what will they think when they find out you set up a mechanism to spy on them?"

She glared at me. The full force of the moving collage that passed for eyes was even more unnerving than usual.

"Shall we move on to the second item?" I suggested silkily. "It's how you might make amends."

"Doonae bother," she sputtered. "I haven't yet sunk so low I require advice from magical inferiors."

"Have you always been this unpleasant?" I growled, taken aback by her overt rudeness.

"Only to you," she shot back.

"Ha! Rude could be your middle name," Cait tossed in her face.

We weren't going to get anything else accomplished. I glanced at the other Sidhe. "Release her."

Death rolled her shoulders, standing straight. "Get

moving." She clapped her hands smartly. "Souls are accumulating out there."

"Already taken care of," Cait informed her tartly.

"How?" Death ground out the question.

"We figured things out on our own. Amazing, huh?" Cait pounded the end of her scythe into the floor, maybe for emphasis.

"We don't need you," Pavel growled. "We never did."

"It's taken us a while to figure that out," Stacia added.

The line of Death's jaw tightened. "Ye'll come to your senses and return to my side. I've taught you everything you know."

"It's long past time for you to step aside. They don't need you any longer," I told her. For the first time since Death had breached Scourie Castle's defenses, I felt sorry for her. Time had marched on. The world had changed, and she'd missed all of it.

"Pffft." Cait shook her head. "We haven't needed you for a long while. It's going to take time for that to sink in—on both sides. We'll still Reap souls. It's what we do. I figure you'll continue to Reap them as well, but just think of all the time you'll save not having to run that sham of a school."

"Speaking of which," Stacia spoke up. "Why'd you quit making Reapers?"

Rather than answering, Death vanished in a cloud of black-tinged magic. Part Reaper but mostly something else. My nostrils flared as I scented the air working to sort it out.

"Has she been hobnobbing with demon kind?" Dena asked.

"Is that what I smell?" Cait sputtered. "That sulfur-copper mix?"

"She's always smelled like that, but usually it's much fainter," Stacia said. "I figured it was because she spent so much time in Hell."

The bar of tension sitting across my upper back relaxed. Stacia's explanation made sense. "Did she really stop creating new Reapers?" I asked Stacia.

"Seems so," Cait answered. "Unless Death's been hiding new recruits from us, she hasn't fashioned more Reapers in at least two hundred years."

"Do you suppose the other gods found out about her magical beacons and forbade her from using that technique?" Krin glanced from Reaper to Reaper.

"No idea," Stacia said. "Information like that would have been way above our pay grade, but Hades and Arawn both told us they'd been expecting a Reaper uprising for a long time."

"Fascinating." A slow smile spread over Krin's austere features. "I feared confronting Death was ill-advised, but mayhap she doesn't command respect among her kinsfolk."

"I have a few more Reapers to fix," Dena said, "but then we need to sit in the same room, compare notes, and figure out what we're going to do first." Turning, she walked toward the door, collecting Reapers as she went.

"Do you still need help?" I called after her retreating back.

"I'll stand in," Krin said and ran after Dena.

Cait shook herself from head to toe. "Damn it. That woman makes me so angry."

"Understandable, given she nearly killed you." I wanted to draw Cait close, but maybe not in front of so many people.

Stacia looked from Cait to me. "And Death wonders why we avoid her. Dealing with her has always made me feel clumsy and useless."

"Aw, sweetie. You're neither." Cait gave her a hug.

Stacia disentangled herself. "We could use happy news after all that. Are congratulations in order?"

For a moment, Cait looked confused, and then color rose from her neck, leaving splotches of pink on both cheeks. "Might be premature," she mumbled.

Stacia furled her brows in my direction.

"I love Cait," I told her. "Hopefully, someday she'll join her life with mine."

Whistles and cheers broke out, along with a bevy of good wishes. When they died down, I added, "We have a lot to deal with first, but once we've dispatched the Vampires and the dark mages—"

"Yeah, and Humans Rule," Cait cut in, but she was smiling. And she hooked a hand under my arm. "This man"—she pointed at me with an index finger—"is a wild-eyed optimist. It's why I'm falling in love with him. If the goddess grants us grace, we'll make a life together."

Reapers closed from all sides offering warm wishes and a bevy of ribald suggestions. Soon all of us were laughing. It felt good after the tension Death had brought into the room, riding on her coattails.

Music cut through the many conversations. It might have been present for a while before I noticed it and scanned the room, seeking its source. Soft and melodic, the volume was growing.

Cait's eyes widened. "Cathbad? He can't be here, but it sure sounds like him."

"Why cannae I be here? Did ye assume I was fettered to the *Dreaming*?" Cathbad broke off singing long enough to ask and stepped through a wall. Decked out in leather with his broadsword and his axe, he looked the same as the last time he'd shown himself to us.

I walked toward him with Cait by my side. Once we were close, I bowed low. "Thank you, bard, for your music. It saved my love's life."

The Druid nodded solemnly. "'Tis precisely why I am here. I gifted both of you—and Padhraic—with my song, and felt a disturbance in its pitch and tone. I came as quickly as I could, but as ye know, time flows differently in the *Dreaming*."

Cait knelt, head bowed. When she regained her feet, she said, "Many thanks from me as well. I understand from the Sidhe, who were instrumental in my healing, that your song made a difference and ensured my survival."

Cathbad dropped a hand onto Cait's shoulder. I both felt and saw power flow into her. "There." He moved his hand. "I've strengthened the binding. If anyone else has the temerity to disturb it, I shall arrive more quickly next time."

Padhraic had glided close. He too inclined his head. "'Tis a rare pleasure to see you again. And so soon."

Cathbad smiled. Power jetted from an upraised hand, coating Padhraic from head to toe. "I did my best to sing away the wickedness whilst ye were in the Dreaming," the bard murmured.

"I heard your song. That you didn't give up on the Leanan meant everything to me. I have no idea why your music didn't touch the others."

"Betimes I would sing to neutralize the wickedness dripping from all of you. In some ways, 'twas self-serving. I dinnae wish it to spread."

Padhraic's dark eyes crinkled at their corners. "No matter what your reasons, your music was always appreciated."

"Why did no one think to alert us when the dark mages released the Leanan Sidhe?" I asked Cathbad.

The bard shrugged. "We had no idea ye dinnae know. Beyond that, 'twasn't our affair."

I winced. "Point taken. You're absolutely correct. No one's fault but our own for not paying closer attention."

"Do you bring news from the gods?" Cait asked.

I would have kept the small talk going a while longer, but maybe Cait's way was best. No beating around the bush meant we'd remain on task.

"I do," Cathbad replied. "'Tis the other reason I was a wee bit tardy reacting to the disturbance in my song."

I waited for more, anxious for information, but he'd tell us in his own way. Cait stood next to me, close enough her shoulder pressed into mine. I'd been beyond ecstatic when she'd told the Reapers she was falling in love with me and shared my hopes for a life together. Delighted. Thrilled. Humbly grateful. But even those didn't cover the gamut of my emotions. I made a vow before the goddess that Cait would never want for anything. I'd cherish her and respect her enough to stand aside while she made her own decisions.

Breathing space would be the hard part. As it was, I wanted to barricade her behind enchantments to keep her safe through the upcoming wars. Even if I could force the matter—and I wasn't at all certain my magic was up to the task—she'd hate me for it.

Her independence and spirit had attracted me in the first place. I'd be an idiot to try to make her over into someone different.

Cathbad raised his hands. Power crackled from his fingertips, and a surprised expression crossed his face. "Reapers. A handful of Sidhe and a roomful of Reapers." Lines spiraled out from the corners of his eyes as he smiled. "Ye've broken free. I sense the alteration in your power. These are exceptional tidings, indeed."

"If you'd been a few minutes earlier, you'd have run into Death," I told the bard.

"She's fortunate to be gone. I doonae take destruction of my music lightly."

Cathbad tipped his head back and began to sing. As before, the melody wrapped around me, encasing me in wonder. Though the song lacked words, I understood the Celts would help us with the dark mages by stripping them of the Celtic portion of their power.

I would have been content for his music to go on forever. Listening to Cathbad held a timeless quality that transcended everything but the joy of his song. If he ever sang of sorrow and loss, I wasn't sure I wanted to hear it. I felt certain it would shred my soul, staining me with anguish.

His voice died away, leaving a hollow silence. Unlike last time, the music didn't replay in my mind.

"Thank you," I told him. "Only dealing with the Norse portion of the dark mages' magic will be an enormous help."

"Doonae underestimate them," Cathbad said. "They will be furious, and anger fuels magic." He glanced about the room at Reapers who'd moved nearer and the few Sidhe who'd helped hold Death at bay. "The same advice goes for Reapers," he said. "Never sell yourselves short. Your power has its roots in the making of the world."

"What do you mean?" Cait asked him.

"Once upon a time, Death was the only Reaper. She maintained a balance point between the living and the dead. She's gone by many names since the dawn of everything, but 'tis been the same goddess wearing different guises."

He exhaled sharply. "None of us understood her rationale in creating Reapers to help her. Granted, there were more dead, but herding shades to the other side only requires a few seconds. Regardless, when she chipped away at her own power to create all of you"—he spread his arms wide—"she gave up absolute control. At first, we saw it as generous, but once we recognized how sharing power pained her, we understood it would only be a matter of time before her need to control every last aspect of your existence exploded in her face."

"Chipped away at her own power? What do you mean by that?" Cait asked.

"Magic isn't limitless. She expended some each time she turned a normal baby into a Reaper," Cathbad explained.

"Which would probably be why she stopped making new Reapers," I muttered.

"Aye, that and many of the gods grew worried. None of them were forever creating minions. In truth, none of them made new magic-wielders at all. While they might have turned a blind eye to a handful of Reapers, when the number drifted north of a hundred, it was a tough nut to swallow."

"Did someone talk with her?" Cait asked.

Cathbad nodded. "Several someones. She told everybody to butt out. Not their business."

"I can see her doing just that," Cait said.

"I shall take my leave." Cathbad drew power around himself where it glistened like a blue-and-violet banner. "Ye havena seen the last of Death. Take good care of my magic, all of you. Our paths will cross again."

A song flowed from his throat as he vanished from Scourie Castle.

"'Twas his music that kept me from completely falling into evil," Padhraic said. "He did his best to rescue all of us."

"So what does it mean, exactly, about the dark gods?" Stacia asked. "Will they lose half their magical ability?"

"Doesn't work that way," I told her. "Blended power is more versatile than magic from a single source. What made the dark mages strong was a composite of Celtic and Norse enchantments. They will lose the advantage of blended power, but they won't lose half their ability. Perhaps a quarter. These things are hard to quantify."

"They'll be furious," Padhraic said. "And they'll blame us."

"Is there someone we could appeal to about the Norse part of their power?" Pavel asked.

It was a good question, but one with a disappointing answer. "I don't believe so," I told him. "Odin isn't particularly approachable, and he has his own problems. Insurrection within his ranks spurred him to shut Asgard to anyone without Norse bloodlines a long while back."

"We haven't yet heard from Arawn and Hades," Stacia pointed out.

"By now Death's probably bent their ears with her tale of woe," Cait cautioned her.

"How do you know they haven't talked sense into her?" I asked.

Cait turned to me, green eyes sparking with anger. "She's moved beyond reason, edged into insanity. It happened a long while back, and I'm pissed at myself for not recognizing how far gone she was."

"Sounds like you saw a whole lot more of her than we did," Pavel said.

"Pffft. After the Vampire assignment that was the beginning of my downhill slide to Worst Reaper Ever, she practically lived on my doorstep," Cait replied.

Dena strode briskly into our midst. "Cathbad was here. I can still hear his song."

"He was, indeed." I nodded. "The Celts agreed to strip their power from the dark gods."

"Good." Dena set her lips in a thin line. "It should help a little. I seem to have run out of Reapers to minister to.

Everyone is gathered in the dining room. Shall we kick this project off the blocks?" Without waiting for an answer, she turned and trotted back the way she'd come.

I looped an arm around Cait's waist; we followed Dena out of the room. "Thanks for giving us a chance," I said low against her ear. "I wasn't trying to be presumptuous, but Death had to understand you weren't in this alone any longer."

"The old me would have turned into a porcupine," Cait admitted.

I chuckled. "Thanks for not tossing quills. And the new you?"

"Is grateful to be cared about. Whatever happens, Liam, thanks for not giving up on me. I'm not the easiest woman to get close to."

"I could say the same thing about myself. We'll get through this." Ferocity threaded beneath my words as a ruthless need to protect her almost flattened me.

"We have to," she agreed. "Because I don't care much for the alternatives."

CHAPTER NINETEEN, CAIT

The meeting had moved well into its second day. We'd split into Sidhe and Reaper groups when it became clear Reapers had serious organizational tasks to achieve before we'd be much good for anything else. Not that we hadn't accomplished a lot. We had. A brand new Reaper council had emerged with half a dozen of us at the helm. Part of our charter was electing new council members every year to give everyone a voice. All important decisions would be put to a vote, not just of the council but of all Reapers. For now, Stacia, Pavel, Lilly, Abby, Davin, and I comprised the council.

I'd been hesitant to take on the responsibility, but the other Reapers had been insistent. Throughout everything, Reapers had ebbed and flowed as some returned from dispatching souls and others were newly arrived. Several of us had healing ability. With the unlocking of our full magic, we no longer needed Dena to clip the ties binding us to Death.

I'm sure it was a big relief to Dena. She'd begun to look a bit frazzled around the edges from the flood of Reapers. I didn't even try to keep track of all of us, but the feel of unfettered Reaper magic surging through the room warmed me.

This was how it was meant to be.

How it always could have been had Death possessed a more generous nature. I finally understood why she'd hidden so much of our innate power, and it didn't have much to do with magic at all. The camaraderie and fellowship linking Reaper to Reaper would have threatened her sovereignty and control over us.

"We're ready to join the Sidhe." I projected my voice to be heard.

Stacia was our self-appointed scribe, and she consulted a list she'd compiled on a tablet. I suppressed a smile. The blend of ancient and modern still astonished me, although it shouldn't have since I'd embraced both worlds too.

She nudged me and spoke low. "We're missing three Reapers."

I frowned. "What do you mean missing?"

She tapped the display and highlighted their names. "They left before we closeted ourselves in here, presumably to catch up with Reaping. They should have returned long before now."

"Do you suppose they could have changed their minds about being part of us?"

"Unlikely." Stacia's voice had moved above a whisper.

"What's unlikely?" Pavel quirked a dark brow.

Heads swiveled our way throughout the generous room. Liam had ushered us into what was clearly a secondary dining area with benches, chairs, and tables, after it became clear we had work to do. We'd tried to be part of the war planning effort, but every question had led to a dozen more. Once we had our magic and structure sorted, we'd be far more useful allies.

Hoping someone might shed light on the missing Reapers, I asked, "Do any of you know"—I glanced at the highlighted names—"Gregor, Rolf, or Anya?"

"Aye, they worked in Australia and New Zealand," someone called.

If it had been only one of them, I'd have assumed their teleport efforts had gone awry. With three, they'd presumably have had magical overlap.

"Where are they?" someone else asked.

"That's the problem," Stacia said. "We're not sure."

"I could go look for them," Pavel offered.

"No!" I clapped a hand over my mouth. "Sorry. For a minute there, I sounded like Death. It's possible she sweetened the pot and offered inducements to make them change their minds." I took a breath and blew it out. "Another possibility is Death is holding them against their will."

"Or they might have ended up prisoners in the realm of the dead. If they let too many of those creepy shades use them as a gateway," Lilly said.

"Aye, well, I don't care for any of those explanations," Stacia muttered.

Liam's timing was almost too good to be accidental as he walked through the door at the far end of the room. "Almost done?" he asked. "We have a meal set out next door, and we're ready to launch a few strategies. We've slotted Reaper magic into them, but of course you'll have the final say as to whether our ideas will be a good fit for your skills."

"Go eat," I urged everyone. Chairs and benches scraped against the stone floor as Reapers got up and walked out of the room.

"I was about to find you," I told Liam after the room was mostly empty. "A meal would be welcome, but we seem to have a problem."

"What kind of problem?" He laced his fingers in with mine.

"Missing Reapers."

He angled his head; a corner of his mouth twisted downward. "How many?"

"Three."

"Could be worse," he said. "I've been expecting some kind of retaliatory action from Death."

"Doesn't have to be that. Not necessarily," I pointed out. "Their teleport spell could have gone off the rails. Or maybe Vampire minions trapped them in the netherworld."

"Eh, I vote for Death meddling. Come on." He tugged at my hand. "We'll hunt for them, but not on an empty stomach."

We walked across the hall and into the larger dining room where someone had piled food on platters sitting on a long table. "What if it's a trap?" I asked.

"Or a diversion," Liam mumbled.

"Kind of amounts to the same thing," I said and layered roasted meat and cheese between two slices of bread.

For a few moments, we choked food down in silence. I hadn't realized how hungry I was until I started eating. My last meal had been breakfast at Liam's two days before. What with the excitement of having so many Reapers together in one spot, and the almost heady glee of escaping Death's harsh oversight, food had been the last thing on my mind.

"Did you tell the Sidhe about the Vampire nest?" I asked between bites.

He nodded. "I did. Our thought was to tackle the dark gods first. We can always storm the seethe if we fail."

Liam strode to the front of the room with me next to him. He whistled shrilly, waiting until everyone had quit talking. "We have a problem to solve," he told the assemblage. "Consider it a testing ground for some of the ideas we've been floating."

"What kind of problem?" Krin asked.

"Three missing Reapers," I told him.

"How do we know they didn't change their minds?" Padhraic called from the center of the room.

"We don't," I spoke up.

"Regardless," Liam said. "One of our questions was how we could mix our magics to allow Sidhe to cross the liminal boundary into the actual realm of the dead. This would be a perfect opportunity to determine if it's possible."

I did a quick nose count. Between Reapers and Sidhe, perhaps three hundred were ranged through the room. "We only need a handful of us," I told Liam.

"Agreed," he said and turned his attention back to the

assemblage. “Four of us will go after the Reapers. Cait and I make two. Who else?”

“I’ll go,” Stacia said.

“And me.” Padhraic shot to his feet.

“While you’re gone,” Krin said, “we’ll home in on precisely which tactics we’ll use and get some hands-on experience with how our magics work together.”

“We’ll split into squadrons,” Dena added.

“Aye, and determine deployment of weaponry,” Padhraic suggested.

I remembered my wonderful Vampire killing blade tucked into my locker back at *Carrick Sky Sports*, but surely the Sidhe had an armory, a roomful of blades better than mine.

“If we’re not back in twenty-four hours, proceed without us,” Liam said. “We’ll catch up as we can.”

“If you’re not back in twenty-four hours, we’ll come looking for you.” Krin eyed Liam.

He shrugged. “You have more important problems. If the missing Reapers are a diversion, you can expect the dark mages to launch an all-out attack. If too many of us are sidelined dealing with trivia, they might succeed.”

“Point taken,” Dena said.

Liam motioned to Stacia, Padhraic, and me, and we walked briskly out of the dining area and into the arched hall. I expected him to outline a plan, but he looked at Stacia and me and asked, “Ideas?”

“If it’s a trap, maybe we should do a little sleuthing in the realm of the dead,” I suggested. “Reapers stand out like sore thumbs, and any shades we run into will know if they've been there."

"Is it a single location?" Padhraic asked.

"Yes and no," Stacia told him. "The realm of the dead has layers. The uppermost one is just beyond the gateways we build. That's where the dead are sorted and sent on their way. No one but the dead and their keepers travel beyond it."

"Every gateway leads to the same spot, more or less," I said. "It doesn't matter where we break through. The realm of the dead doesn't follow Earth's contours."

"Rather akin to the corridors just beyond Earth's boundaries," Liam said. "No time like now to determine if blending our two strains of Earth magic will mean Sidhe can transit the gateway."

"Ready?" Stacia tapped my arm.

"Ready to get this over with," I mumbled and opened my grave vision. The castle hallway faded, replaced by gray mist. No ghosts in Scourie Castle. It surprised me. I'd expected at least one or two holdouts from much earlier times.

Stacia raised an arm, power flowing from her as a shimmering gateway took shape. Padhraic stood next to her, and I felt as much as saw him weaving his magic in with hers. Liam did the same. I welcomed the touch of his magic. It enhanced my own, made it ever so much more multifaceted.

But would it be enough.

"Ready to give this a try?" I asked. At his nod, I glided toward the gateway and stepped through. At first, I was alone, but then Liam popped into view.

"Had to make a few adjustments," he said. "The gateway

still recognized I had no business here, but I'd borrowed enough of your Reaper Earth-linked power, it allowed me passage."

Stacia and Padhraic joined us. She aimed more magic at the gateway to hold it open. The half-light of my grave vision illuminated this side of the barrier as well, but Death had done a number on all of us. I'd never be comfortable in the realm of the dead. No matter what she'd said about our enhanced magic bailing us out, I'd always be afraid if I remained too long, I'd be screwed. I still remembered how hard it had been to find my way back when Vampire shades in Malin had tricked me.

Ghosts came into view, floating and gliding. "Have you seen Reapers?" I called.

"Nay. Only you," a man with long, tangled hair answered.

Stacia and I repeated the question to every passing shade and received the same response. After maybe half an hour had passed, she said, "We need to leave."

A tall, thin shade with hair the color of midnight hurried toward us. Garbed in black robes, he glowed in a very unghostlike manner. And then I understood this was no ghost.

"Arawn!" Stacia called.

He stopped next to us and growled, "How is it Sidhe crossed beyond the gates?"

"Forgive us." Liam bowed his head. "Reapers are missing. We were only trying to help."

"We will talk, but outside." Arawn made shooing motions with both hands. He had a high forehead and a hawk's beak of a nose. Deep-set dark eyes glared at us.

It was a relief to pass through the gateway. Stacia held it until all of us were through. I wasn't certain whether to hang onto my Reaper magic, so I kept it flowing.

Arawn glowered at the four of us, and I girded myself for a lecture on how badly we'd treated Death. "The Reapers are with Death at the home she maintains in the frozen northlands," Arawn told us.

"Not by their own design." Stacia stood tall.

"Nay, but she will not harm them." Arawn's tone softened.

"You can't know that. We have to go after them," Stacia insisted.

Arawn thumped her chest with his index finger. "Hades and I will assist with the dark mage problem, but we will not intervene between Death and her minions. 'Twas a mistake to fashion so many of you. We told her. She didn't listen. Now she's sinking beneath a mess of her own making. She must find her own way out."

I felt torn. Arawn had just said he'd help with the dark mages, but could I sit back and do nothing while Death did goddess only knew what to Gregor, Rolf, and Anya? After the way she'd nearly killed me, I had zero faith in her ability to restrain her lethal side. If any of the Reapers mouthed off to her, she was as likely to kill them as she was to vanish in a cloud of furious magic.

After she'd shackled the Reapers so they couldn't run away.

"We are deeply appreciative of your assistance," Liam was saying. I dragged my attention out of the hollow pit my thoughts had become.

"It comes with a price." Arawn's gaze moved from one to the other of us.

"Which is?" Padhraic asked.

"Leave Death to her own devices. Mayhap those three Reapers will get through to her when the rest of us could not."

I narrowed my eyes to slits. "So the agreement is we do nothing to rescue Gregor, Rolf, and Anya?"

Arawn nodded. "Chose quickly. The dark ones are on the move. I feel it."

"Do you have a plan for them?" Liam asked.

"We do," Arawn said. "Lacking Celtic magic, they will be susceptible to our power."

"Where do the Sidhe come in?" Padhraic furled his brows.

"And Reapers?" I tossed out.

"What we're counting on," Arawn said, "is if we can knock out one or two, the others will leave."

"Mmph. Same thing we'd thought," Liam told him. "But we could be wrong. Besides, we can't kill them, so it's a matter of making them so miserable they choose to go away."

"We can swathe them in death-imbued cloth," Arawn said. "Shrouding that will hold them for centuries because it clouds the mind, condemns them to wander in Purgatory."

"How?" I asked. "It's not like they're going to sit still while you drape them in winding cloths."

"Which is where we would require a mix of Sidhe and Reaper magic. We won't hit it right the first few times, but there's got to be some cocktail that will render them insensible long enough to get the job done."

"We'd have to get it right," Stacia said. "If we muff it, and they escape, we'll never get close enough for a second try."

"Then I suggest you find something to practice on." Arawn pulled the hood of his robe over his black hair. "What about it? Do we have a deal?"

"Why are you protecting Death?" I asked him. I came within an angstrom of netting him in a truth spell, but he was a god, and I was just a Reaper. It would have been impudent as fuck to assume he'd lie to me.

He turned the full force of his eyes on me. Thank Christ they didn't change like Death's. "She dinnae use to be this way," he said in Gaelic. "Once, she was reasonable. I haven't abandoned hope she can find her way back."

"May I ask a boon?" I lowered my head, expecting him to yell at me, but he didn't. "Might someone keep an eye on the Reapers?" I went on. "To make certain they're all right."

"We will send messengers. They will be discreet."

Stacia nodded my way. She didn't like the terms, but neither would she fight them.

"We accept," I said.

"Indeed we do," Liam seconded. "And if ever the Sidhe can do anything in return, you've only to ask."

"Fight bravely. The dark ones are a scourge. If we canna stem their evil, I fear for our future."

I kept my eyes on the ground, the misty world of Reaper magic swirling around me. If one of the gods of the dead was worried enough to say what Arawn just had, it was grim tidings indeed.

"Meet in the second corridor spanning Earth in two turns of the glass," Arawn said. "Hades and I will be there."

"Just us?" I asked.

Arawn laughed, and the sound set off a cascade of ice spilling down my spine. "Nay, child. Bring an army and pray it is enough."

Power buffeted me. When it cleared, we were back in the corridor inside Scourie Castle. I hadn't sheathed my Reaper magic, but Arawn had apparently done it for me. Wrested it from me without me even realizing it.

I felt guilty about abandoning three Reapers, but Arawn had been convinced Death wouldn't harm them. Maybe it was like with children. Once you lost one or two, you valued the others more. Somehow, I couldn't quite view Death capitulating so easily to anything that smacked of emotion, but perhaps Arawn knew her far better than me.

"We have to trust him," Padhraic said.

"Not much choice," I mumbled.

Padhraic shrugged. "I parleyed with the dark mages for a long while. It touched me in ways I still struggle with. By comparison, Arawn is solid."

"Why would you suggest trusting him might be a gamble?" Liam asked.

"I didn't. Not exactly. Him having joined forces with the dark ones is quite the longshot. He meant it when he said that bit about fearing for the future."

"You used a truth net?" I stared at him.

"Maybe a wee one. He didn't notice."

"He said to bring an army," Liam said. "Let's alert everyone and get moving."

Something occurred to me, and I said, "Wait."

"Aye?" Liam nodded encouragingly.

"How do we know the dark mages will be in this corridor?"

"Presumably, Arawn has a plan," Liam said. Breath rattled from him. "I don't want to get lost in conspiracy theories. Maybe Arawn wants all of us out of commission so he can offer the dark gods free rein to Earth, but I don't believe that's true. I stopped shy of a truth spell, but everything he said sounded sincere."

"He even has a soft spot in his heart for Death, though I'll be damned if I know why," Stacia muttered.

"Anyone who could give her a fiftieth chance can't be all bad," I said and mostly meant it. "We have to decide if this is a go or no go. Let's put it to a vote with everyone."

"Already happening." Liam nodded. "I raised Krin via telepathy as soon as we got back." He tilted his head as if listening and said, "The vote was a clean sweep in favor of moving forward. Next stop is the armory. Let's hope the dark mages are as wary as we are and only one of them shows up."

I ran lightly along the stone walkway, following Liam to the castle armory. Privately, I didn't think we'd be lucky enough to face only one of the dark gods. They traveled in packs. But I kept my fears to myself. They had no place here.

An hour later, I was decked out in mail that looked like something out of *Lord of the Rings*. A short sword hung from a waist belt, its handle well wrapped with wood to dull the pain metal caused me. My shirt and jacket offered protection from the hauberk's interlocking rings.

We'd organized into battalions of fifty. Each contained more Reapers than Sidhe. Liam headed up ours. He drew me aside. "Try not to take chances." He grinned crookedly. "Please."

"I'll do what I have to," I told him.

"I know." He kissed my forehead. "I love you, Cait. Let's get through this."

My heart swelled with longing for him, for a life that was something other than endless warfare. "We will." I tried for reassuring and fell short. "We have to. There'll be no peace until it's done."

"Done is a long way off," he told me solemnly. "Today's battle is a start. If we prevail, it will make tomorrow's and the next day's easier."

"Someday, there won't be any more," I said fiercely. I refused to contemplate a future peppered by endless conflict.

He dropped a hand onto my mail-clad shoulder. "I hope you're right, Cait. Truly, I do."

CHAPTER TWENTY, LIAM

The second corridor came into view, shaping itself around us. A barren place, it lacked much of anything to hide behind, but that might be why Arawn and Hades had chosen it. Cracked black dirt spread as far as I could see, unbroken by trees or bushes. The sky was dirty white, and a pallid orange sun hung partway to the far horizon.

As promised, the two gods were waiting for us when we arrived. Arawn had traded his robes for black-tinted armor. Apparently, metal didn't bother him. Good to know. A saber swung from one hand, and a broadsword was strapped across his back.

I'd never come face to face with Hades before. He reminded me of Odin. Tall and broad-shouldered, he had silver hair gathered into a queue low on his neck. Battle-scarred leather covered him along with a mail hauberk and vambraces. A battle axe was slung across his back. I shook his hand, feeling the weight of his sky-blue eyes.

"Nice to get out of Hell for a bit," he growled in a deep voice.

"Aye, we should leave more often, and under better circumstances," Arawn agreed. I remembered Abby had intimated they were lovers. What an unlikely couple, and then I barricaded my thoughts behind staunch wards.

Sidhe and Reapers continued to emerge until all of us were ranged in our six battalions. Every Reaper carried a scythe. Made sense since their magic had been fully restored.

"Thank you for heeding my advice," Arawn said.

"Aye, we might have enough combined magic to finish this." Hades sent an approving glance skittering over the assemblage.

Finishing anything seemed overly ambitious. I wanted to ask what their plans were for luring the dark gods but didn't. In a tiny, shuttered corner of my mind, I still wondered about traps and diversions and other nefarious schemes. I'd had a conversation with Krin in deeply shielded telepathy. Both of us had decided we had to trust someone, and if we couldn't trust the gods of the dead, we may as well do what Hollis had wanted and move the Sidhe off-world.

Arawn was part of the Celtic pantheon, Hades part of the Greek one. By contrast, Death had never declared allegiance to any of them. It made her a wild card with no loyalty to anyone beyond herself.

A deep woof brought my head snapping around in time to see Cerebrus, Hades' three-headed dog, running our way.

Short black hair covered his body, and he stood perhaps a meter tall. Muscular shoulders and a stocky build supported his heads.

"Damn it. I told him to stay behind," Hades muttered.

"Like he ever listens to you," Arawn retorted.

Cait sank to her knees, cooing over the dog. He clearly appreciated the attention and nuzzled all three heads into her hands, licking furiously.

I smelled rot before I saw the dark mages. "Cait. On your feet. They're coming."

She sprang to my side, sickle at the ready. "Yeah. It would be a they, wouldn't it."

"Fight what's in front of you."

"Funny. Death always said the same thing."

"She wasn't all bad," I murmured. After everything that had happened, my words surprised me. Perhaps in the face of a real adversary, Death's shenanigans paled by comparison.

Cait trained her green gaze on me. "I have to believe that. If she hurts those Reapers in a fit of pique, I'll never forgive myself."

"Cait. I love you, but you have to focus. You can't afford to be diverted by guilt or worry or anything else. We have a shitstorm to get through first."

"Got it." Her words were terse. "I needed a boot in the butt."

"Anytime, sweetheart."

My prediction about a shitstorm was prophetic. D'Chel leapt through a jagged gash in the thin air of this place, followed by Perrikus and Adva. I waited, but the other three didn't follow. Slototh had never been much of a threat, but I was glad not to have to deal with Majestron Zelia or Tokkhots with his poison bite and blood. Maybe they were hovering just out of sight, waiting to see how things went.

Until proven otherwise, I'd assume the other three gods were somewhere near.

Krin roared orders. Two battalions took on each dark god. We had them outnumbered so badly, it should be a rout.

Should being the operative term.

The sounds of screeches and metal rose around us as Sidhe and Reapers engaged with the dark mages. Winged horrors had tracked after them, a string of malevolent atrocities. And they were still coming. More than a meter long with a wingspan double that, they were part bat, part flying dinosaur. Long snouts contained rows of wicked-looking teeth. At first, I thought they had to be illusion, until one spat a stream of poison.

It ate right through a Reaper's jacket, leaving it a smoking ruin. He had the good sense to shrug out of it before the venom ate completely through the fabric and started burning his flesh. "Ward yourselves," I shouted using magic to amplify my words.

Damn it. None of the Reapers knew the first thing about fighting. Why would they? Except for Cait and her crash course battling Vamps, none of them had ever had to defend themselves.

Cerebrus was apparently immune to the poison. He leapt high into the air, snapped a bat-thing into one of his three mouths, twisted, and snared another one. For something as large and ungainly as he was, he must have had springs in his feet, or an endless supply of magic. He dropped the two unnatural creatures after breaking their necks and went back for two more.

I sent jets of destructive power winging skyward, taking out swath after swath of the fuckers. They died too easily, so they had to be a diversion.

Aye, a deadly diversion that could kill the unwary.

We'd just barely surrounded Adva when he slapped up a gateway and vanished through it. Big surprise. He was the god of portals, and he'd lead us on a merry chase.

"What now?" Cait shouted, staring at the still-glowing hole in the air, scythe clutched in an upraised hand.

Waiting for him to show himself was a ridiculous waste of manpower—and time. But jumping through after him was folly and exactly what he wanted. Adva was famous for losing his enemies in a maze that rivaled the Minotaur's labyrinth.

Cait twisted to face me. "He's getting away."

"It's what he wants you to think."

"I don't care. I'm going after him. Don't worry. The mirror with blue edges leads out."

"Cait!" I screamed her name. Before I could tell her announcing Adva's secret to the world had been foolhardy, she was gone. It would take very little for the god of portals to switch things up. Blue only worked if no one knew about it.

Above me, the gateway was closing. I had no choice. I couldn't let her face Adva alone, so I jumped through, but I was almost too late. The gateway scissored around me, trapping my legs. I sent gout after gout of power at the damned thing before I found a combination that forced it to release me.

Fire and air.

I filed it away in case I had to defeat another of Adva's castings. Clearly, he hadn't wanted me to charge after Cait. Too bad. I was here now.

I fell through a mirror into a hall lined with them. It extended as far as I could see in every direction, but some of it was reflection from the multiple surfaces. Where was Cait? I couldn't see her.

I called her name, but my voice echoed back at me. I've always had a methodical nature, particularly where magic is concerned. It was how I'd freed my legs from the scissoring effect of the gateway. The glass I'd fallen through was obviously the way out. It's edges were clear, not blue, and I took note of its relative shape and size.

I set a magical marker at my entry point. Once it glowed a soft blue, I started in one direction, determined to follow the passage to its endpoint. If I didn't find Cait, I'd traverse every side channel until I did.

I took care to count my steps, making notations on my palm as I went. I lacked a pen, but magic worked just as well.

Surely, Cait wouldn't have gone through one of the mirrors. She was smarter than that.

I reached one end of the cavernous chamber and began to backtrack. Whenever I located a side corridor, I checked it thoroughly and set another marker. I used red for these to distinguish them from the first ones I'd established. I reached my starting point and headed in the opposite direction. Partway down the main corridor, Cait bounded out of a side hall. Her sickle glowed silver in the muted light of this place.

Relief was a visceral thing, pounding me in the guts. I closed my arms around her. "Didn't you hear me calling you?"

She clung to me and shook her head. "It's...odd down here. My vision comes and goes. I tried my Reaper vision, but light blasted me from every side. And shades clawed at me. Fuck. How could there be thousands of dead in this place?"

"There aren't." I traded off holding her close to gripping one of her hands, and we trotted along the main mirror-lined passage. "Have you seen Adva?"

"Yeah. He was here right at first. He ran off but looked back to make sure I was following him. I knew better than to play that game. So after a couple of attempts, he vanished."

"He's still in here. I feel him."

"I'm sorry," Cait said. "What I did was ridiculous and impulsive, and now we're trapped in here when we should be outside helping everyone."

"We'll get out."

"I've examined every single mirror. None of them have blue edges."

Telling her she'd blown that clue wouldn't make her feel any better, so I just led us toward where my first beacon glowed blue. It wasn't as pure as it had been when I'd set it. Yellow streaks ran through it, but it was easily distinguishable from my line of red markers.

"Here," I said. "This was the way in, so it has to be the way out."

Movement flashed in my peripheral vision. I turned, prepared to face Adva. Sure enough, he strolled toward us. Red-gold curls framed his green-gold eyes and boyish features. He still favored his uptown lawyer look with navy slacks and a cream-colored button-down shirt.

"Nice of you to drop by," he purred. "I so rarely get visitors."

"Skip the crap," I told him. "We were just leaving."

"Really? Do you actually think I would have left your beacon where you placed it? I'm not that stupid. Besides. You're who told the Celts to withdraw their magic. They offered us that gift thousands of years ago. You had no right."

"It's kind of a two-way street," I shot back. "You had no right to free the Leanan. Or to teach magic to humans. Or to dabble in Vampire affairs."

He shrugged. "Don't quibble, Sidhe. Two wrongs don't make a right and all that. Hey. Maybe two rights make a wrong." He laughed like a mad thing.

"Let me guess," I narrowed my eyes as I sought to divert him and buy us a bit of time. "Odin kicked you and the others out of Asgard. That was when you decided to free the Leanan and stir up shit."

"You'll never know. Chase me. If I'm in a charitable mood, I may lead you out of the maze." Turning on his heel, Adva took off at a slow jog, but he didn't look back over his shoulder.

Cait fisted a hand and punched the air. "Damn him and his arrogance."

I leaned toward the mirror nearest my marker, taking a closer look. Adva was right, it wasn't the same mirror. This one was shorter, squatter, and it didn't have as much distortion. But the way out had to be close. I consulted the figures I'd inscribed on my hand and backtracked to the first red marker, keeping Cait next to me.

I had to get this right. The magic I'd imbued in my beacons was winding down. Forcing what I hoped was the same stride I'd used earlier, I counted steps and ended up two mirrors up from where my blue light sputtered. This mirror looked right. Rather than clear edges, they'd shaded to blue, but I'd take my chances. Maybe they'd always been blue, and my first take had been powered by Adva's illusions.

I wrapped an arm around Cait, holding tight. "This one," I told her.

Where she pressed against me, her body was like a tightly wound spring, but she didn't question my choice. Neither did I. Wrapping us in a protective cocoon of air, I jumped through.

The sound of Adva's outraged yowls behind us told me I'd guessed right. Not that we couldn't have tried again. And again, but this was better. The second corridor swam into view around us.

A startled intake of breath from Cait was followed by. "Aw shit. Look at that."

Perrikus and D'Chel were nowhere to be seen, but a behemoth the size of a skyscraper was mowing through Sidhe and Reapers. Shrieks, cries, and the acrid stench of expended magic filled the air. Three spinning eyes the size of platters topped a sinuous neck. Metal scales covered the creature from stem to stern, lending it the appearance of an armored tank with short legs and a long tail. It opened its mouth and bellowed, displaying triple rows of fangs.

Two sets of arms jetted out from its body at right angles. They functioned like blades, slicing through everything in their path. I'd heard of monsters like the one confronting us, even seen a few, but nothing to rival this one.

Arawn and Hades were circling around behind the thing, while Cerebrus pranced in front, probably to divert it. Whenever the bastard got close to the dog, it disappeared. Good. I liked Cerebrus, and clearly he knew what he was doing.

So far, the monstrosity hadn't noticed us. Good. I'd take any advantage I could. *"Open your magic to me,"* I spoke into Cait's mind and erected an invisibility casting around where we stood. I'd have to dismantle it at the last minute, but first I had to create a blend of air to drill through the thing's scales and fire to explode its heart.

Cait figured out quick enough what I was doing and added her own touches. It didn't take long before I was ready. *"Once I drop the ward, it will know we're here."*

"Do it."

I wanted to tell her how much I loved her, how much her faith in me meant, but it would keep. In one fell swoop, I dismantled the ward and sent the magical brew I'd concocted straight at the monster's chest. Had I used enough air? I added more at the last minute, and the plates over the thing's heart disintegrated.

I wanted to cheer, but I kept power flowing. Adding Cait's magic to my own was the key to this because the blended product was so much stronger than anything I could have conjured up. The behemoth bellowed in pain. Its stubby legs folded. I'd forgotten about Hades and Arawn, but a shiny black lattice crashed down on the creature, effectively trapping it.

It bawled and hollered and writhed.

"We did it," Cait screeched. "Us and Hades and Arawn."

The gods rushed forward, winding length upon length of more of the black netting around the struggling abomination. The air thickened with the scents of Sidhe and Reaper magic as the fallen regained their feet. Clearly, the bastard had only immobilized them. A burst of powerful magic battered the behemoth. Both Hades and Arawn stood over it, chanting like madmen as jets of black lightning crackled from their hands. Cerebrus pranced from side to side, barking from all three mouths.

I hurried toward them with Cait by my side, intent on helping. Before we got there, the monster morphed into Perrikus and D'Chel, firmly snared in winding cloths.

It took a moment before it sank in that the beast had been illusion powered by the two dark gods mixing their magic. D'Chel had provided the shapeshifting, but the addition of Perrikus' power had raised it to the nth degree.

"Ha! Gotcha!" Hades crowed.

"Nice work," Arawn called our way. "An inspired bit of enchantment considering you came up with it on your own."

I swallowed a snort and a few hot words. Victory was hard to argue with, and the gods would never view Sidhe as other than magical inferiors. I could live with that.

"Do you think capturing two of them will be enough?" Cait asked. Her scythe had taken on a golden hue.

"For now, it is." I hugged her. The others would be out for our blood, but we didn't have to address that problem today.

Krin and Dena ran toward us sporting broad grins. "What happened to the two of you?" Krin asked. "You were gone for a while, but you returned at just the right time."

"It's a long story," I told him. "One best saved for a winter evening sipping port around a fire."

He slapped me across the back. "I'll hold you to it."

"I'd expect nothing less of you."

Cait had bent and buried her free hand in Cerebrus' short fur. The dog clearly adored her. When she looked up, she asked Arawn, "Any word about Death and the Reapers?"

He removed his helm and tucked it under one arm. "Aye. Today is one for unexpected outcomes. She released the Reapers. They're waiting for you back at Scourie Castle."

Stacia whooped. Cheers rose from many Reaper throats.

"Thank you," Cait said solemnly. "But why was it unexpected?"

"We thought she'd want to keep a few Reapers close by." Hades shrugged, and his hauberk rattled. "Guess we were wrong."

"Shall we get these two miscreants out of here?" Arawn kicked D'Chel in the side.

"Aye, we have a nice, cozy cell in Hell staked out for you," Hades said and bent to punch Perrikus in the chest.

"Why aren't they fighting back?" I asked.

"The mesh contains a spell," Hades explained. "Remember? We described it. These two will wander through dreams and mists for the next thousand years. Mayhap by then they'll have gotten past the worst of their evil."

Cerebrus woofed.

"You can come visit anytime," Cait told the dog. He woofed a few more times as if he'd understood, which he probably had.

Dark-tinged magic smelling of the sea burbled around the two gods. When it cleared, they were gone, along with Perrikus and D'Chel.

"Time to go," Krin told everyone.

"See you back at Scourie Castle," Dena told the Reapers and Sidhe.

"We'll be there in a day or two," I told Dena and turned to Cait. "Where would you like to go. We've earned a few hours of rest."

She smiled at me. "Is my houseboat a possibility?"

"You bet," I told her and summoned a journey spell to take us there. What I'd said earlier about today being only the first of many battles was true. But we'd fought well. A few more victories, and maybe, just maybe she could get back to running *Carrick Sky Sports.*

"About my flying lessons," I said once my teleport casting was well underway.

"What about them?" She smiled, and my soul cracked wide open with loving her.

"Maybe before we go back, we could work in one more."

Cait threw her arms around me. "I'm sure that could be arranged."

I hugged her back and waited until the walls of her living

room glowed into being around us. A hasty scan with still more magic assured me no one had been here since we'd left. "You're home," I murmured.

A muted clunk from behind us told me the scythe had joined my journey spell. I'd come to recognize its unique magical signature.

"Home's not a place anymore. It's wherever we are," Cait said.

I liked the sound of that. A lot. We were still tangled in each other's arms, and I lowered my mouth to hers. I had my priorities, and loving her sat at the tiptop of my list.

You've reached the end of *Rebel Reaper*. *Untamed Reaper* will be along in a month or so. Two of the dark mages are out of the way, but four remain. The Vampires haven't gone anywhere, and Humans Rule is still raising hell. Read on for a teaser from *Untamed Reaper*, possibly the last book in this series, but maybe not. You never know about these things.

BOOK DESCRIPTION: UNTAMED REAPER

I did it! I'm free. Well, sort of. Freedom isn't as cut and dried as the word implies. In this case, I'm at the top of Death's Worst Reaper Ever list. What it signifies remains to be seen.

I broke free from Death because there wasn't any other way out of Reaping Vampires. She refused to let me off the hook or consider other arrangements. I'd have been content leaving it at that, but word about my choice got out. Other Reapers clamored for independence too.

Death's fury expanded another notch with every defection until nowhere is far enough away for me to run to. If I was only fighting her, it might be manageable. Toss in Vampires who hate my guts, a phalanx of dark gods who want my hide, and a bunch of bigoted mortals who've decided magic is holding them back.

Pah. They're their own worst enemy, but they're the least of my problems.

It's been a rocky journey. Along the way I've uncovered allies and even a man who loves me. Will we be enough to slam the gates and send darkness packing?

We have to be.

No prisoners.

No choices.

UNTAMED REAPER, CHAPTER ONE, CAIT

The Cessna 172 dipped and banked to counteract a stiff wind. I sat in the right seat keeping a close eye on Liam. He'd asked for flight lessons, and he had real aptitude, but only because he cheated.

"Uh-uh." I resisted shaking a finger at him.

He turned his arresting hazel gaze my way and asked, "Uh-uh, what?" as if he was the soul of innocence. White-blonde hair streamed down his back, secured by a length of leather at the nape of his neck.

I smothered a snort. "You're using magic to keep the plane straight and level. An infusion of air beneath the right wing, to put a finer point on it."

His lips parted in a "so sue me" smile. Damn, it was hard to be angry with him when he looked like that. "Does it truly matter how I master this?" He furled his blond brows and cast a sidelong glance my way.

I lacked a ready reply, so I said, "Turn sixty degrees left and take us up another thousand feet."

The little plane responded so readily to him, it almost made me jealous. I have magic of my own, but it had never occurred to me to employ it while I was learning to fly. Now, sure, but not a hundred years ago.

I fell in love with the concept of flight not long after the Wright brothers' historic trip above Kitty Hawk, and I've been hanging around one airstrip or another ever since.

Liam trimmed up the plane and asked, "What's next?"

"Stall it," It said.

He frowned. "You have to say more than that."

"Tip the nose up until the plane starts to shudder, then return to straight and level flight."

"Like this?" He tugged the yoke toward him, and the nose floated upward. Soon the stall horn blared a warning. "Handy," he muttered and tapped the yoke.

"Indeed. The plane lets you know before you fall out of the sky."

"Would that really happen?"

"What do you think?" I countered.

He scrunched his forehead. "Seems like at some point the wings would work as airfoils again."

"You guessed right."

He made a rather male sound that reminded me of a grunt. "Why do you suppose it was a guess?"

Rather than answering, I grinned and asked, "Ready for your first landing?" At his nod, I outlined the mechanics of flying a pattern. "Once you get better," I said, "you'll be able to set a flight path and come in straight, but it's simpler to judge speed and height when you fly downwind, crosswind, and final legs."

I stopped talking and left it to him to figure things out. We were a little lower than I'd have liked on our final approach, but he figured things out and added a cushion of air to fix things.

"You did really well." Enthusiasm lined my words.

"Coming from you, I bet that's high praise." He taxied the plane off the runway and headed for the hangar.

"I thought about what you said," I murmured as we buttoned up the aircraft. It needed fuel before its next flight, but I could take care of that later. Who knew when I'd have this plane in the air again. For that fact, who knew when I'd get back to Seattle and *Carrick Sky Sports*.

"Which thing?" Liam stepped close and wrapped his arms around me.

"You addle my brain when you're that close." I dipped from beneath his embrace. "I've been thinking about employing magic to help you control the plane. There's nothing wrong with it, except it kind of feels like cheating."

"How so?"

I clasped my hands together. "What if something really went wrong?"

"If I couldn't fix it, I'd teleport out of there."

"How hard would you try to fix it?" I pressed.

He nodded, his smile fading. "Point taken," he rumbled in his deep, rich voice.

"Don't get me wrong," I went on. "Not much that magic can't repair, at least temporarily. Air provides float, and water will cool an overheated engine. What it won't do is tell you precisely what's wrong. If you don't know—because you never bothered to learn the mechanics of flight and how each part of the airplane keeps it airborne—the magic you apply will be a Band-Aid. It might get you on the ground, but then you won't have the first idea how to fix your bird."

He curled a hand around my forearm. His touch felt amazing. That's the thing about brand-new lovers, everything about them is intoxicating. I could look at him forever, breathe in his sandalwood and damp greenery scent, listen to the music of his voice.

And hunger for more.

"How about if I do both?" he suggested. "Learn the traditional way but keep the door open to filling in with magic."

"Perfect. It's exactly what I do." I angled my head and regarded him. "Do you want to get licensed?"

"Is it like getting a license to drive a car?"

"More or less," I replied. "There's a written test and an in-the-air test and a few tasks in between like a flight physical and getting a student pilot certificate."

"How long would it take?"

"Minimum is forty hours," I told him. "At least twenty with an instructor and ten solo hours."

"Looks like I have my first hour. Do I get credit for when we flew to Canada?"

"It might be arranged. As I recall, I did a bit of teaching on that flight too."

His forehead crinkled in what I'd come to recognize as his thoughtful expression. "Sure. I'll give it my best shot, but it might not happen for a while."

This time it was me who tossed my arms around him. He laughed and stroked hair back from my face. "Most women want gemstones and flowers."

"Airplanes, all the way for me," I murmured from where my face was buried in the crook of his neck.

"I'll keep in in mind."

Almost as if it had heard me and was jealous, my scythe clattered to the ground next to me. I picked it up and propped it over my shoulder. Up until recently, I hadn't seen the Reaper tool for months. Something about me claiming the full spectrum of my power had encouraged the silver-gray implement to not only become visible, but to follow me around.

"I noticed it behind the rear bank of seats," Liam murmured.

I had too, even though I hadn't carried it aboard.

We strolled out of the hangar, arm in arm; I locked it behind us. "Have you heard from anyone?"

He shook his head. "It worries me a little. This is our second day here, and I have checked my email a couple of times. Unless there's anything else pressing you want to attend to, we should head back to Scotland."

I'd been surprised we hadn't seen Death, but I kept my thoughts buried. Saying her name out loud might encourage her to show up.

"Taking the plane up wasn't urgent. It was an indulgence," I murmured.

"Maybe not."

Something about his tone caught my attention. "You've been expecting Vamps to show up, haven't you?"

He nodded. “It’s a reasonable expectation since they’ve swarmed your office every other time we’ve been here. Humans Rule knows about you too.”

I winced. After a plane got into trouble, I’d engaged in a very public display of magic to ensure no one got hurt. A few people thanked me, well more than a few, but shortly afterward delegates from HR—a bunch of bigots who badmouth magic by day and practice it by night—showed up in my office accompanied by Vamps and one of the dark gods.

Probably hadn’t helped I’d outed myself, announcing I was a Reaper to whoever might be on the field that day. “Surely someone has figured out we’re here,” I muttered.

“My assessment as well,” Liam said. “Not sure what it means they’ve left us be.”

I sent a jolt of magic to open the door of the Quonset hut I use for an office, intent on grabbing my bag so we could leave. “Do you want to teleport from inside?” I kept my voice low.

“Better than vanishing in plain sight,” he growled.

The sound of footsteps slapping against asphalt sent me spinning to see who was running straight toward us.

Kiko Tanaka, one of my closest friends, ran as if demons dogged her heels. Slight, with mounds of dark, straight hair, she’s a pharmacist who loves to fly. I met her years ago at a mixer for pilots and the various businesses peppering the airstrip. Usually, she wore jeans and sweaters, but today she hadn’t taken the time to change out of her scrubs from the pharmacy.

The scythe winked out of sight.

"Thank God you're here," she panted and skidded to a stop in front of Liam and me. "I've tried and tried to call you. Must've left you twenty messages."

I took one look at her and grabbed an arm, dragging her inside the Quonset hut. Liam followed us inside and shut the door. I felt the bite of his magic as he erected a hasty ward and sound screen around us.

"Sorry," I said. "First I was away, and recently I haven't been checking my phone. I closed my business for two weeks, so It didn't seem as important."

The harsh rasp of her breathing pounded against me. I've known Kiko for years, and she's not the excitable type. Like most pilots, she's normally stoic and unflappable. I waited until she stopped gasping for breath before I asked, "What happened?"

Her pupils were so dilated, I wondered if she'd sampled some of her own wares. More likely, she was just frightened.

"This is going to sound nuts," she said in a high, thin voice that didn't sound much like her, "but someone's been following me, watching me."

Breath hissed from my lungs. Crap. Fuck. Were Vampires going to start targeting everyone who knew me? So much for my flight school. One of my concerns had been putting my students at risk.

"Tell us more," Liam urged, clearly not immobilized by my worries about *Carrick Sky Sports.* Good thing one of us was rational.

Kiko blew out a long, noisy breath. "Maybe a week ago I got a creeped out feeling when I went from my car into the pharmacy. I was working the late shift, so it was just getting dark. I tried to tell myself I was being foolish, that nothing was out there, but"—she trained her dark eyes on me—"you've taught me magic is real."

"Why'd you think it was something magical?" I asked. "And not some creep stalking you?"

"Same thing I asked myself all through my eight hour shift. Never did come up with anything definitive. It was past midnight when I got off, and I requested one of the security guards to walk me to my car."

"Good call," I murmured.

"Yeah, except I felt like a total wimp." She shut her eyes for a moment. When she opened them, she kept talking. "Driving home was okay, but once I'd parked near my unit I had the same feeling, a sense I was being stalked. My apartment complex has security too, so I called and waited for one of the guys to escort me into the building. Told him I was worried about being shaken down for drugs."

Kiko straightened her back until she stood as tall as her five-feet-two-inch frame allowed. "Every day, it's gotten worse until I have to psych myself up to leave my house. Whatever it is doesn't feel human. There's a smell..."

I battled a sinking sensation and leaned closer. "Describe it."

She crinkled her nose. "It's horrible. Fetid. Rotten."

"Vampires," Liam growled. "Has to be."

Kiko's eyes widened. "Erm, they're real? They're not on the list with witches and druids and the rest of them."

I still had hold of her arm. "It's not a them," I reminded her. "It's an us."

She blinked and looked at Liam. "Figures you'd be

something too. What are you?" She made a face. "Sorry, that didn't come out quite like I wanted."

"Stop worrying about being politically correct," I said. "Liam is a Sidhe."

"Like a faery?" She directed her gaze at her feet. "Don't you guys have wings?"

"That would be the Fae and only a few varieties of them," he told her with only the slightest hint of humor riding beneath his words.

"Not important," she said. "I've been drugging myself to sleep. By earlier today, I almost had myself convinced I'd hallucinated the whole thing."

Oh-oh.

"What happened?" Liam and I blurted almost in unison."

Kiko swept a hank of hair to one side displaying obvious fang marks over one of her jugular veins. "They were there when I woke up. Freaked the fuck out of me. When you said Vampires, everything clicked. One of them came into my house. While I was asleep. Don't locks keep them out? Christ, Cait. Am I going to turn into one of them?" Her dark eyes sheened with tears.

"No to both questions." Liam kept his voice soothing. "Locks aren't much of a deterrent to anything magical, and you won't turn into a Vampire. That's a two-stage process. They'd have to drain you to the point of death—and you wouldn't sleep through that. Then you'd have to drink their blood. Right now, the biggest problem is they've marked you."

"Ewww." Tears spilled over. "Why me? What did I ever do?"

I felt like crying too. "Nothing. You did nothing. Your only crime was associating with me," I told her. "It's me they want."

"Can I get rid of this mark thing?" She turned toward Liam. I did as well since I didn't have an answer for her.

"Maybe. The question is where we should go. It will be dark soon, and Vampires know about this spot."

They knew about my houseboat too. And obviously, Kiko's apartment. "Why do we need a spot they haven't discovered?" I looked Liam's way.

"To give us time to undo their actions. They put a ball into play. They won't take kindly to me dismantling it."

"Even if you do," Kiko wailed. "What's to stop them from sneaking into my house again." She dropped her head into her hands. "I can't stay there anymore. I don't feel safe."

"What will we need to fix Kiko?" I glanced at Liam. "And how long will it take? Hey. Would that deserted storefront work?"

He snapped his fingers. "I'd forgotten about it. Aye, 'twould be perfect. I'll require about an hour."

"Death knows about that spot," I reminded him.

"Aye, but she doesn't have a pony in this race," he said.

"What deserted shop?" Kiko asked in a strangled sounding voice. If she was freaked out now, things weren't going to get better for her over the next hour or two.

I bent so we were more or less at eye level. "It's an empty shop maybe half a mile from my houseboat. We need a spot the Vampires don't know about, which rules out my home, your home, and this place." I swung an arm wide.

Before she could say anything else, I continued. "We will use a magical spell to move us from here to there. The moment we arrive, Liam and I will ward—er, protect—the place and shield it from prying eyes and ears. Then he will use magic to hopefully undo what the Vampire did last night."

"If we're fortunate, I can shield you from future attacks, but I'm not as certain of that," Liam said.

Kiko's eyes had grown big. "I don't have to do any of this, right?"

I nodded. "It's your choice, but if you don't let us help you, what will you do instead?"

"Run away," she said in a small voice.

"Vampires are everywhere," I murmured. "They have a way of communicating with one another."

"Damned if I do, damned if I don't, huh?"

"About the size of it. I'm sorry," I told her.

"I know you are. You were honest with me, and being friends was my choice. I could have walked after you told me you were a Reaper."

"If we're going to leave, we have to go now," Liam's voice was uncharacteristically sharp.

"Why?" Kiko asked.

My nostrils twitched, picking up the roadkill stench of Vamps. They were closing on us. "Because Vampires aren't far away."

Her head swung from side to side. "But I don't see any."

"They're traveling through channels not accessible to

mortals," Liam said. Magic crackled around him as he called a teleport spell.

I grabbed my shoulder bag and snatched my silver-and-iron infused Vampire killing blade from my locker. A stifled gasp from Kiko said more than words would have. She was about to plummet headfirst into a world she'd had no idea existed.

Apologies died on my lips. We had to get out of here. I cracked my magical center open, offering Liam assistance, and the Quonset hut dropped away, replaced by the dusty deserted shopfront where he and I had taken refuge one night. We'd been spying on Humans Rule and had needed a spot to regroup.

"Why do Vampires hate you?" Kiko asked, keeping her voice low as she turned in a circle and examined the empty store.

"Because part of my job is sealing them behind the veil separating Earth from the realm of the dead. They might be dead, but they like it here and have no intention of leaving. Not under their own steam."

"Sorry I asked," she muttered. "Geez. What else don't I know about?"

"Lots," Liam said succinctly. He moved next to Kiko, but didn't touch her. "Do you request my magical intervention of your own free will?"

"What is this?" She came as close to smiling as she had since she'd run up to us. "A disclaimer in case shit goes awry?"

"Nay. Working magic on mortals is forbidden unless they specifically request us to do so."

"Got it," she said, followed by, "Yes, I want your help. Please."

"Good enough." He dropped one hand on her shoulder, the other on her head. "This won't hurt, and you shouldn't remember anything."

"I don't like the not remembering part," she murmured just before she sagged against him.

He laid her on the floor and knelt next to her. Power flowed from his fingertips, and a numinous shroud took form, encasing her from head to toe.

"Tell me what you need from me," I murmured.

"Keep your magic accessible."

I wanted to ask what he was doing but was afraid to interrupt his concentration. Minutes clicked by. I felt a tug on my power from time to time. The shroud changed colors. Sometimes Liam chanted, sometimes not. I kept tabs on Kiko's soul. It looked healthy to me, and firmly tethered to her body. Somewhere along the way, my scythe returned, leaned against a wall where it glowed softly.

Gradually, the fang marks vanished, replaced by smooth, ivory skin.

Liam rocked back on his heels, and the shroud dissipated into blue and violet streamers. Kiko opened her eyes with a start. "Was it successful?"

"You're no longer marked," Liam said.

Kiko reached for her neck, trailing fingertips over the spot the indentations had been. She struggled to sit. "Thank you so much."

"You're welcome," Liam replied and helped her to her

feet. “It wasn’t too bad. Healing isn’t one of my natural talents, but I had a fallback position.”

“Dena?” I furled my brows.

He nodded.

“Who’s she?” Kiko glanced at me.

“A Sidhe in the Scottish Highlands. Fortunately, we don’t need to travel there.”

“Not sure how fortunate it is. I’ve always wanted to see Scotland,” Kiko mumbled. She sounded tapped out.

Liam scooped up a chunk of what looked like quartz from a spot where the shroud had been. He handed it to Kiko. “I’m not certain how well this will perform, but I’ve matched it to your energy. Keep it with you at all times, and it should offer protection against Vampires.”

“Will this make it okay for me to return home?” She took the stone from Liam and zipped it into her jacket.

“How about if you stay in hotels for a week or two?” I jumped in, not wanting anything else to happen to her.

“I can do that,” she said. “I’d been considering it anyway. Um, guess I can take a taxi back to my car.”

“Where exactly did you park?” I asked.

“Down by *The Tailwind.*” She named the small restaurant at the far end of the airfield.

“I’ll take you back to your car,” I told her.

“And then meet me at the houseboat,” Liam said. “We can leave from there. I’ll transport the blade.”

“Leave for where?” Kiko’s dark eyes skipped from him to me. She was a proud woman, but I could tell she was wondering what would happen if she needed us again.

"We'll be gone for a while," I told her. "If you run into problems, text me or email me."

"Neither works where we're going." Liam reminded me.

"Not right away," I corrected him, "but I'll be checking messages every day or two."

"Good enough," Kiko said. "I sure won't be talking with anyone else about any of this. They'd commit me."

I didn't know what to tell her. Apologies were inadequate, and shy of dragging her across the Atlantic, we'd done all we could. I draped an arm around her and visualized the airfield. My spell spit us out between two buildings not far from *The Tailwind*. I swathed us in invisibility and walked her to her car.

When we got there, she threw her arms around me. "Thanks, Cait. Don't blame yourself, please."

I hugged her back and smiled and said the right words while I made certain she got into her car and drove off without incident. When you cut to the chase, her run-in with Vampires was my fault. All my fault. Only my fault.

I shook my head and slid behind a hangar. My scythe took up its customary spot hooked over one shoulder. I wasn't competent enough to teleport from behind an invisibility casting. Not yet, so I dismantled it.

Kiko was safe for the moment, but any of the remaining dark mages could undo Liam's good work.

Fuck. Who else would I put at risk before this was done?

ABOUT THE AUTHOR

Ann Gimpel is a USA Today bestselling author. A lifelong aficionado of the unusual, she began writing speculative fiction a few years ago. Since then her short fiction has appeared in many webzines and anthologies. Her longer books run the gamut from urban fantasy to paranormal romance. Once upon a time, she nurtured clients. Now she nurtures dark, gritty fantasy stories that push hard against reality. When she's not writing, she's in the backcountry getting down and dirty with her camera. She's published over 75 books to date, with several more planned for 2020 and beyond. A husband, grown children, grandchildren, and wolf hybrids round out her family.

Keep up with her at www.anngimpel.com or http://anngimpel.blogspot.com

If you enjoyed what you read, get in line for special offers and pre-release special reads. Newsletter Signup!

ALSO BY ANN GIMPEL

SERIES

Alphas in the Wild

Hello Darkness

Alpine Attraction

A Run for Her Money

Fire Moon

Bitter Harvest

Deceived

Twisted

Abandoned

Betrayed

Redeemed

Coven Enforcers

Blood and Magic

Blood and Sorcery

Blood and Illusion

Demon Assassins

Witch's Bounty

Witch's Bane

Witches Rule

Dragon Heir (Summer and fall, 2019)

Dragon's Call

Dragon's Blood

Dragon's Heir

Dragon Lore

Highland Secrets

To Love a Highland Dragon

Dragon Maid

Dragon's Dare

Dragon Fury

Earth Reclaimed

Earth's Requiem

Earth's Blood

Earth's Hope

Elemental Witch

Timespell

Time's Curse

Time's Hostage

Gatekeeper (Winter 2019 and spring 2020)

Shadow Reaper

Rebel Reaper

Untamed Reaper

GenTech Rebellion

Winning Glory

Honor Bound

Claiming Charity

Loving Hope

Keeping Faith

Ice Dragon

Feral Ice

Cursed Ice

Primal Ice

Rubicon International

Garen

Lars

Soul Dance

Tarnished Beginnings

Tarnished Legacy

Tarnished Prophecy

Tarnished Journey

Soul Storm

Dark Prophecy

Dark Pursuit

Dark Promise

Underground Heat

Roman's Gold

Wolf Born

Blood Bond

Wolf Clan Shifters

Alice's Alphas

Megan's Mates

Sophie's Shifters

Wylde Magick

Gemstone

Lion's Lair

Unbalanced

STANDALONE BOOKS

Branded, That Old Black Magic Romance (paranormal romance)

Edge of Night (short story collection, paranormal and horror)

Grit is a 4-Letter Word (nonfiction)

Heart's Flame (post-apocalyptic romance)

Icy Passage (science fiction romance)

Marked by Fortune (post-apocalyptic coming of age story)

Melis's Gambit (historical paranormal romance)

Midnight Magic (paranormal romance)

Red Dawn (post-apocalyptic paranormal romance)

Shadow Play (historical paranormal romance)

Shadows in Time (Highland time travel romance)

Since We Fell (contemporary romance)

Warin's War (paranormal romance)

www.ingramcontent.com/pod-product-compliance
Lightning Source LLC
Chambersburg PA
CBHW051010180726
48291CB00006B/2045
9781948871587